PANDA MAN to the RESCUE!

BOING-OING! IT IS I, PANDA MAN!
NICE TO MEET YOU!

STORY by SHO MAKURA art by HARUHI KATO

Meet Panda Man, the greatest martial artist in the world.

That may not be quite true, but Panda Man thinks so, and that's what matters.

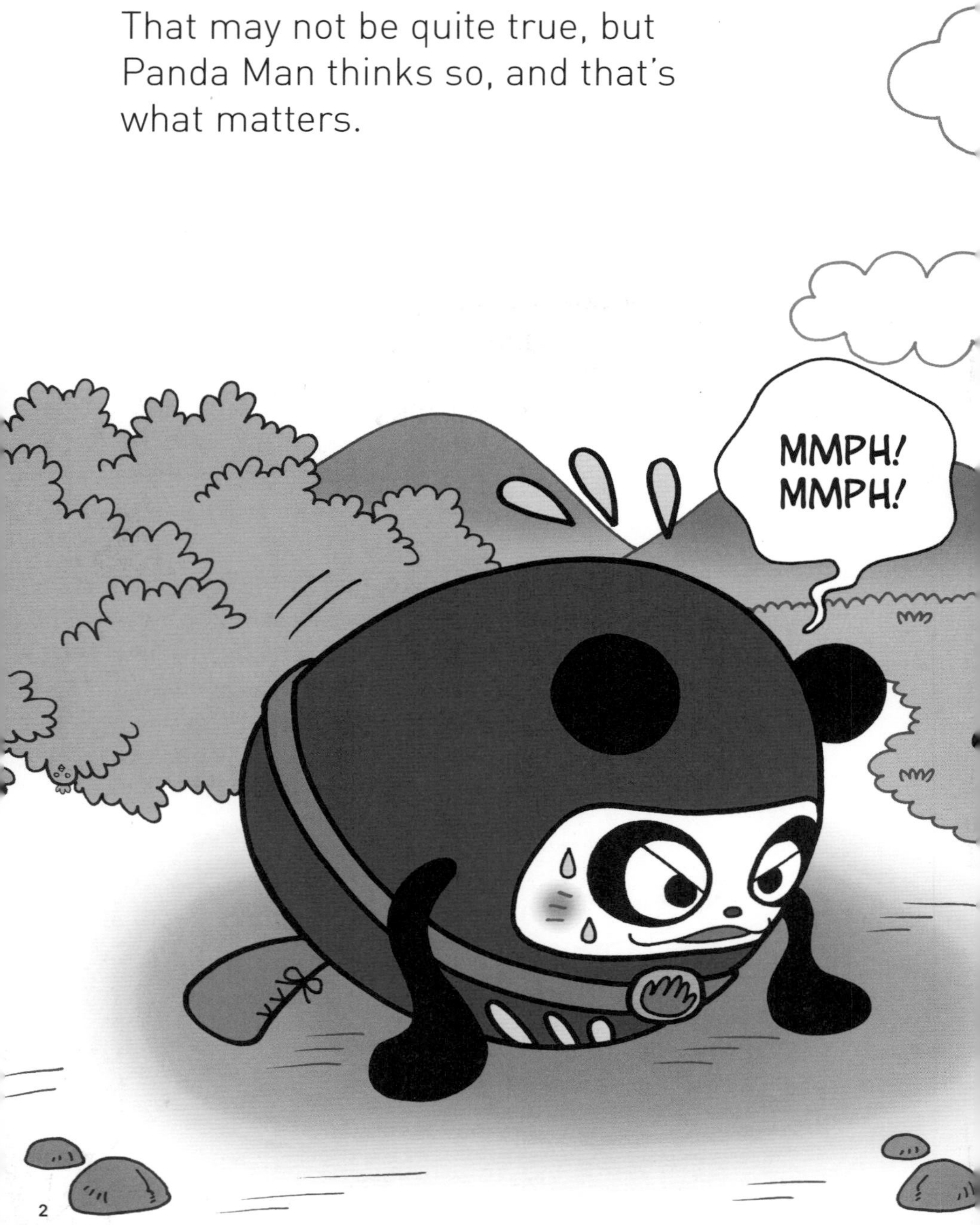
MMPH! MMPH!

Every day, deep in the mountains,
Panda Man puts himself through
a rigorous training routine.

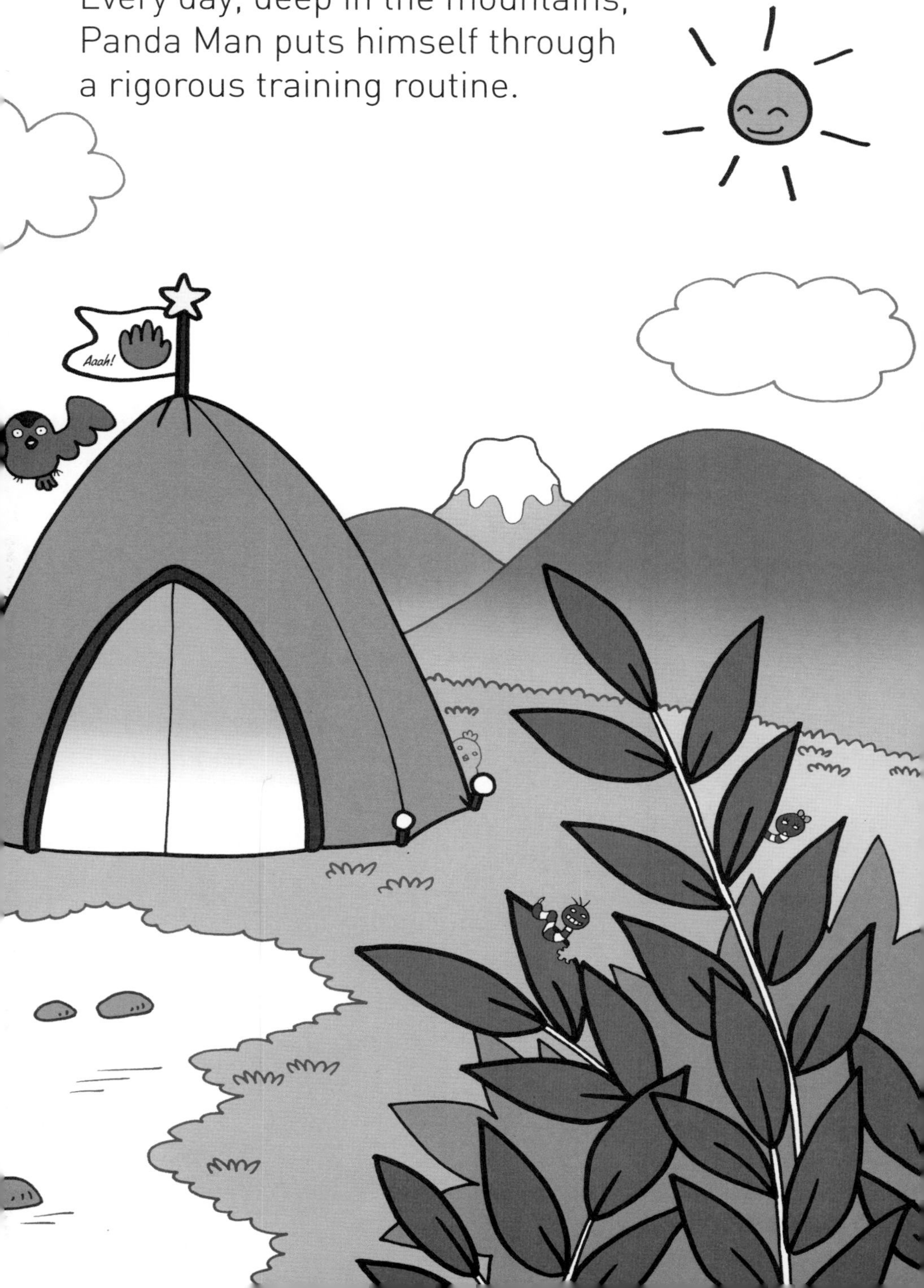
Aaah!

Would you look at that! Today's training has already begun. Let's watch.

First Panda Man punches his punching bag 100 times. Then he lifts weights 200 times.

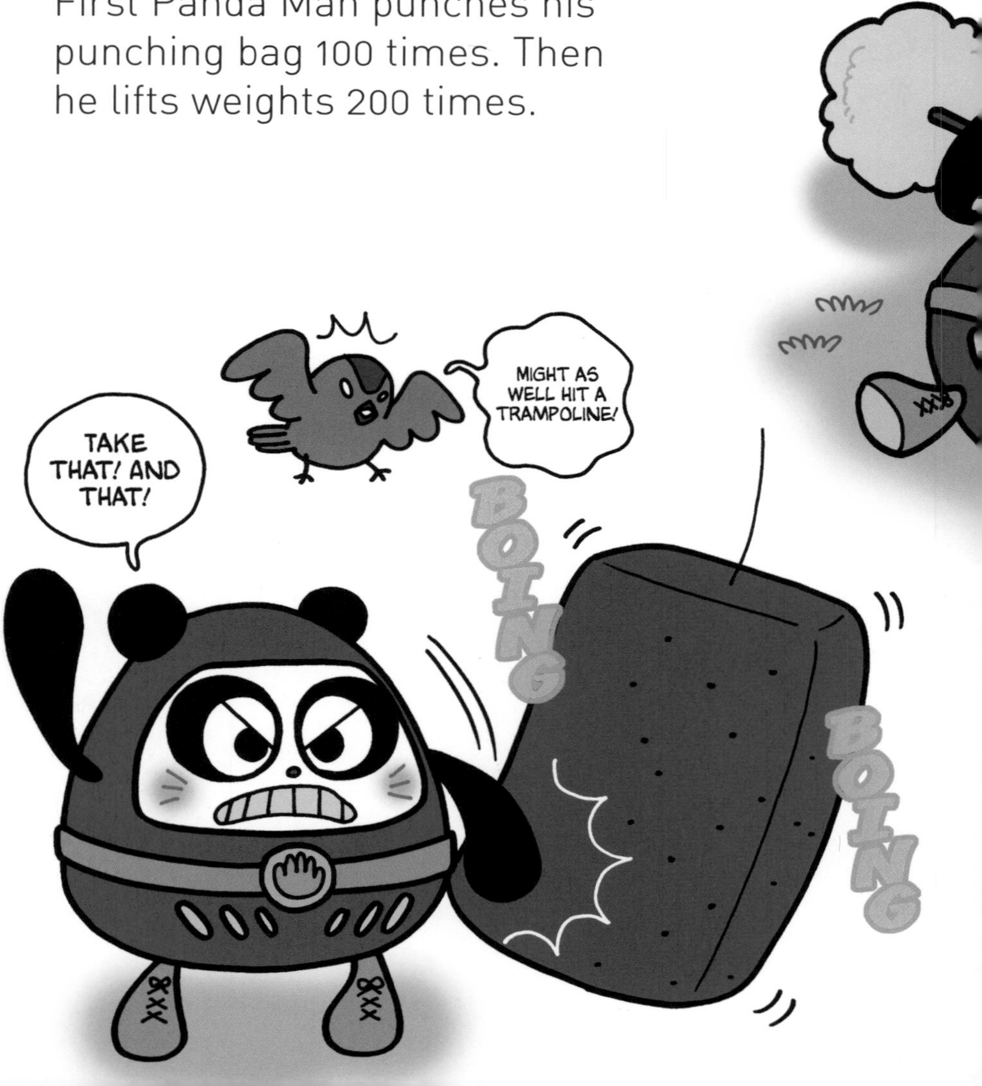
MIGHT AS WELL HIT A TRAMPOLINE!
TAKE THAT! AND THAT!
BOING
BOING

Finally, he sharpens his mind by sitting under the rushing water of an icy-cold waterfall.

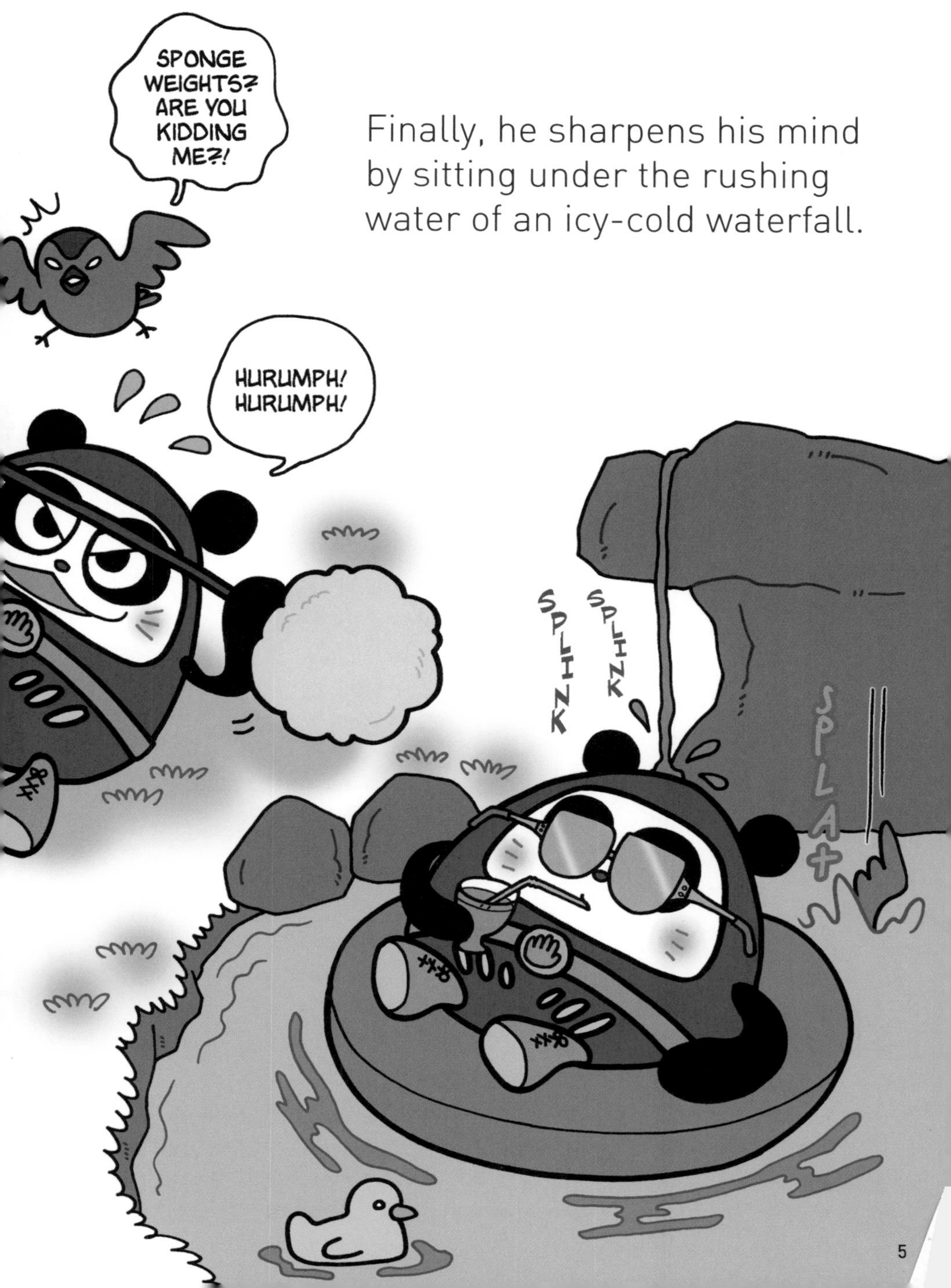
SPONGE WEIGHTS? ARE YOU KIDDING ME?!
HURUMPH! HURUMPH!
SPLINK
SPLINK
SPLAT

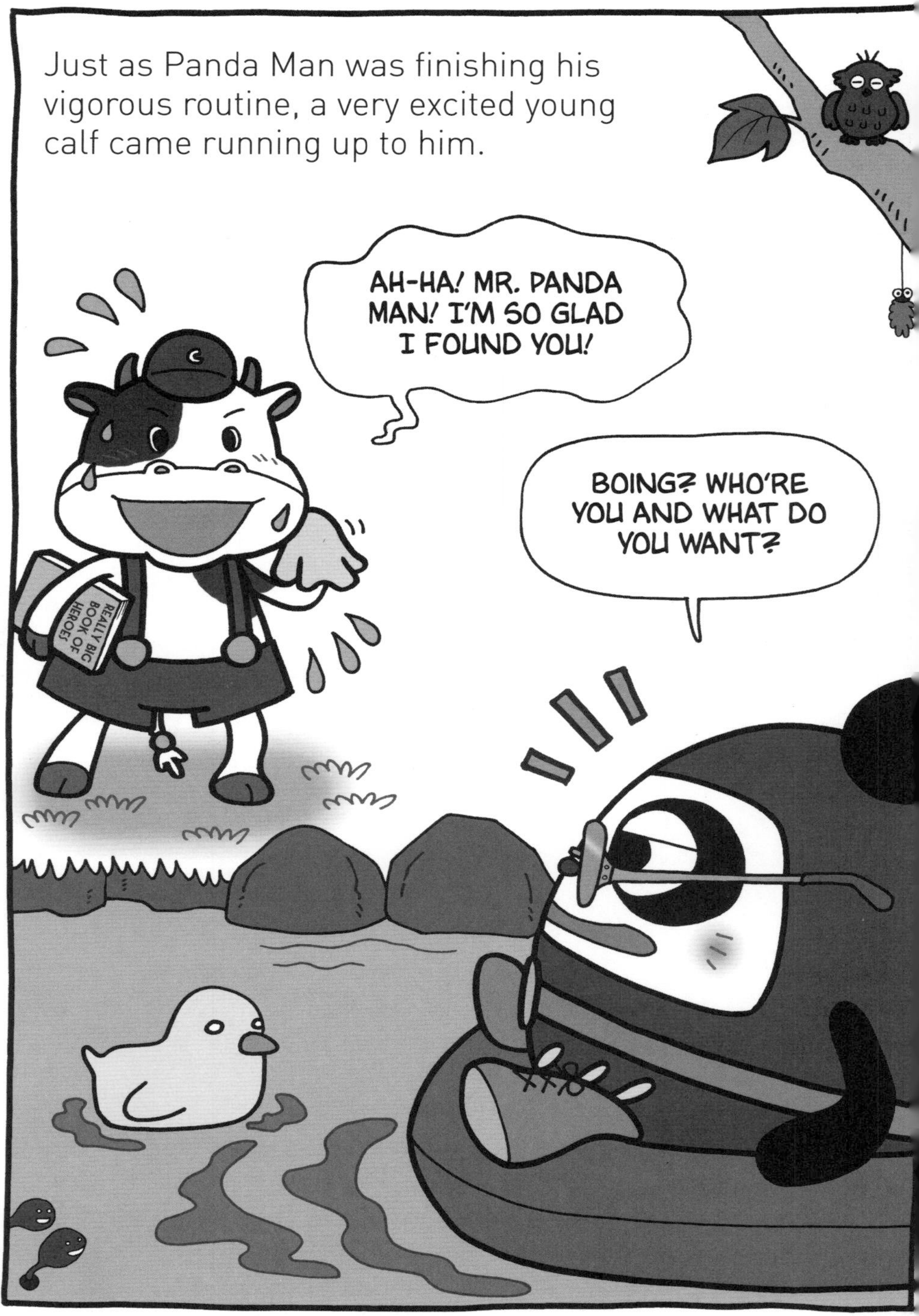
Just as Panda Man was finishing his vigorous routine, a very excited young calf came running up to him.
AH-HA! MR. PANDA MAN! I'M SO GLAD I FOUND YOU!
REALLY BIG BOOK OF HEROES
BOING? WHO'RE YOU AND WHAT DO YOU WANT?

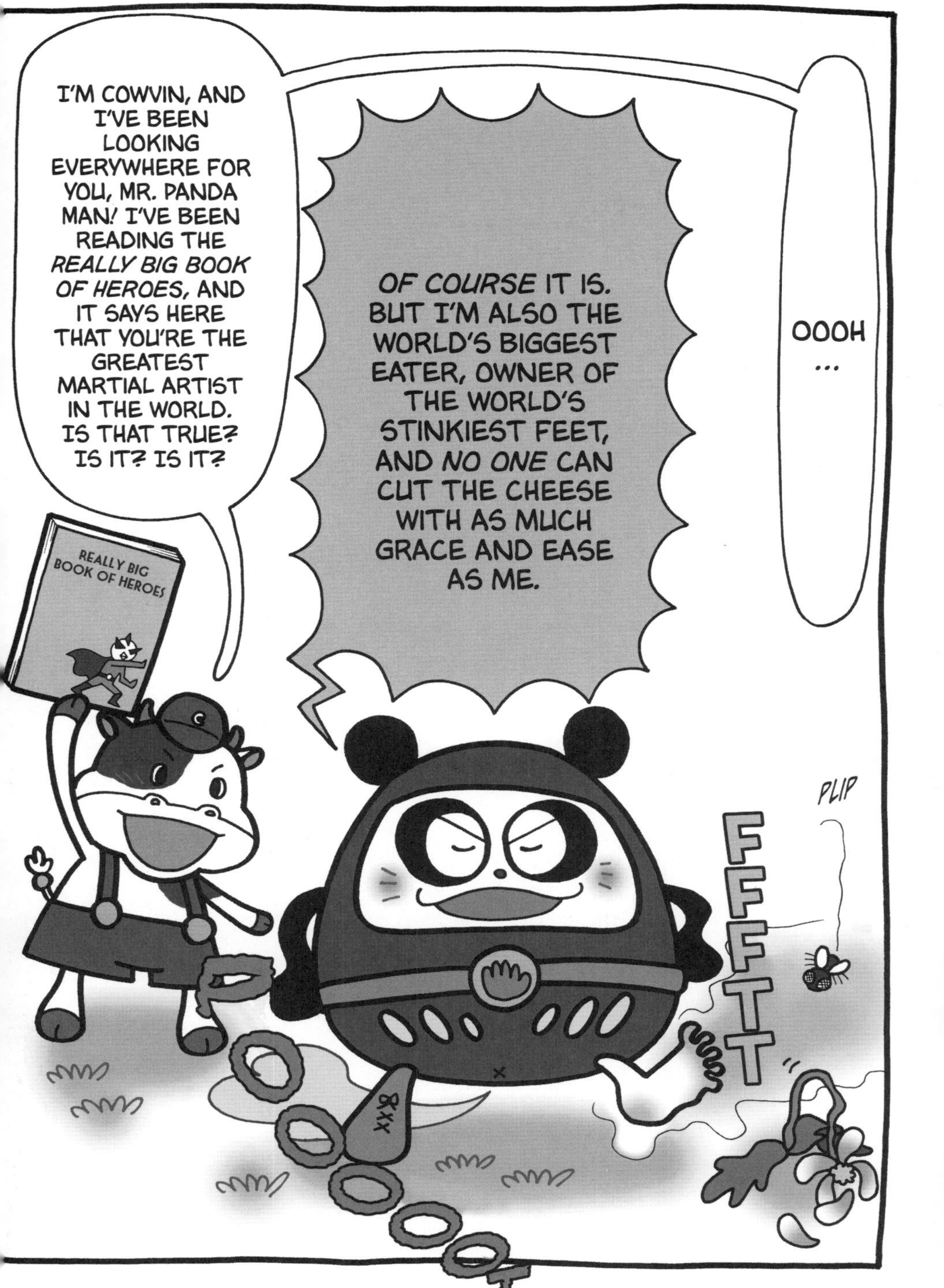
I'M COWVIN, AND I'VE BEEN LOOKING EVERYWHERE FOR YOU, MR. PANDA MAN! I'VE BEEN READING THE *REALLY BIG BOOK OF HEROES*, AND IT SAYS HERE THAT YOU'RE THE GREATEST MARTIAL ARTIST IN THE WORLD. IS THAT TRUE? IS IT? IS IT?
REALLY BIG BOOK OF HEROES
OF COURSE IT IS. BUT I'M ALSO THE WORLD'S BIGGEST EATER, OWNER OF THE WORLD'S STINKIEST FEET, AND *NO ONE* CAN CUT THE CHEESE WITH AS MUCH GRACE AND EASE AS ME.
OOOH ...
PLIP
FFFFTT
POOOOOT

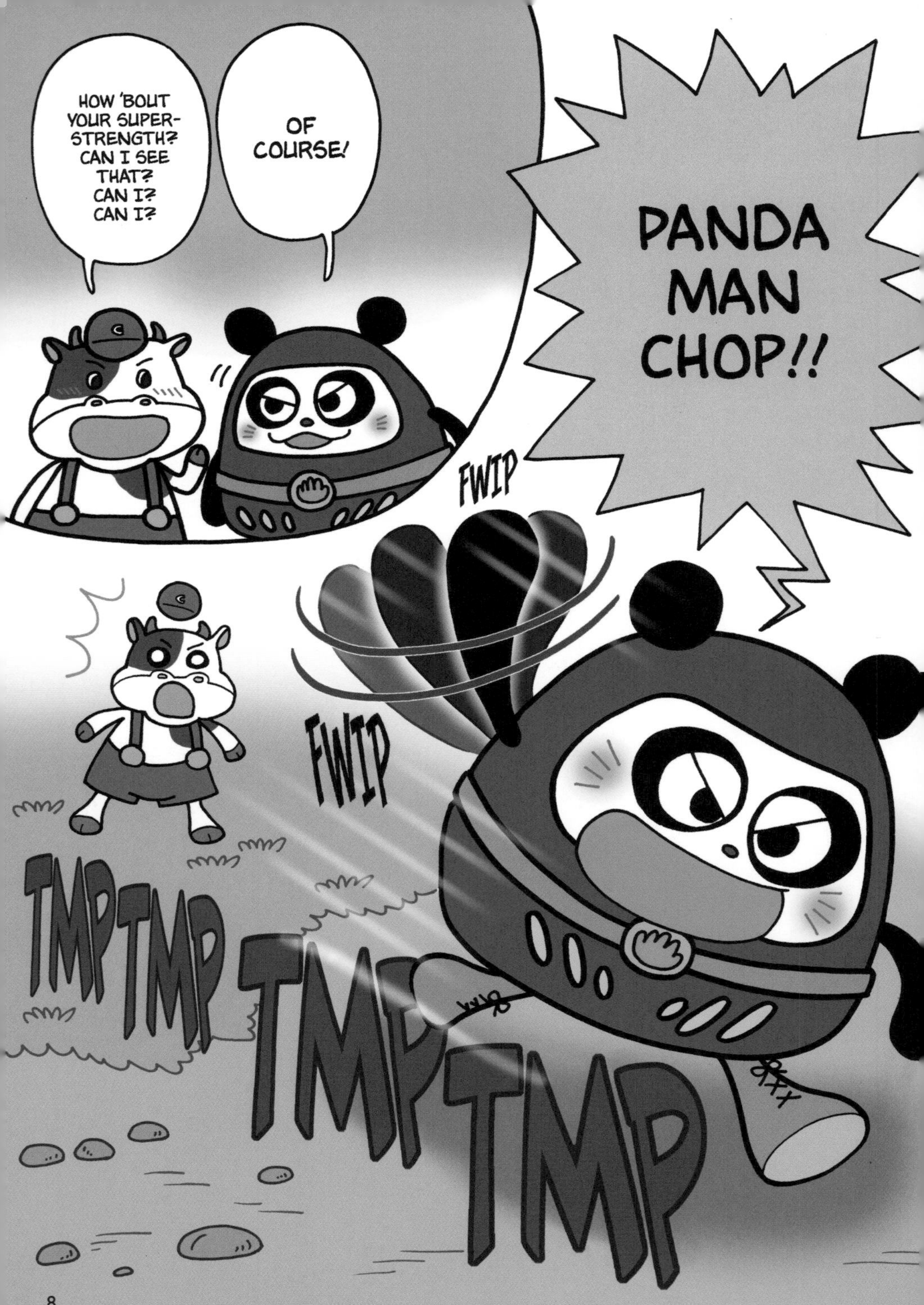
HOW 'BOUT YOUR SUPER-STRENGTH? CAN I SEE THAT? CAN I? CAN I?
OF COURSE!
PANDA MAN CHOP!!
FWIP
FWIP
TMP TMP
TMP TMP

Waving his arm with all his might, Panda Man ran full force toward a nearby log.

Unbelievable!

Can Panda Man really chop through the log with his bare hands?

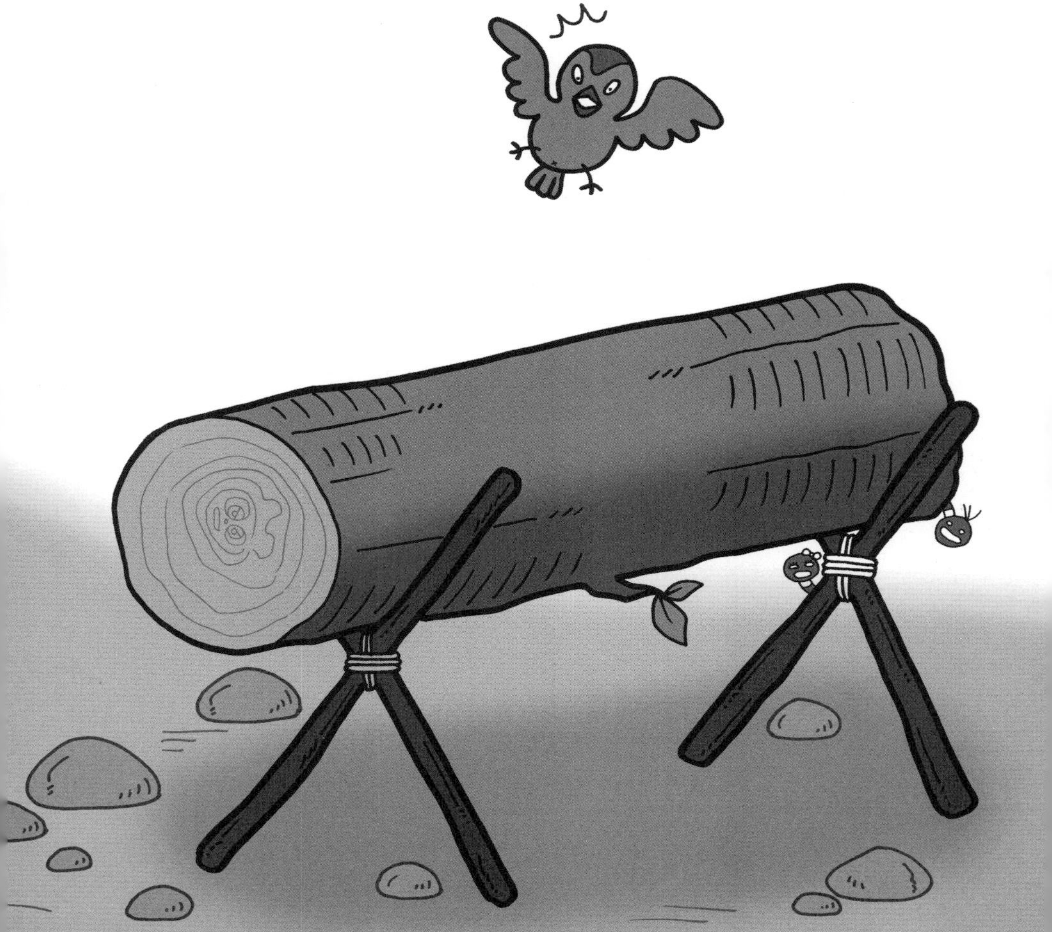

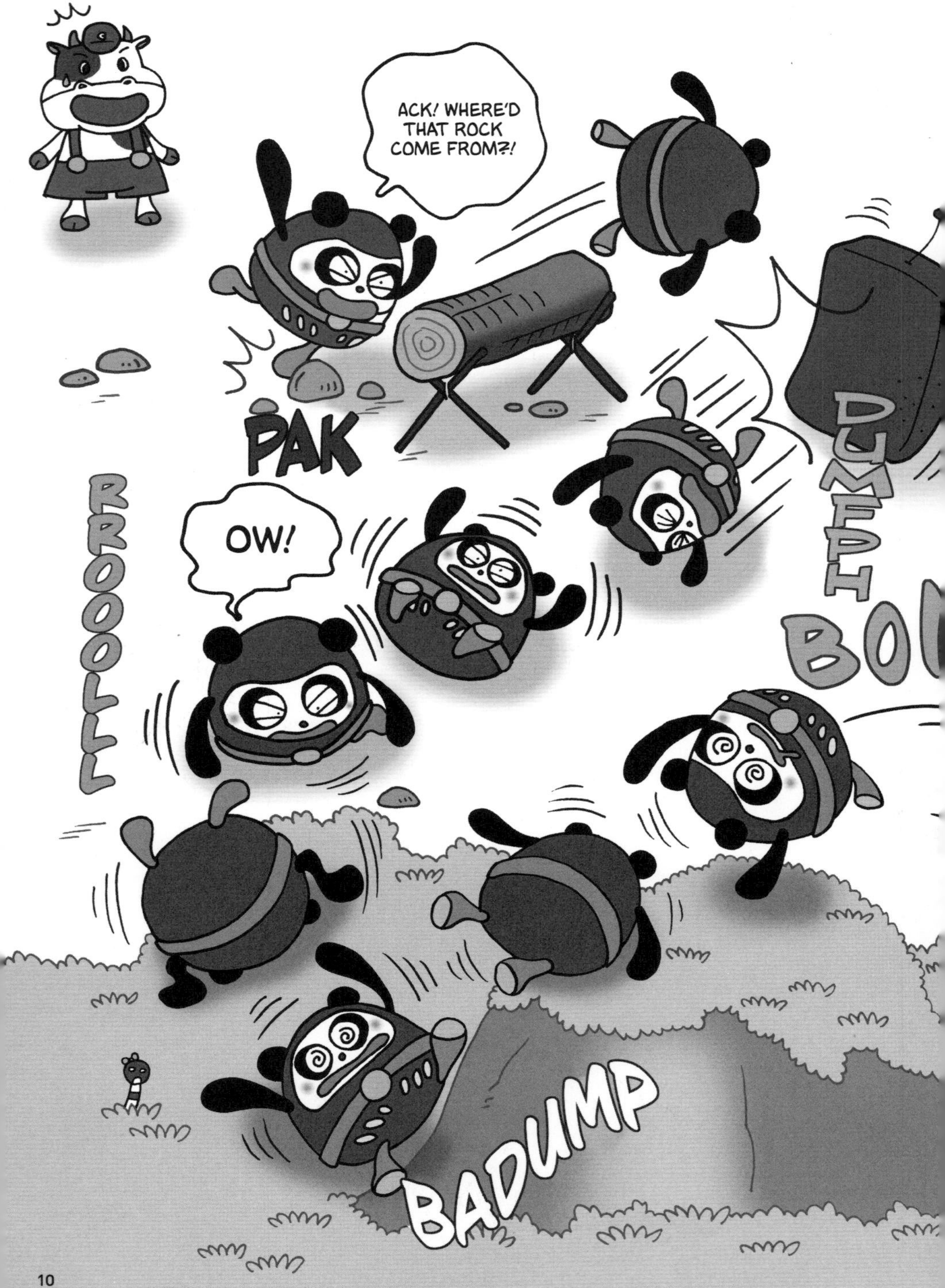
ACK! WHERE'D THAT ROCK COME FROM?!
PAK
DUMFPH
BO
OW!
RROOOOLLL
BADUMP

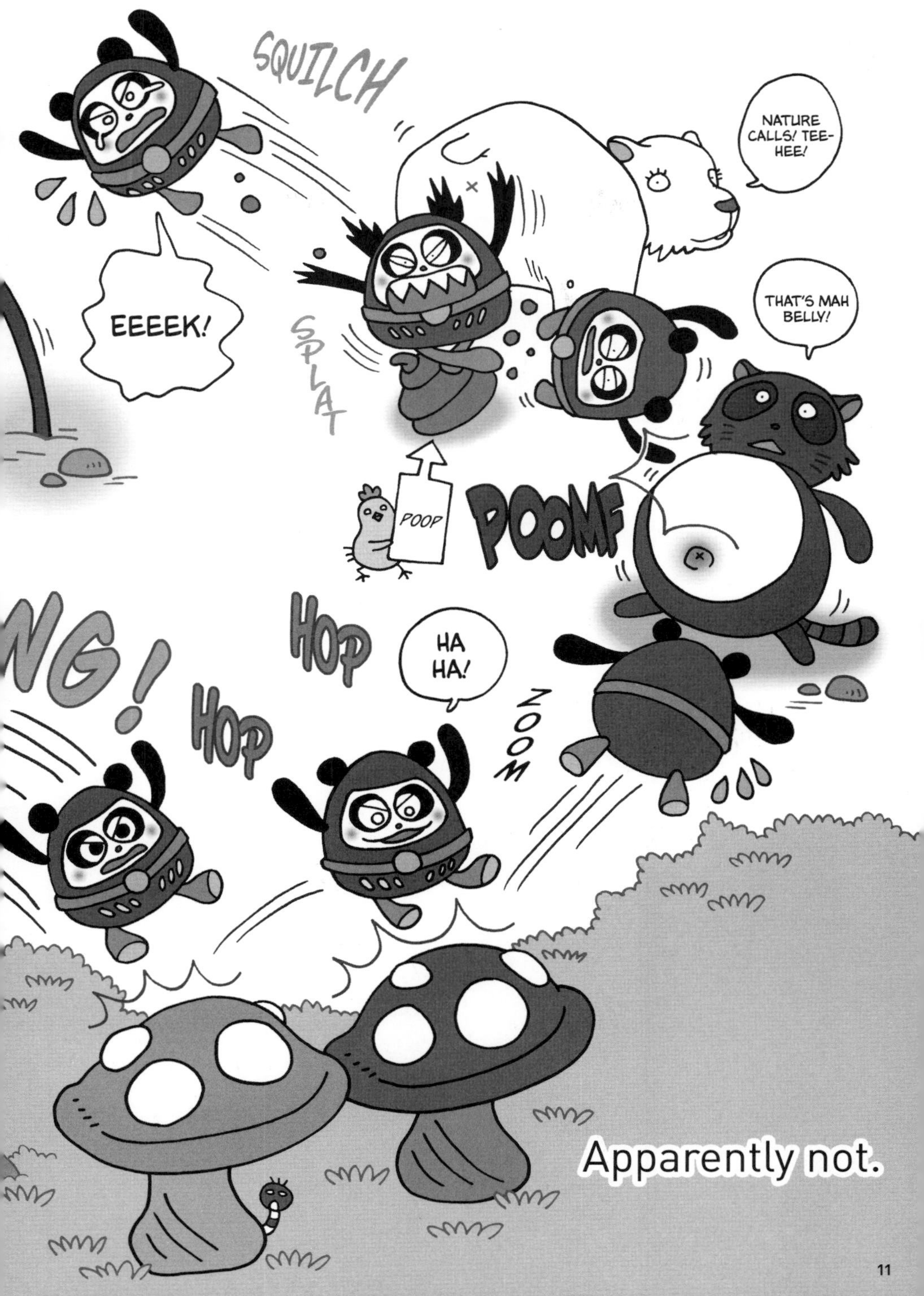
NATURE CALLS! TEE-HEE!
SQUILCH
THAT'S MAH BELLY!
EEEEK!
SPLAT
POOMF
POOP
HA HA!
HOP
ZOOM
HOP
NG!
Apparently not.

But wait! Panda Man managed to break the log after all! Cowvin applauded wildly.

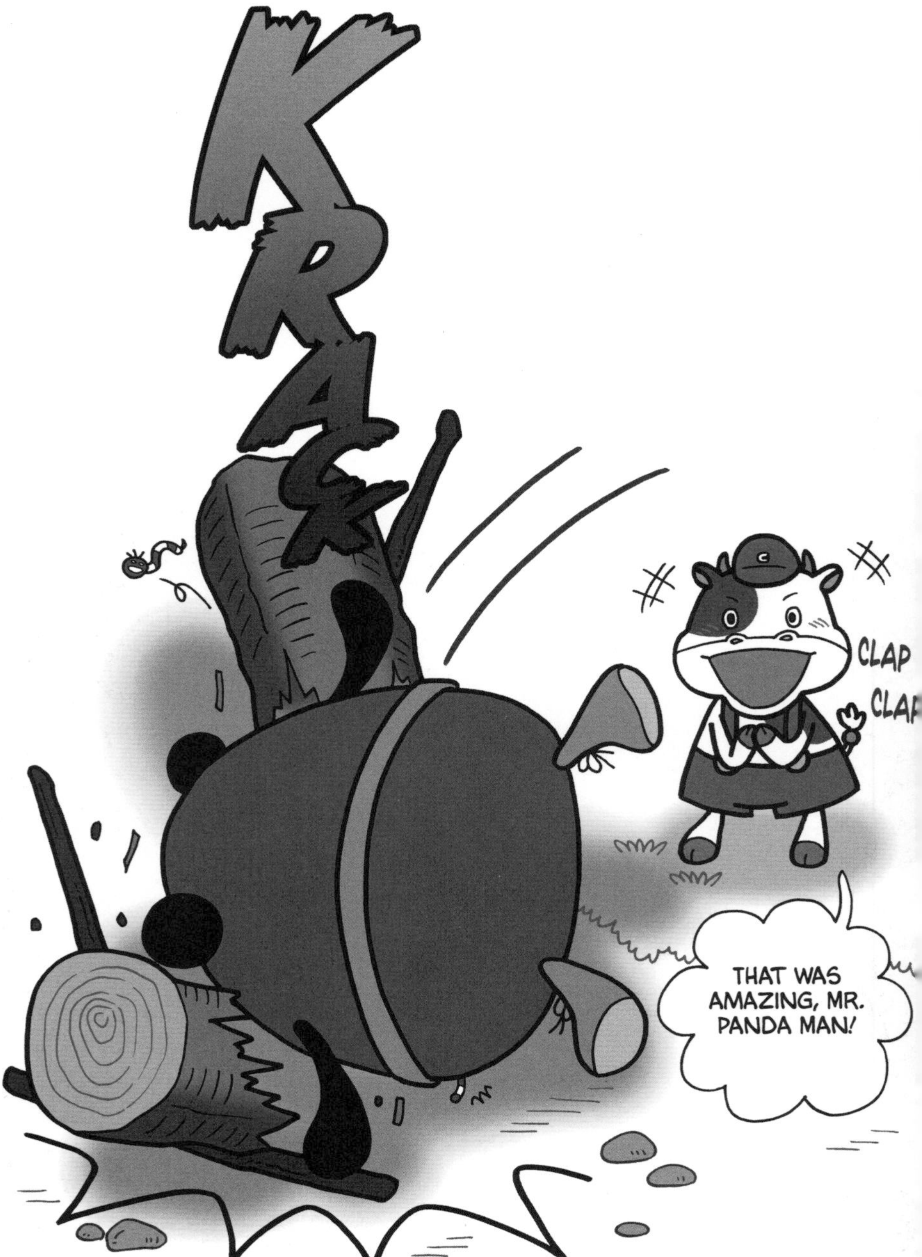
KRACK
CLAP
CLAP
THAT WAS AMAZING, MR. PANDA MAN!

Then he grew serious.

"Mr. Panda Man," he said. "I didn't just come to see your super-strength. A ruthless band of thieves is attacking my village! You're the only one in the world who can stop them!"

"Boing?" Panda Man replied. "A band of thieves? Oooh, that makes me mad! The world's maddest! These cowards need a dose of justice. The world's justest justice. Yes. I, Panda Man, will save your village!"

Of course, there was a catch.

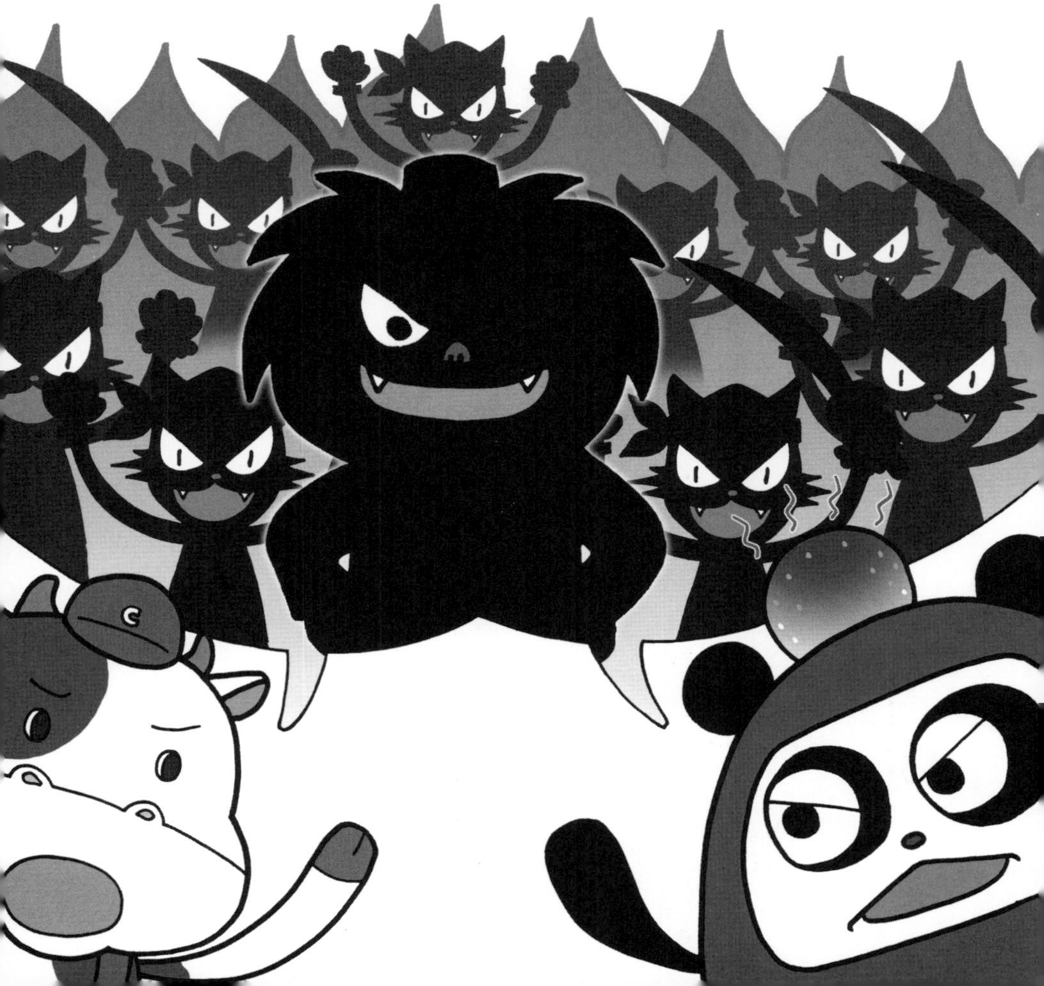

“I must warn you,” Panda Man continued. “My services don’t come cheap. My fee will be... one *million* dollars!”

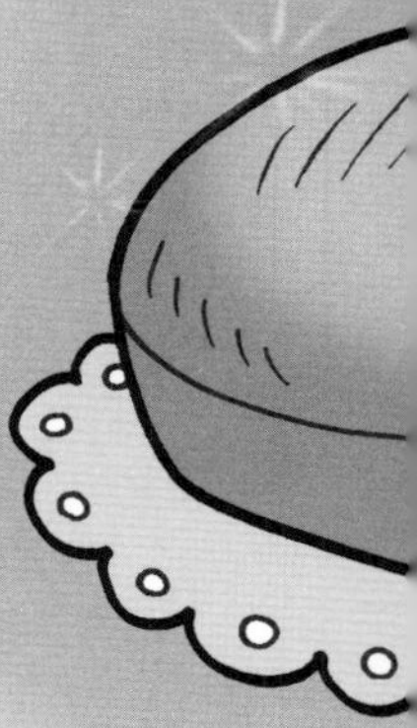

Poor Cowvin.
Poor, poor little shorthorn.

“One...m-million...?” Cowvin gasped. “Our village can’t afford that much.”

“It’s nothing personal.” Panda Man shrugged. “I just make it a point to be the world’s most... well, everything. So I have to have the world’s most expensive protection fees. I have no choice.”

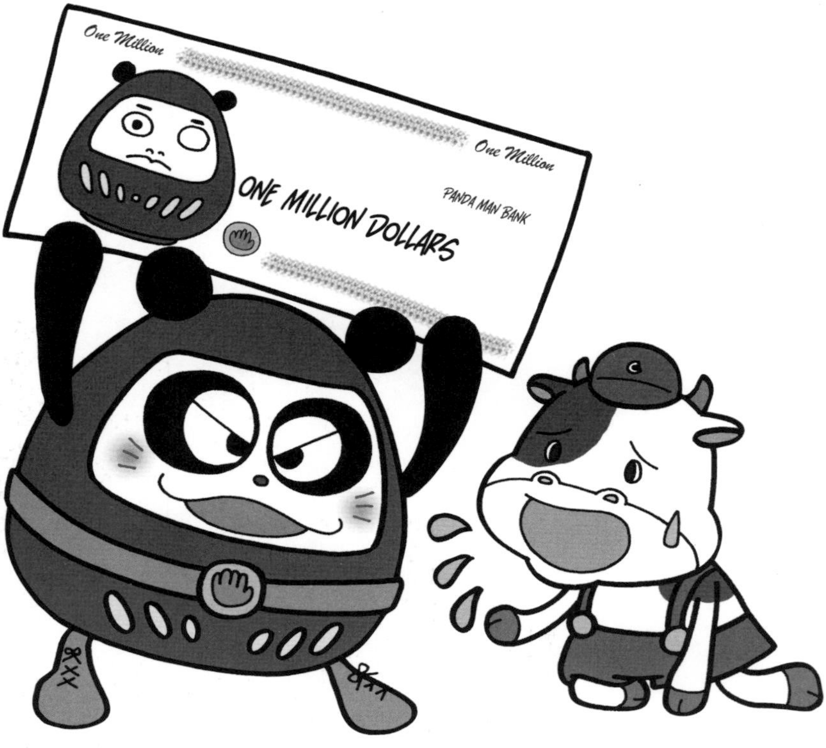
One Million
One Million
ONE MILLION DOLLARS
PANDA MAN BANK

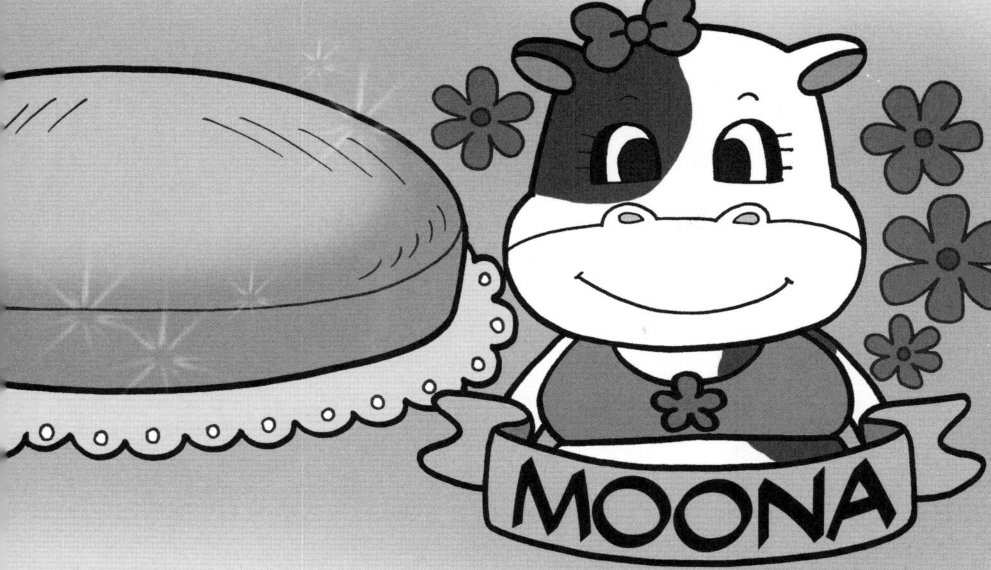
MOONA

Suddenly, Cowvin had an idea.

"Hey! I have an idea! My sister Moona is really famous for making the world's yummiest butter cake. If you helped my village, you could eat all the butter cake you want!"

"Did you say the world's *yummiest* butter cake?" Panda Man asked. "In that case, I'll waive my fee...just this once."

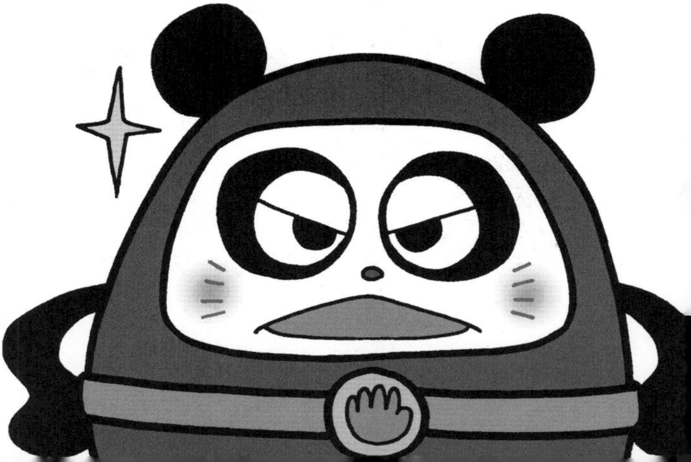

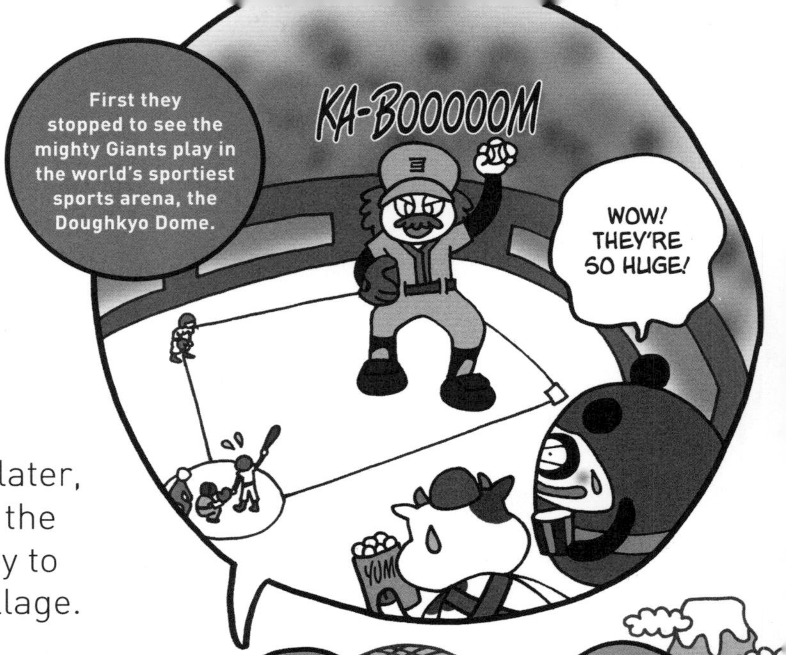
First they stopped to see the mighty Giants play in the world's sportiest sports arena, the Doughkyo Dome.
KA-BOOOOOM
WOW! THEY'RE SO HUGE!
YUM

A moment later, they began the long journey to Cowvin's village.

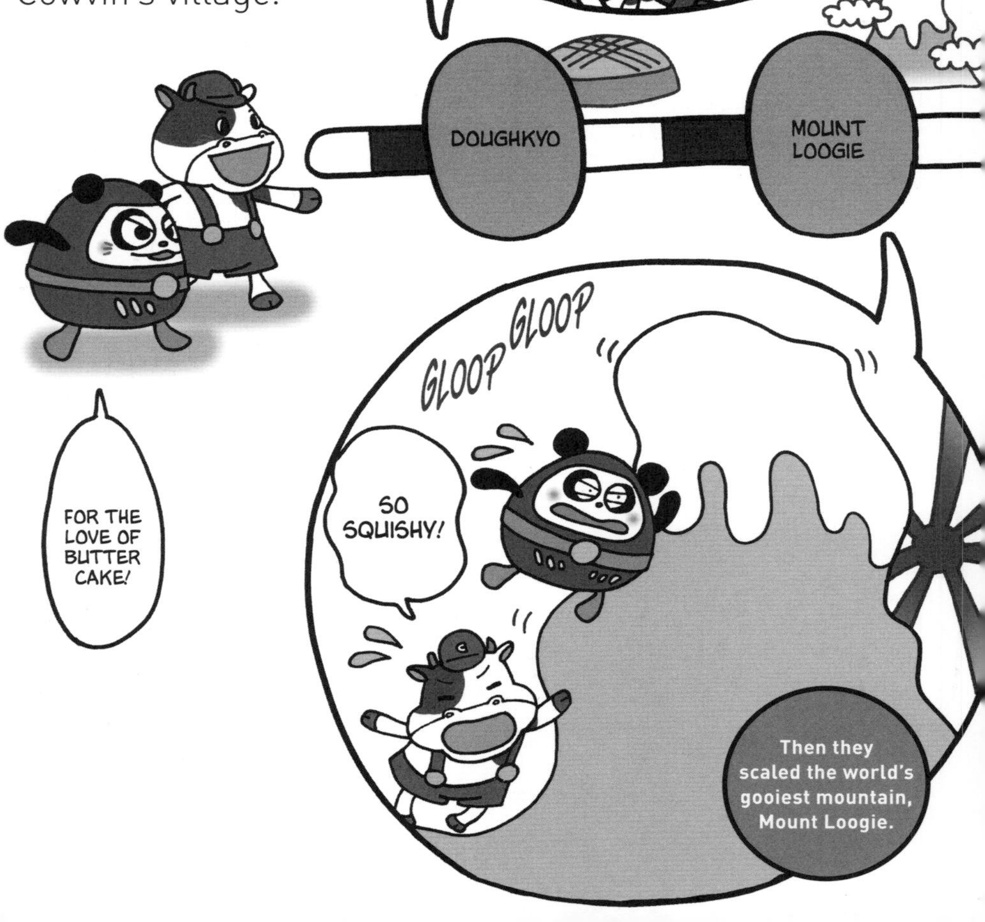
DOUGHKYO
MOUNT LOOGIE
FOR THE LOVE OF BUTTER CAKE!
GLOOP GLOOP
SO SQUISHY!
Then they scaled the world's gooiest mountain, Mount Loogie.

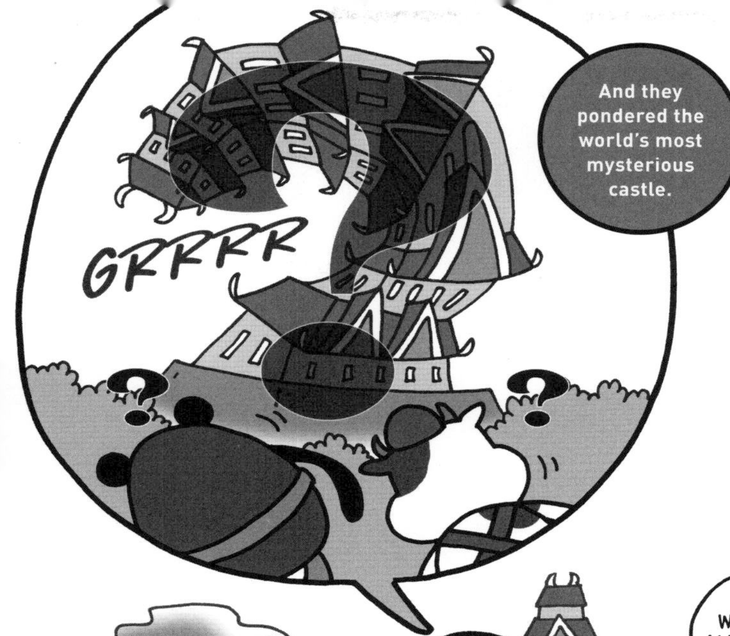
And they pondered the world's most mysterious castle.
GRRRR

And since they visited so many of Panda Man's favorite world-famous sites, for Cowvin, their trip became the world's longest.

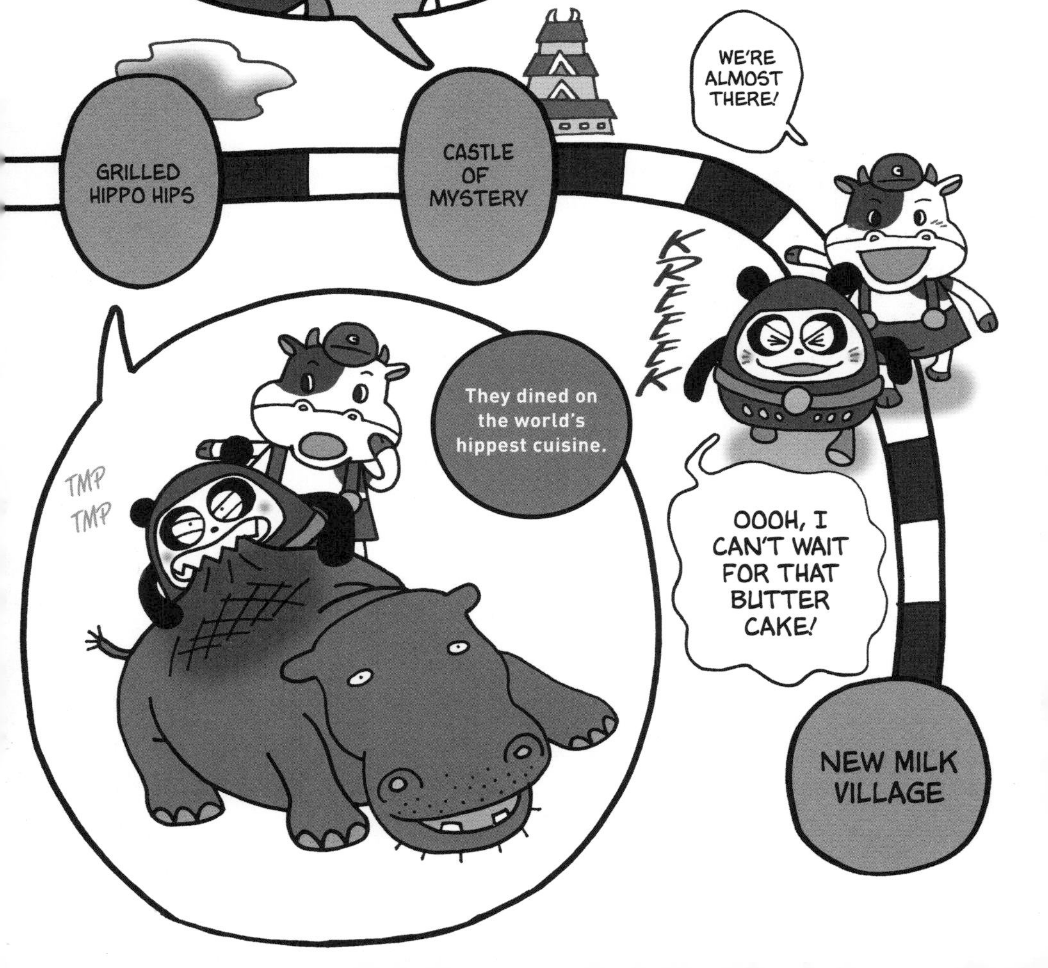
GRILLED HIPPO HIPS
CASTLE OF MYSTERY
WE'RE ALMOST THERE!
KREEEEK
OOOH, I CAN'T WAIT FOR THAT BUTTER CAKE!
NEW MILK VILLAGE
They dined on the world's hippest cuisine.
TMP TMP

Finally, Panda Man and Cowvin arrived in New Milk Village.

But something wasn't right.

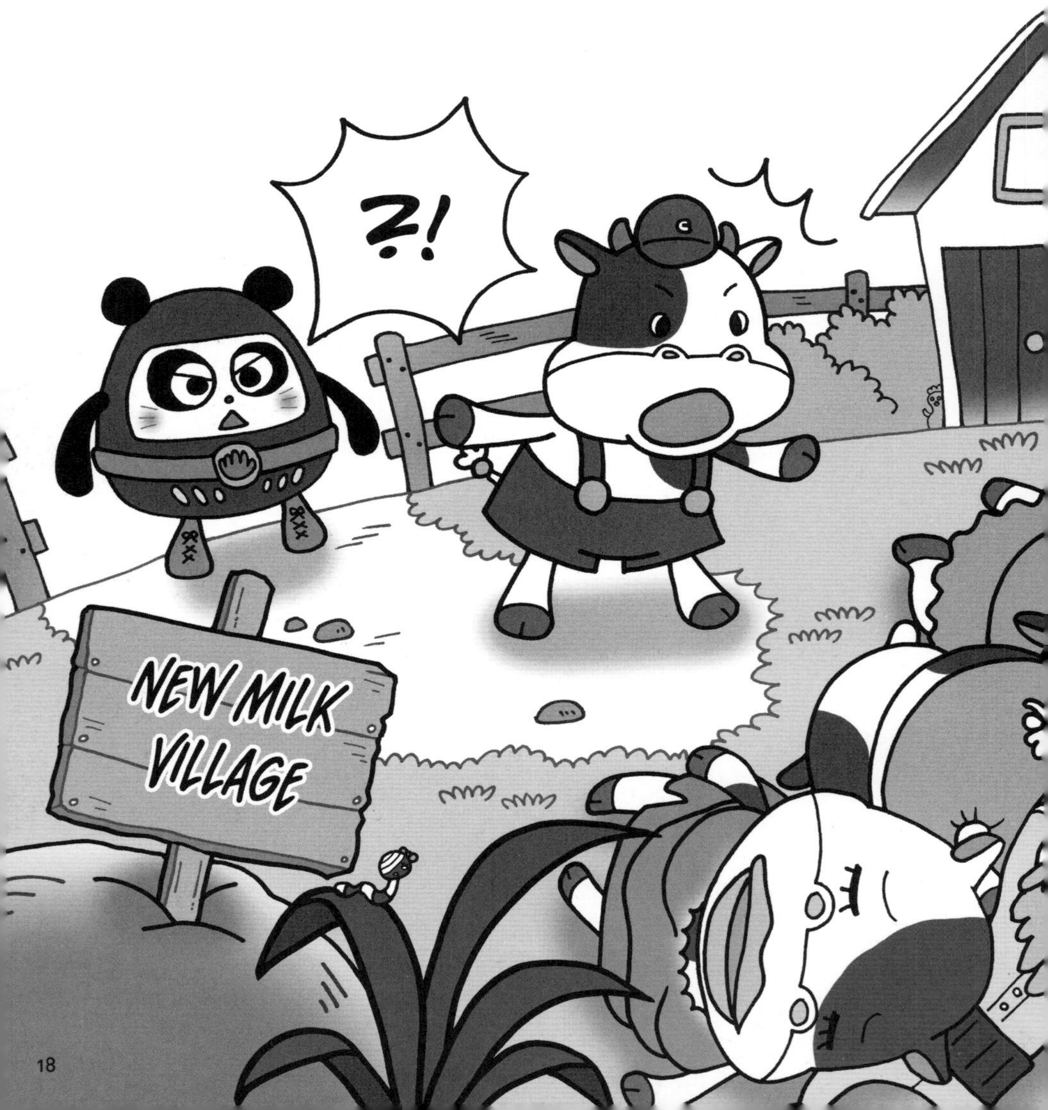
?!
NEW MILK VILLAGE

All of the townsfolk had fallen to the ground! Cowvin's sister was somewhere among them.

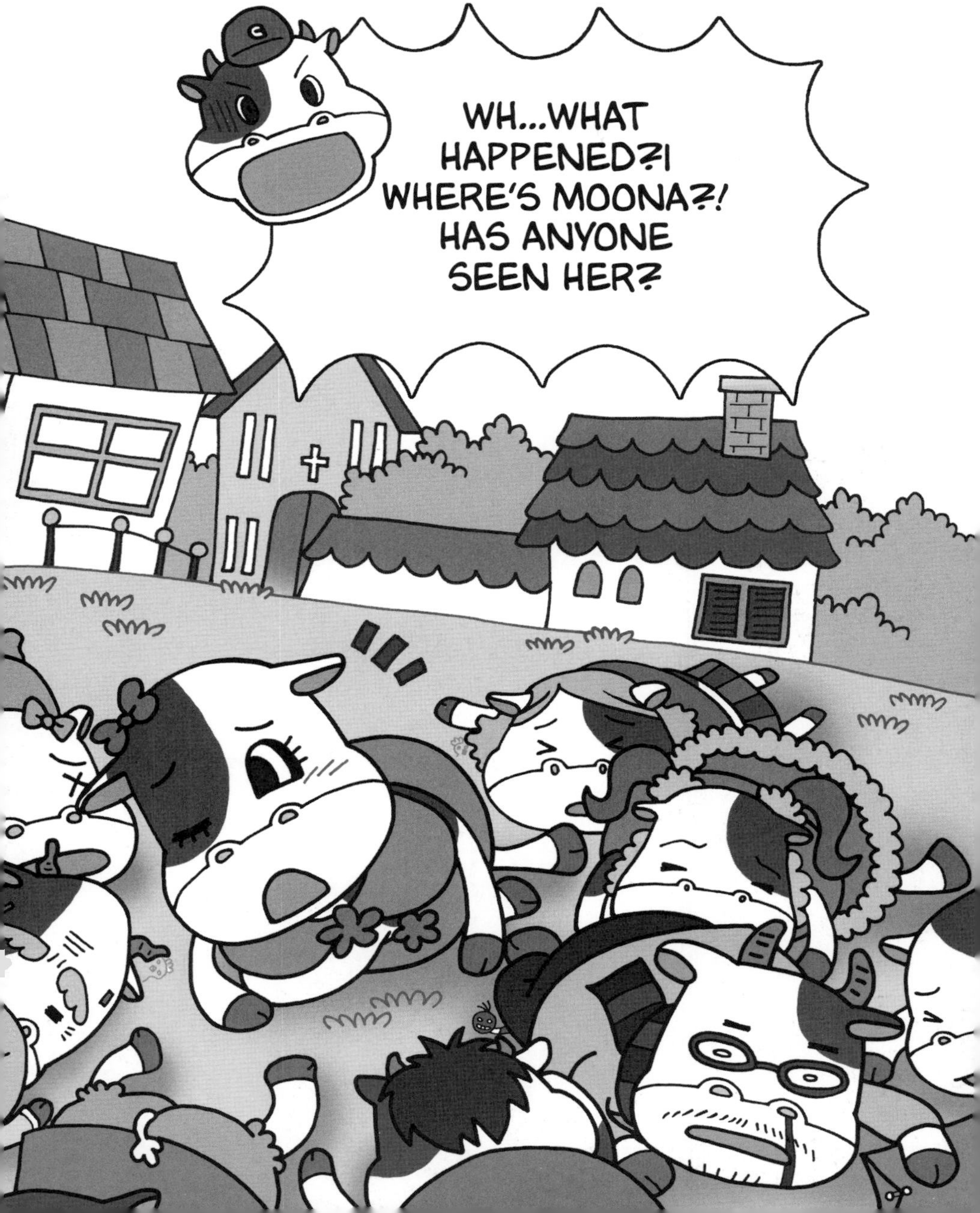
WH...WHAT HAPPENED?! WHERE'S MOONA?! HAS ANYONE SEEN HER?

"Oh, Cowvin... You did it!" Moona cried, rising slowly to her hooves. "You found Mr. Panda Man! But I'm afraid you're too late."

"What happened, Moona?" Cowvin asked.

"Well, we had just begun the day's milking when...

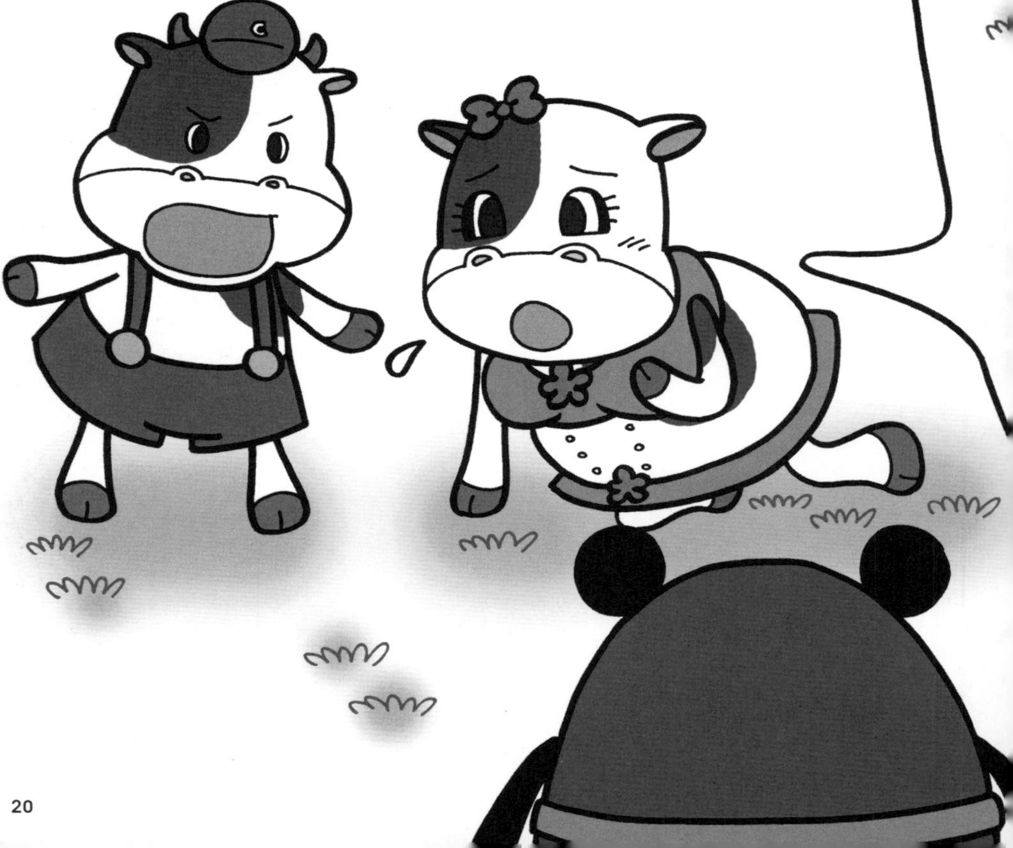

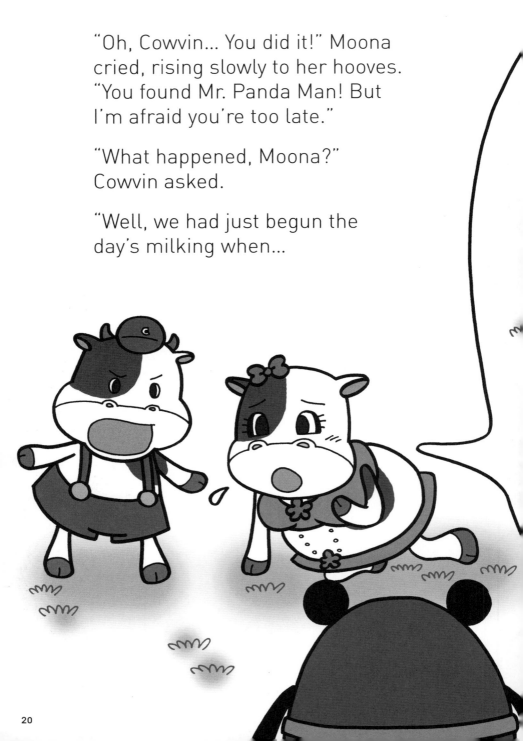

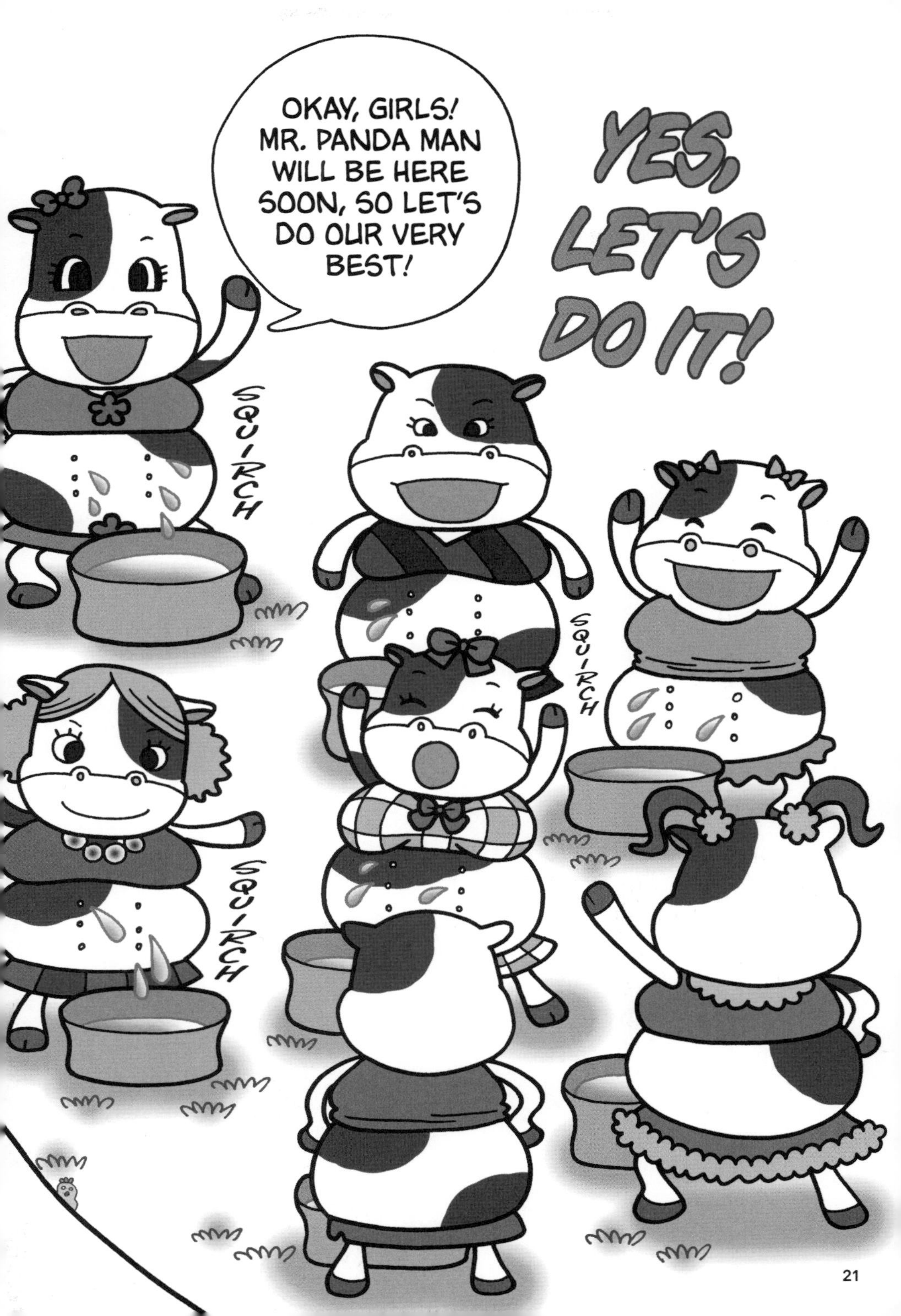

YES, LET'S DO IT!
OKAY, GIRLS! MR. PANDA MAN WILL BE HERE SOON, SO LET'S DO OUR VERY BEST!
SQUIRCH
SQUIRCH
SQUIRCH

...those awful thieves showed up!"

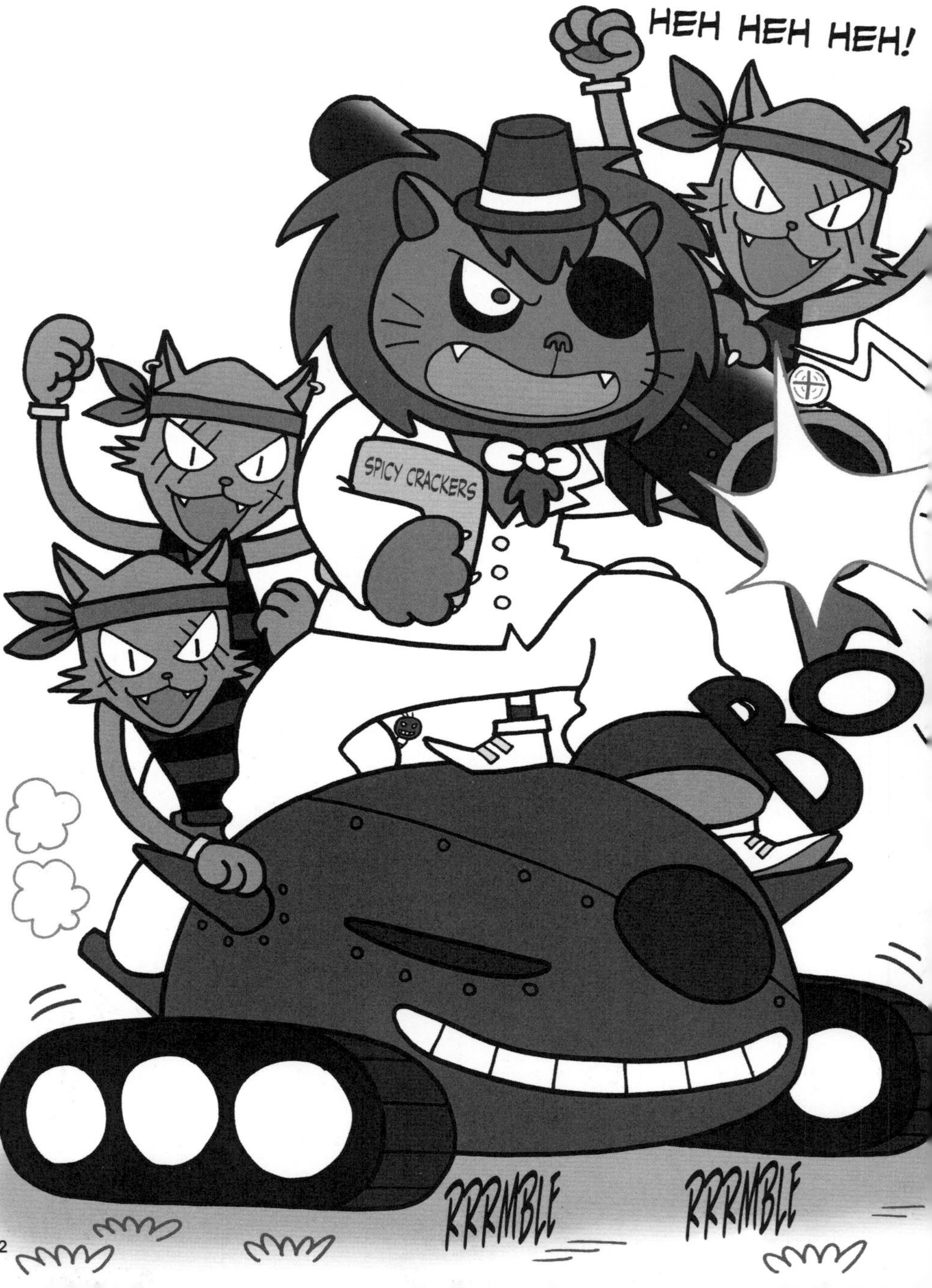
HEH HEH HEH!
SPICY CRACKERS
BO
RRRMBLE
RRRMBLE

Moona explained that the chief thief was a spicy-food-loving lion named Leo Pepperpot.

"He attacked us with seasoning!" Moona cried.

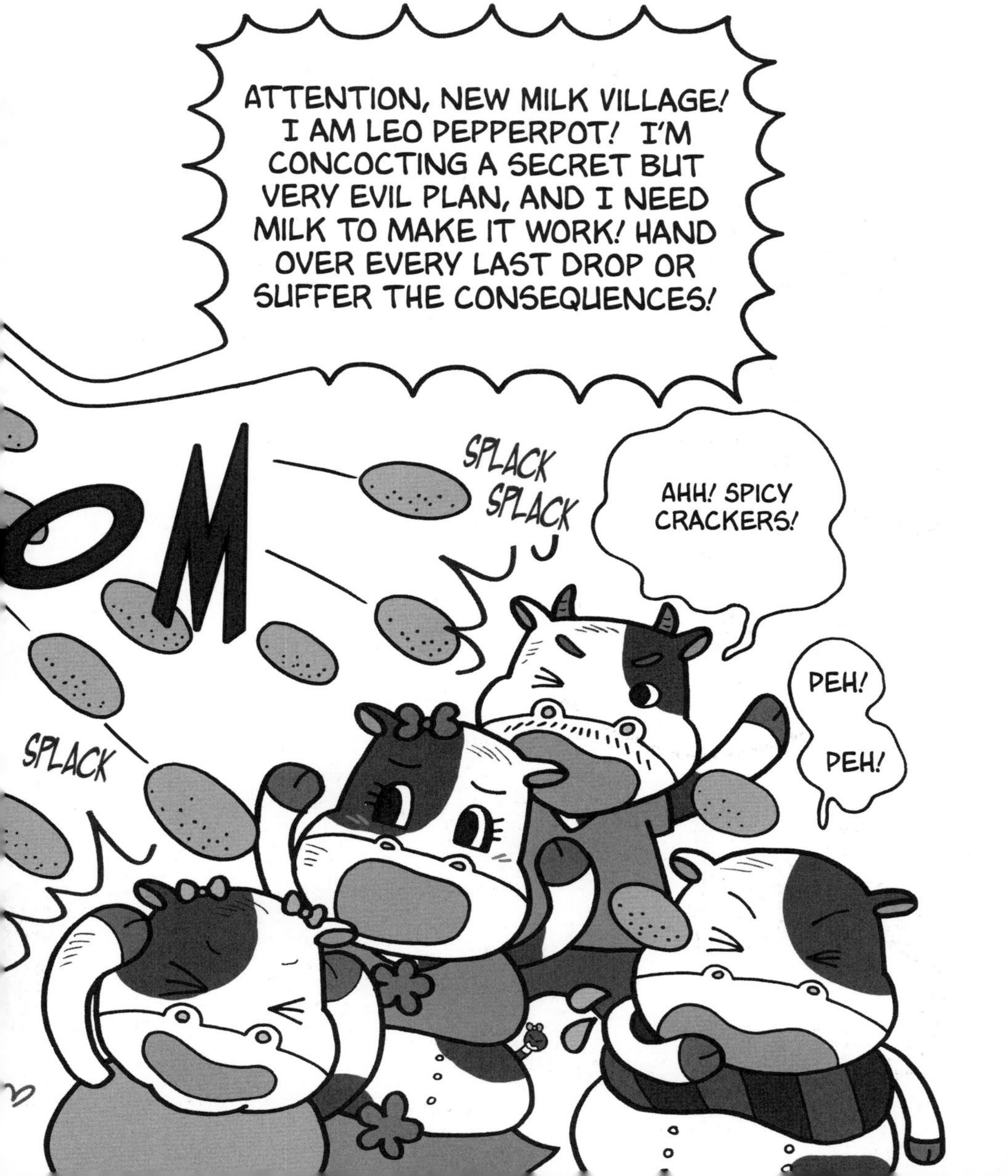
ATTENTION, NEW MILK VILLAGE! I AM LEO PEPPERPOT! I'M CONCOCTING A SECRET BUT VERY EVIL PLAN, AND I NEED MILK TO MAKE IT WORK! HAND OVER EVERY LAST DROP OR SUFFER THE CONSEQUENCES!
PEH!
PEH!
AHH! SPICY CRACKERS!
SPLACK
SPLACK
SPLACK

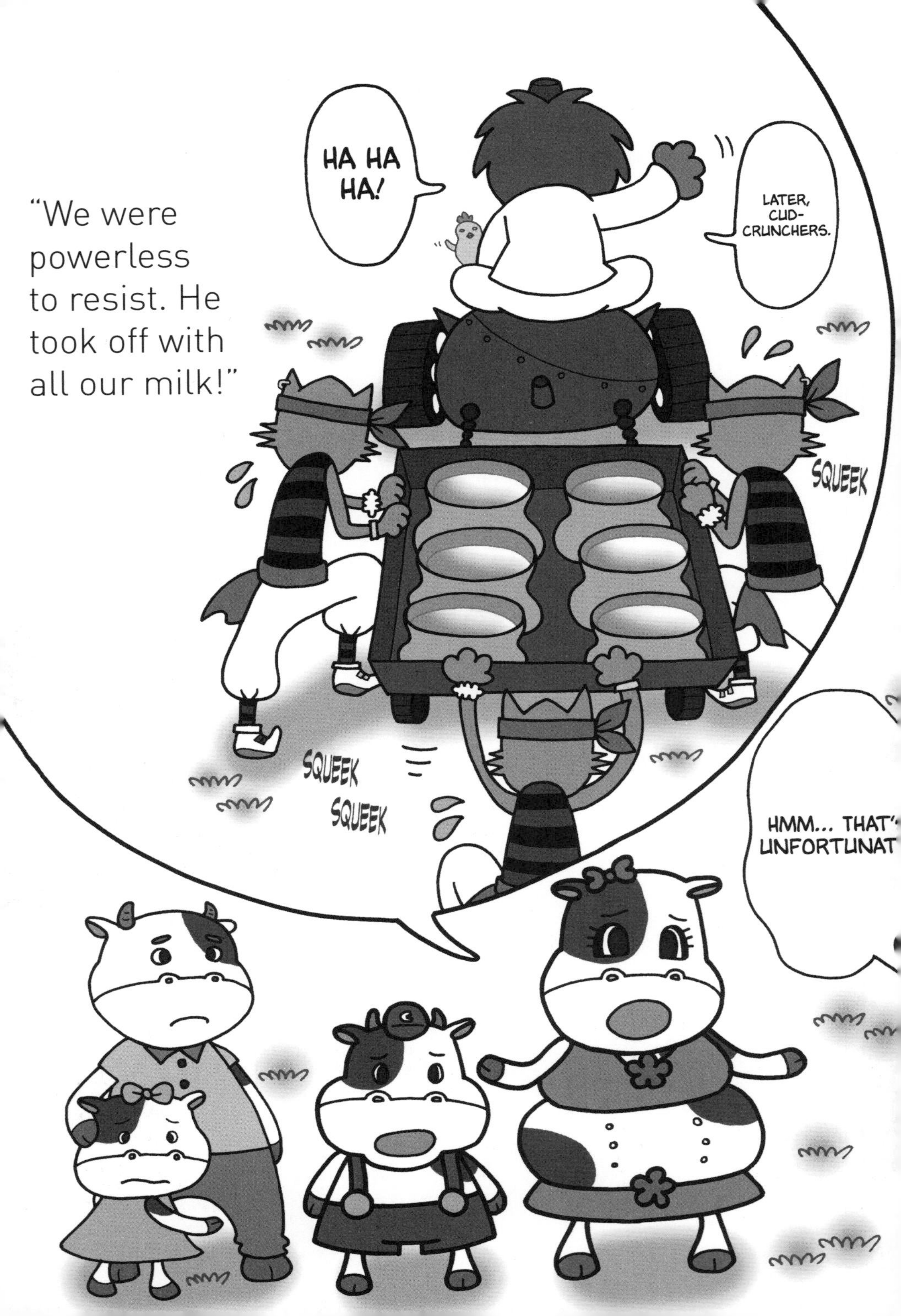
"We were powerless to resist. He took off with all our milk!"
HA HA HA!
LATER, CUD-CRUNCHERS.
SQUEEK
SQUEEK
SQUEEK
SQUEEK
HMM... THAT'
UNFORTUNAT

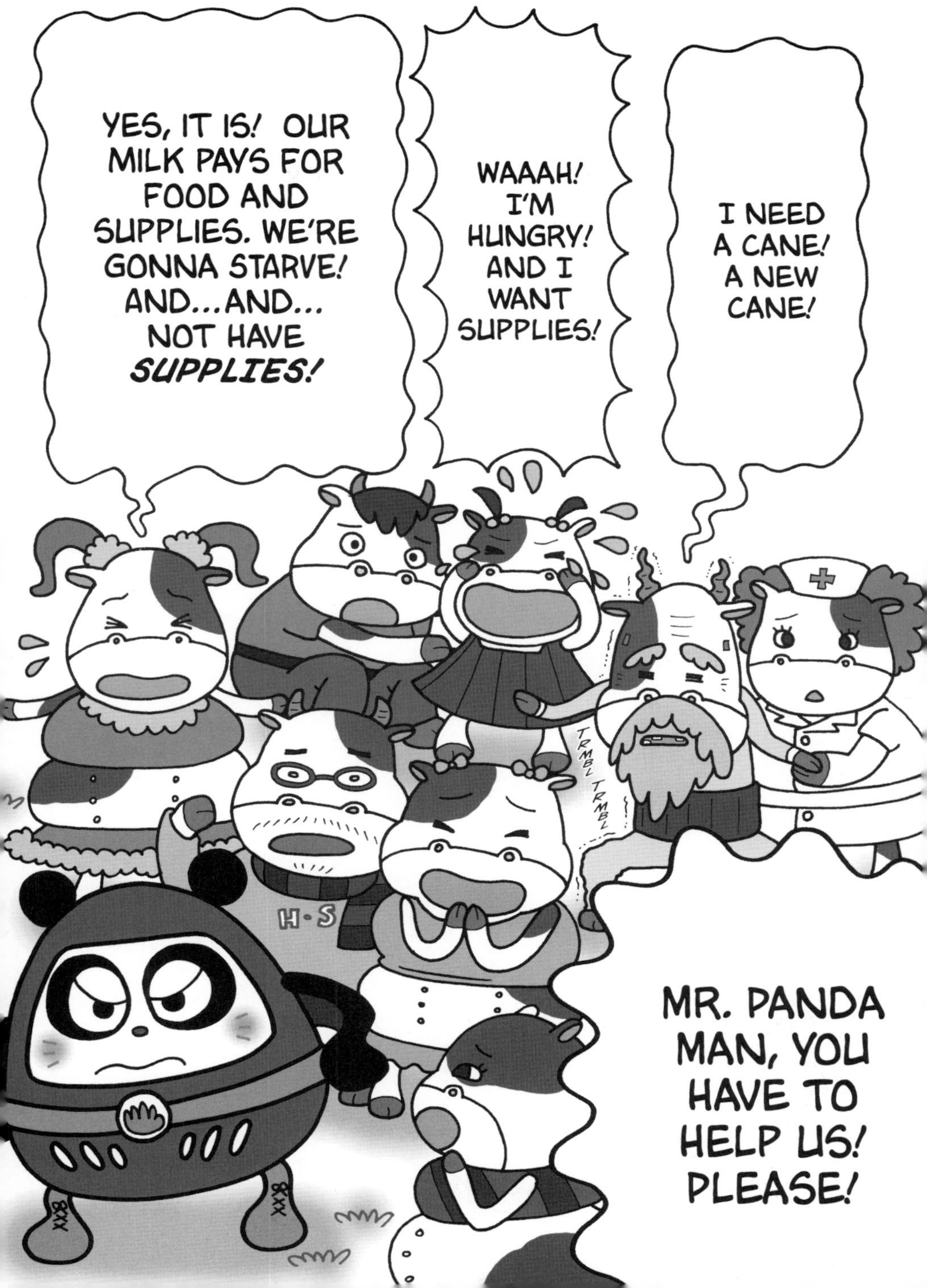
I NEED A CANE! A NEW CANE!
WAAAH! I'M HUNGRY! AND I WANT SUPPLIES!
YES, IT IS! OUR MILK PAYS FOR FOOD AND SUPPLIES. WE'RE GONNA STARVE! AND...AND... NOT HAVE SUPPLIES!
TRMBL TRMBL
H·S
MR. PANDA MAN, YOU HAVE TO HELP US! PLEASE!

"All right, all right already," Panda Man said. "I'm here, so you have nothing to fear. But before I do anything, I must have a taste of the world's yummiest butter cake!"

Just thinking about the cake made Panda Man drool.

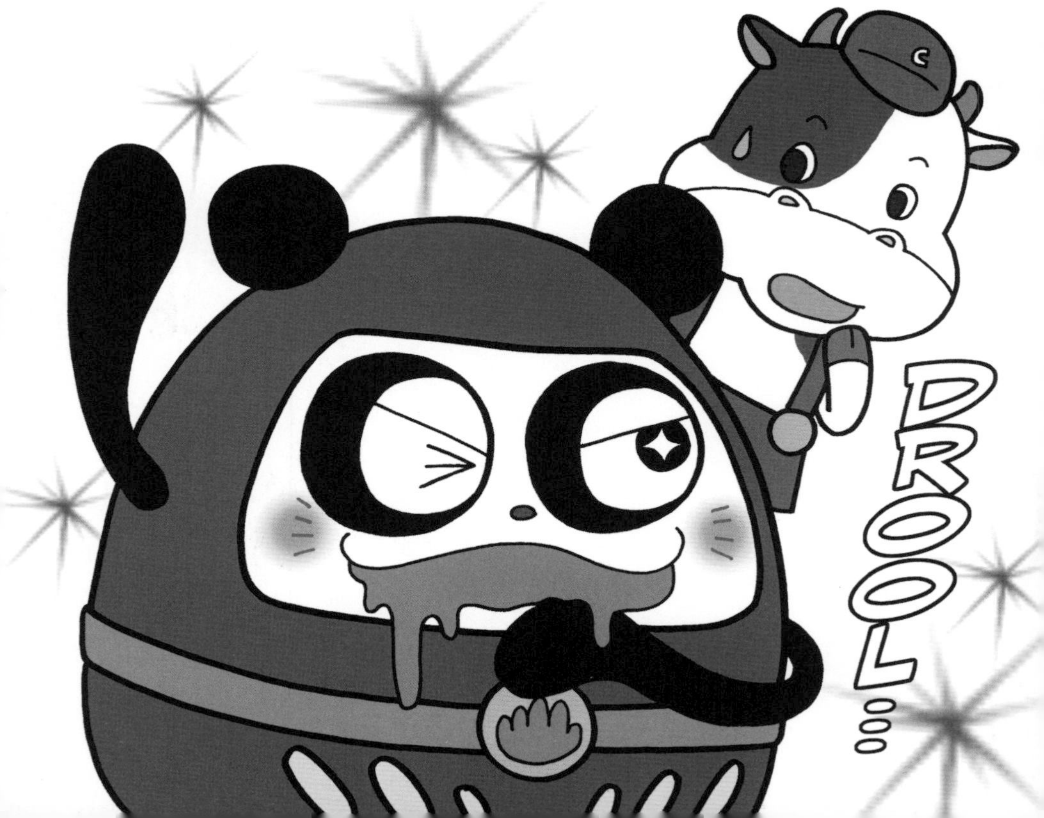
DROOL...

"B...butter cake...?" Moona gasped. "But, Mr. Panda Man, butter is made with cream. And since Leo Pepperpot has taken all of our milk..."

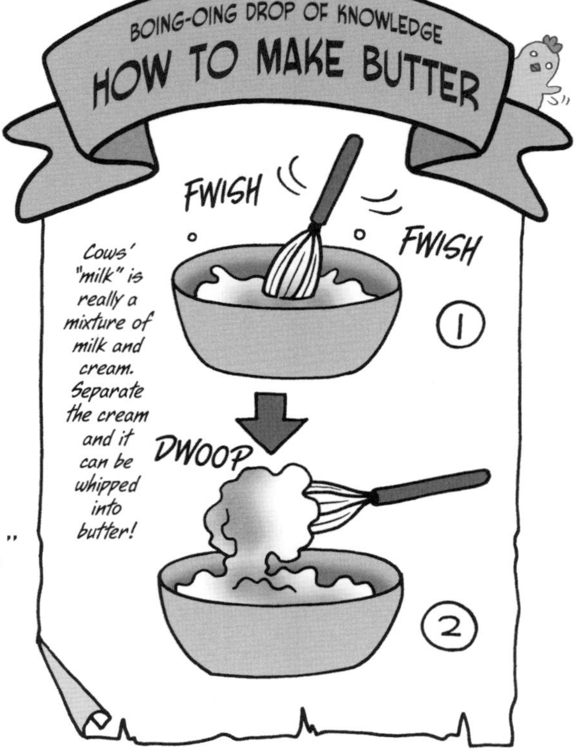
BOING-OING DROP OF KNOWLEDGE
HOW TO MAKE BUTTER
FWISH
FWISH
Cows' "milk" is really a mixture of milk and cream. Separate the cream and it can be whipped into butter!
1
DWOOP
2

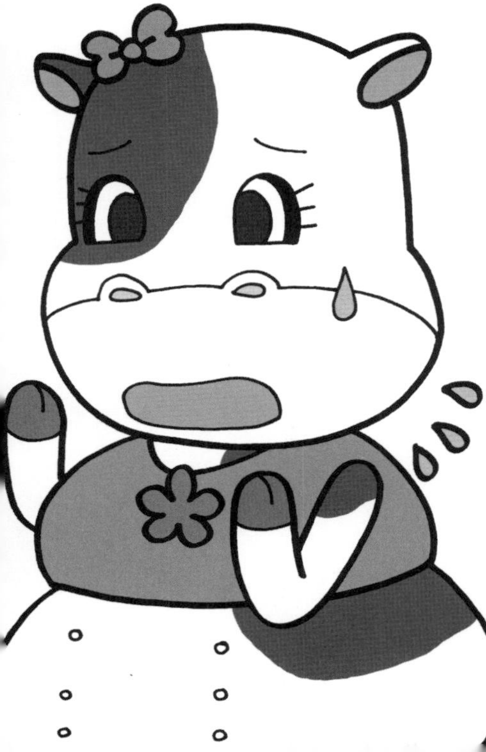

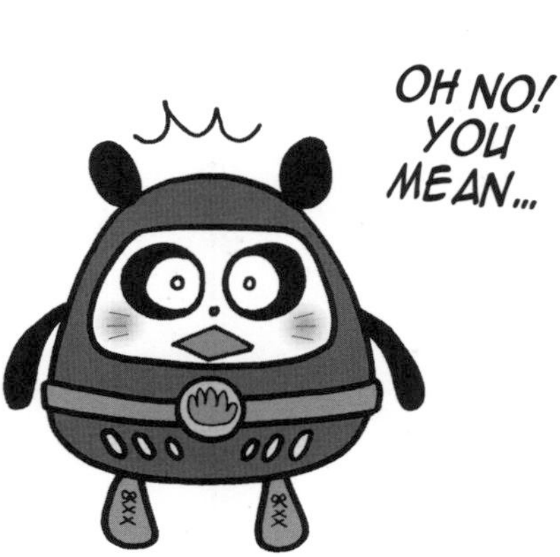
OH NO! YOU MEAN...

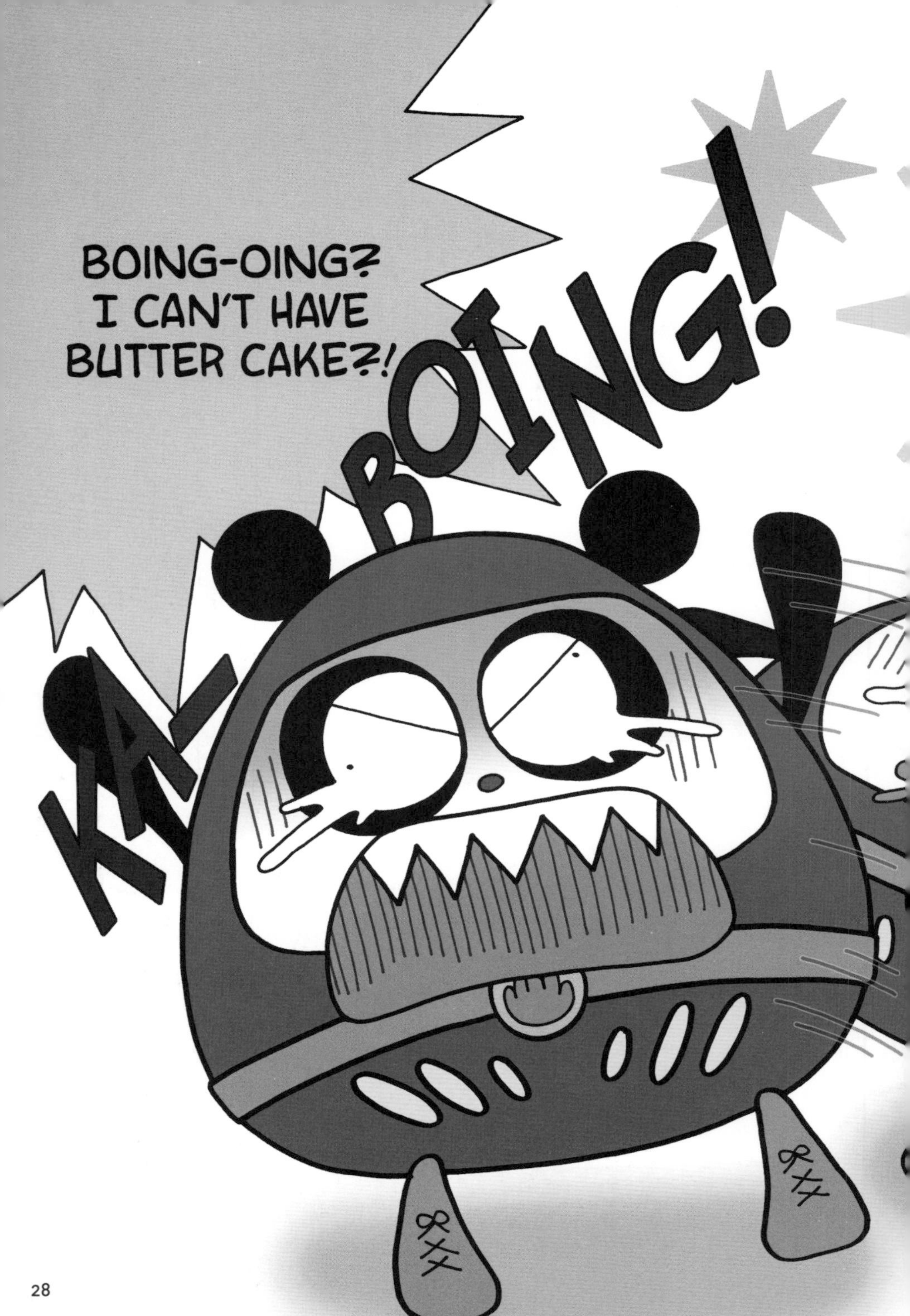
BOING-OING?
I CAN'T HAVE
BUTTER CAKE?!
KA-BOING!

Poor Panda Man. This was more than he could bear.

The shock made him dizzy. His eyes went blank, and he fell to the ground.

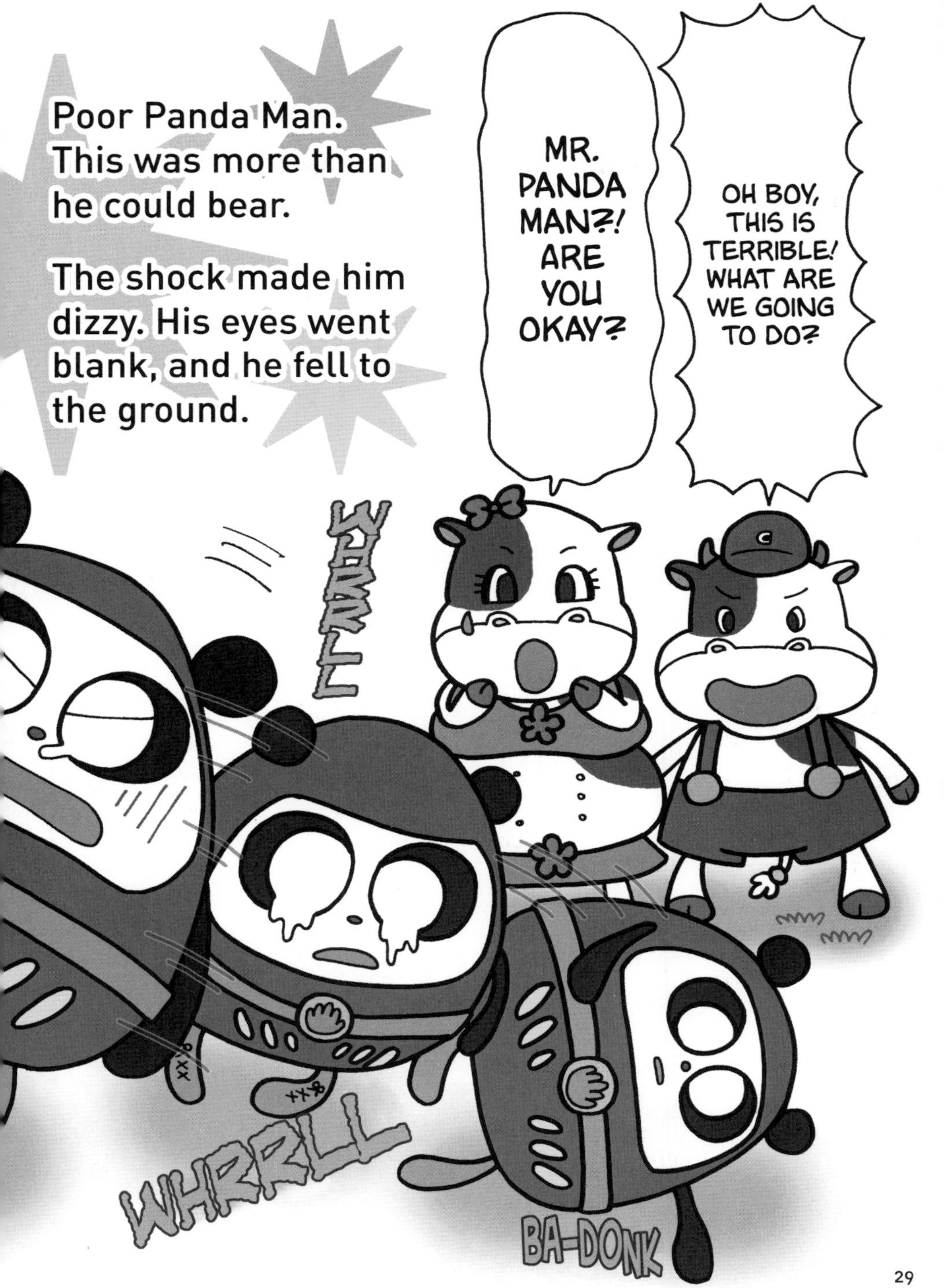
MR. PANDA MAN?! ARE YOU OKAY?
OH BOY, THIS IS TERRIBLE! WHAT ARE WE GOING TO DO?
WHRRLL
WHRRLL
BA-DONK

Thinking quickly, Cowvin pulled the *Really Big Book of Heroes* out of his pocket and read aloud:

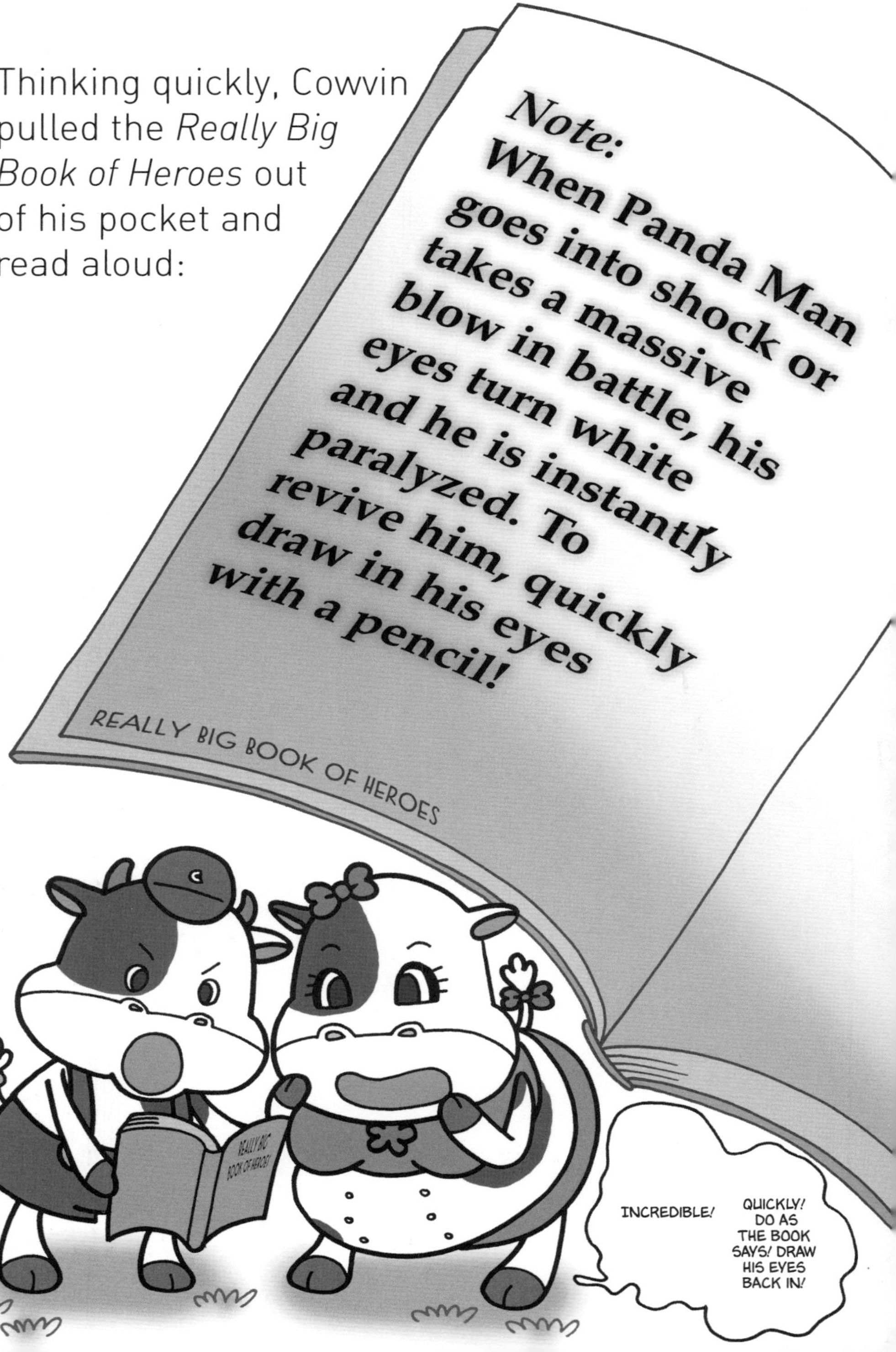
Note:
When Panda Man goes into shock or takes a massive blow in battle, his eyes turn white and he is instantly paralyzed. To revive him, quickly draw in his eyes with a pencil!
REALLY BIG BOOK OF HEROES
REALLY BIG BOOK OF HEROS!
QUICKLY! DO AS THE BOOK SAYS! DRAW HIS EYES BACK IN!
INCREDIBLE!

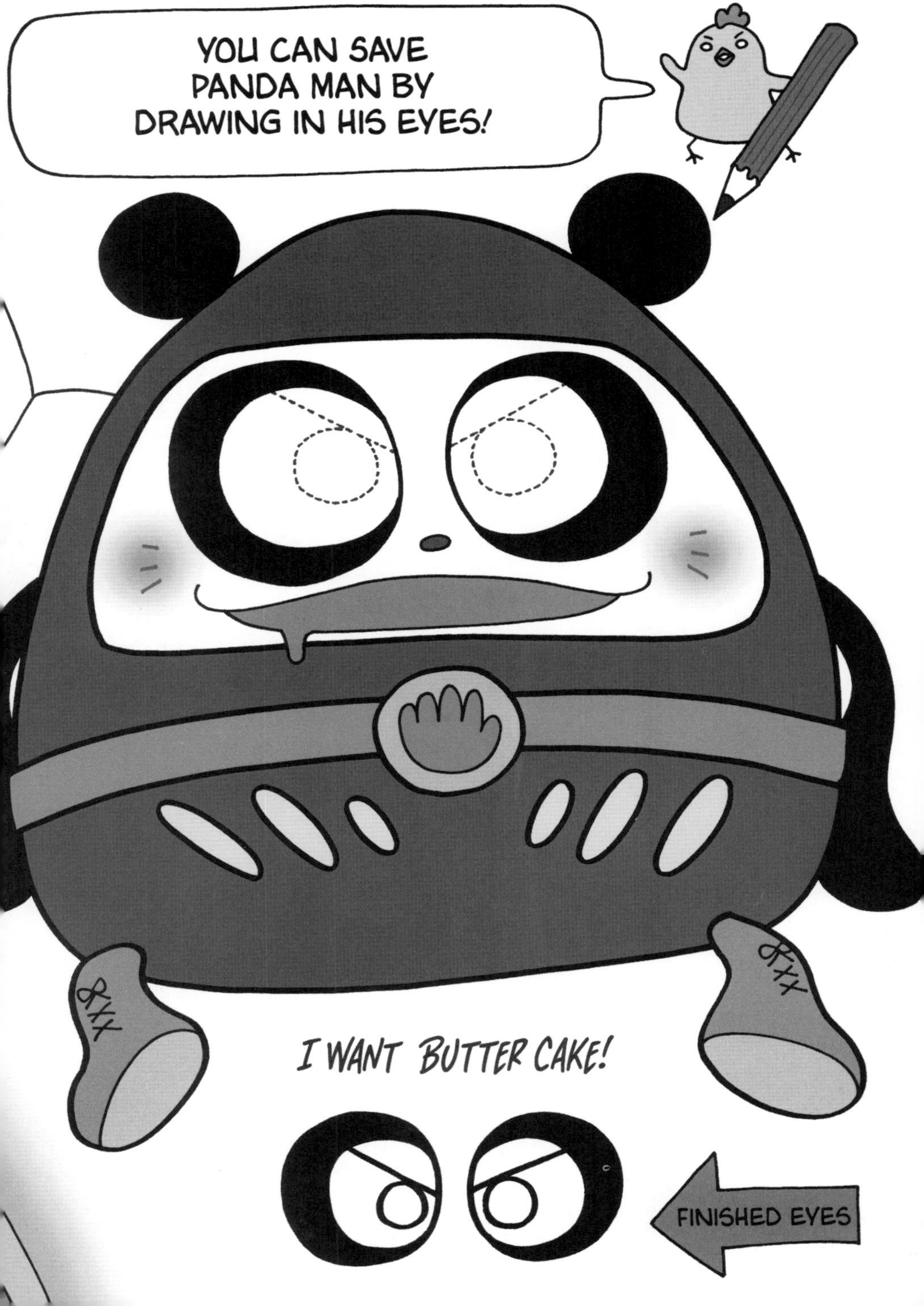
YOU CAN SAVE PANDA MAN BY DRAWING IN HIS EYES!
I WANT BUTTER CAKE!
FINISHED EYES

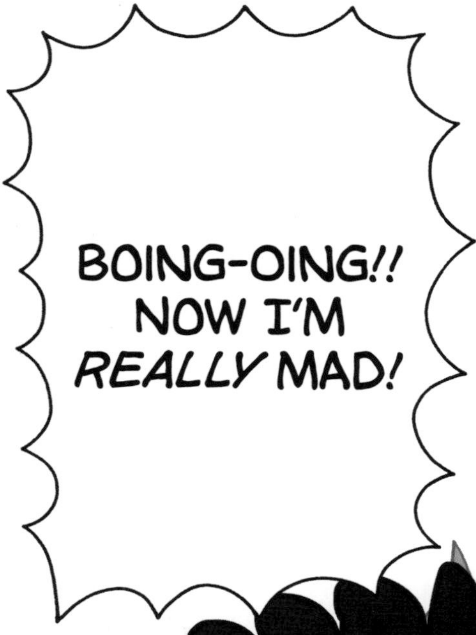
BOING-OING!! NOW I'M *REALLY* MAD!

As Panda Man sprang to attention, his eyes burned with rage. Rage over the butter cake, mind you, not the great injustice that the villagers had suffered.

But...let's just keep that to ourselves.

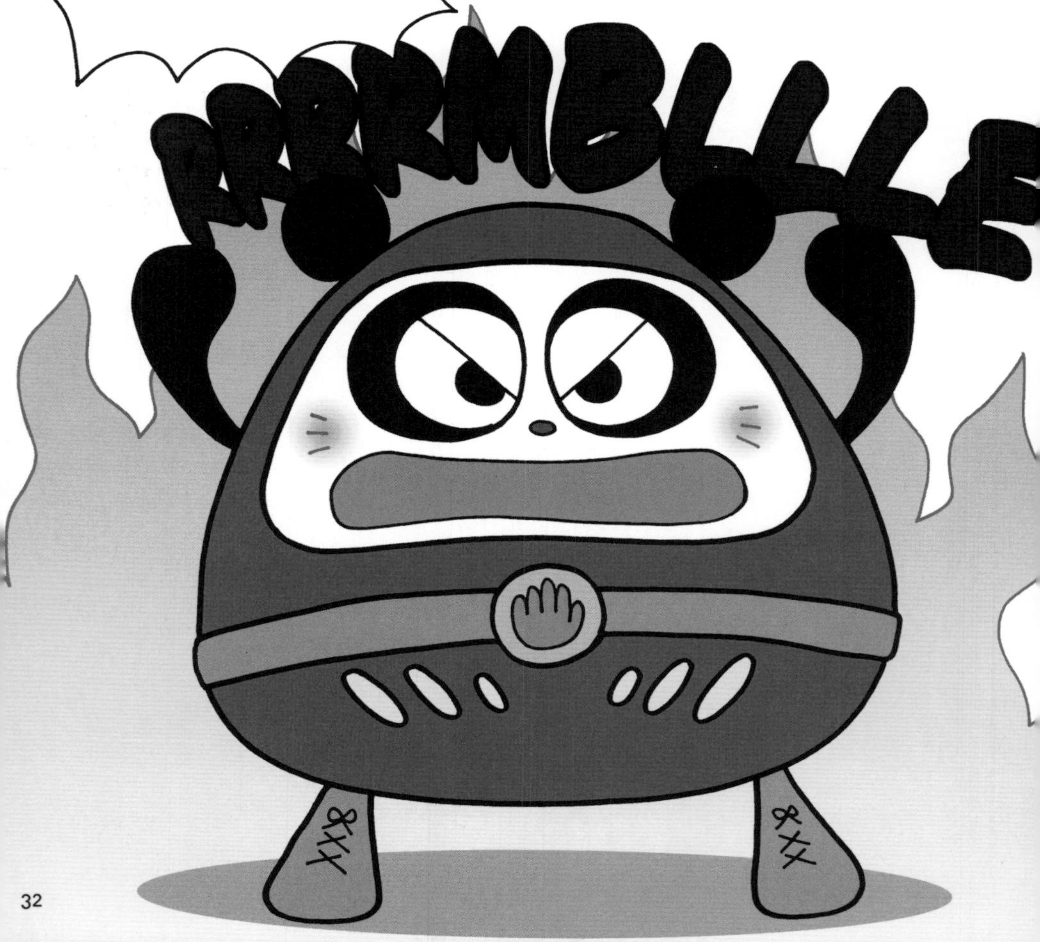
RRRMBLLLE

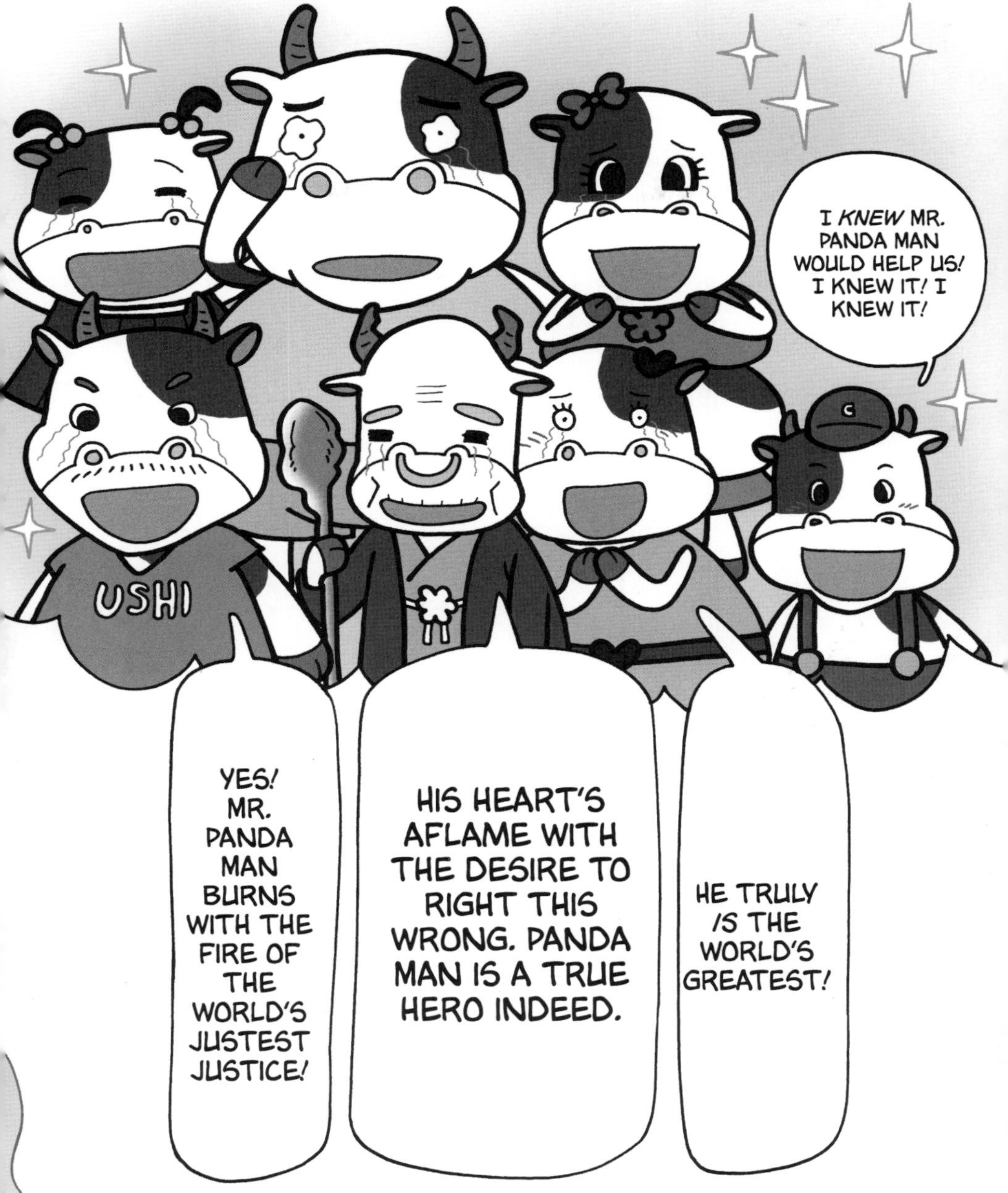
I KNEW MR. PANDA MAN WOULD HELP US! I KNEW IT! I KNEW IT!
HE TRULY IS THE WORLD'S GREATEST!
HIS HEART'S AFLAME WITH THE DESIRE TO RIGHT THIS WRONG. PANDA MAN IS A TRUE HERO INDEED.
YES! MR. PANDA MAN BURNS WITH THE FIRE OF THE WORLD'S JUSTEST JUSTICE!
USHI

Panda Man's passion moved the villagers to tears.

With the hope of the whole village behind him–and the promise of butter cake in front of him–Panda Man went off in search of the thieves.

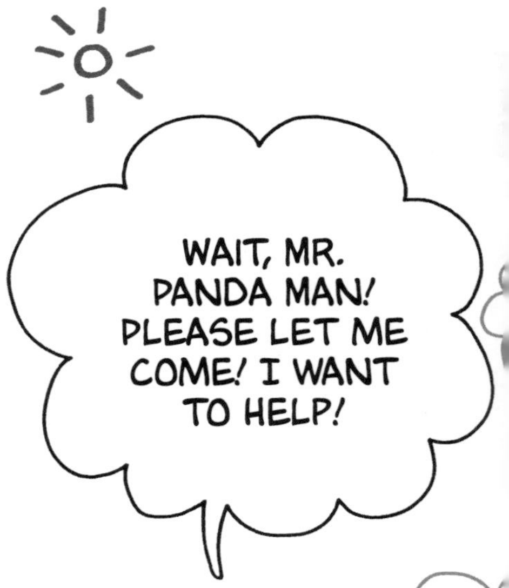
WAIT, MR. PANDA MAN! PLEASE LET ME COME! I WANT TO HELP!

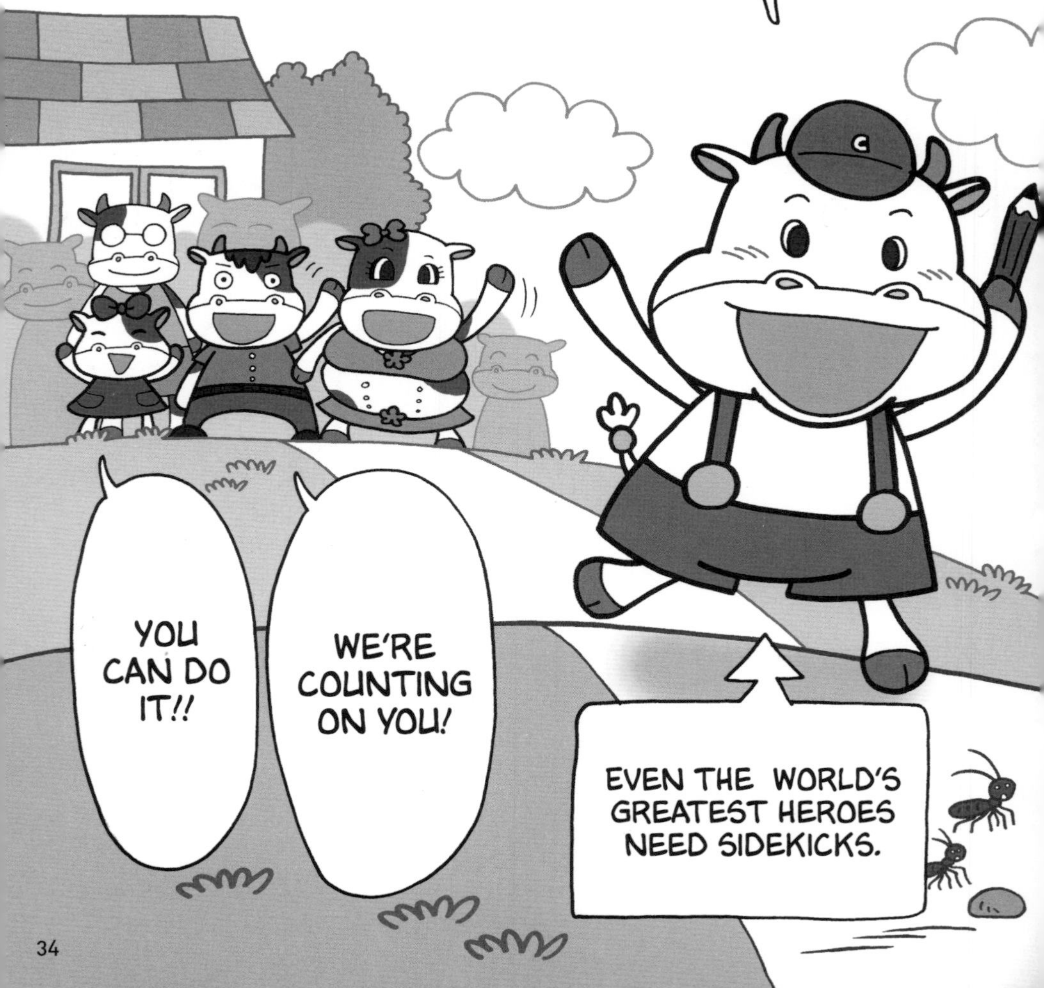
YOU CAN DO IT!!
WE'RE COUNTING ON YOU!
EVEN THE WORLD'S GREATEST HEROES NEED SIDEKICKS.

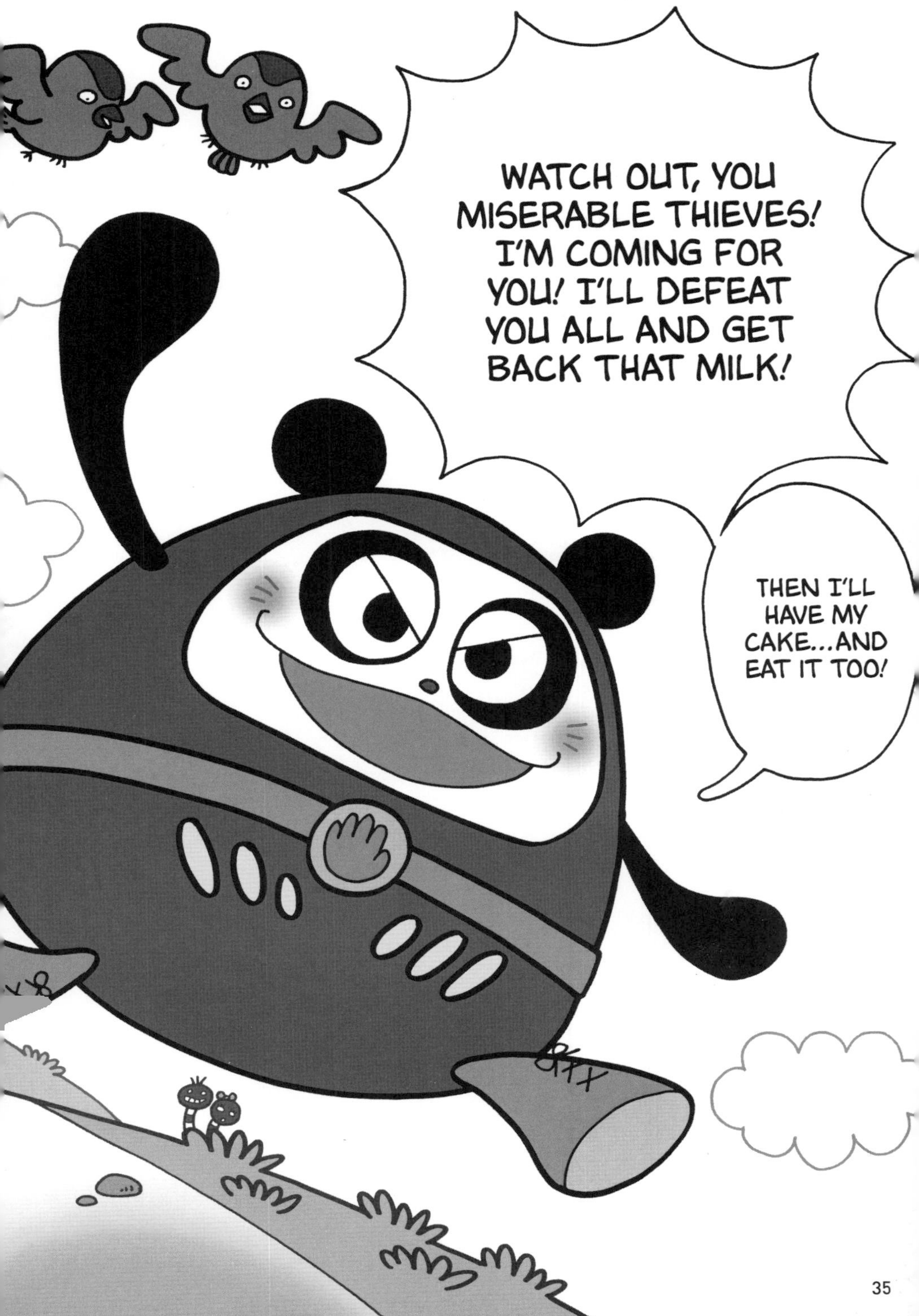
WATCH OUT, YOU MISERABLE THIEVES! I'M COMING FOR YOU! I'LL DEFEAT YOU ALL AND GET BACK THAT MILK!
THEN I'LL HAVE MY CAKE...AND EAT IT TOO!

A moment later, Panda Man was extremely bored. To pass the time, he told himself a story.

Use these images to create a story of your own!

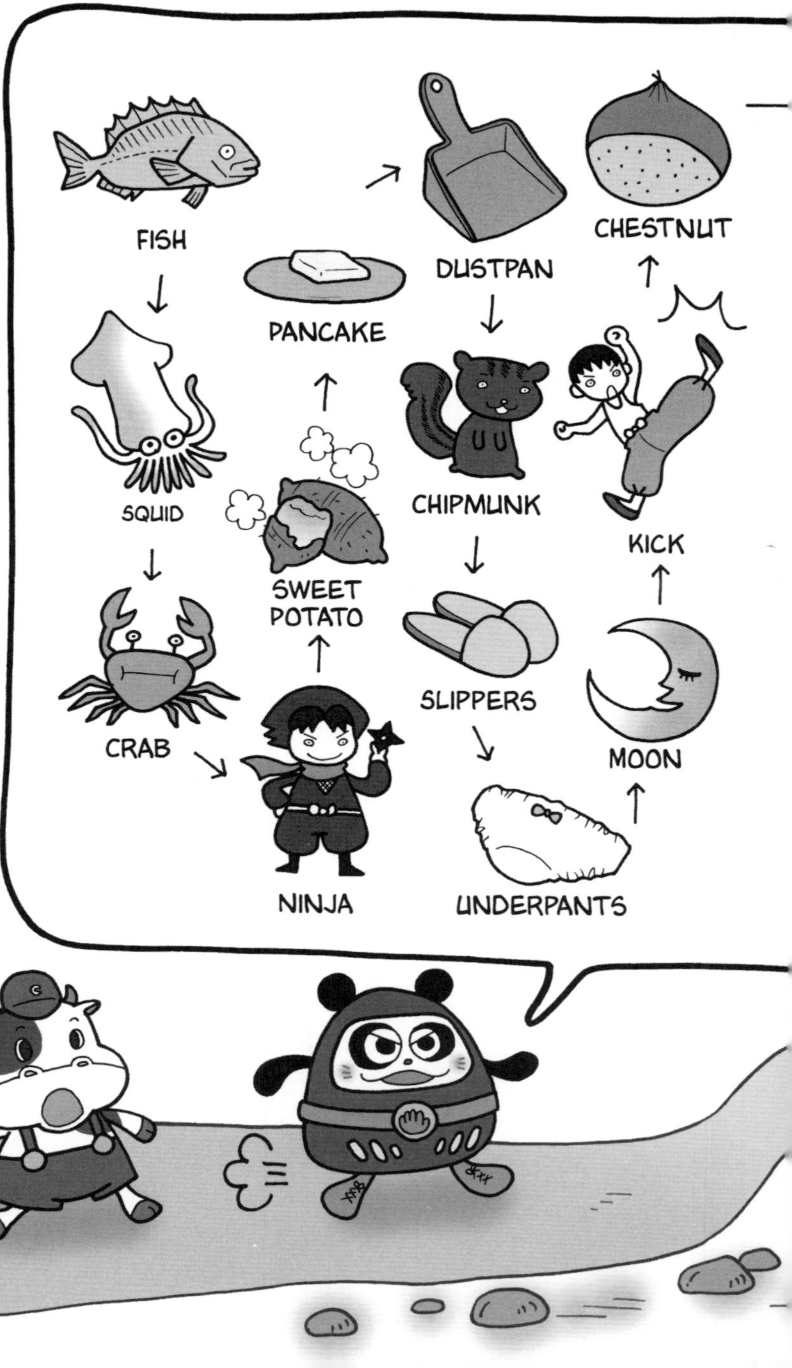
FISH
SQUID
CRAB
NINJA
SWEET POTATO
PANCAKE
DUSTPAN
CHIPMUNK
SLIPPERS
UNDERPANTS
MOON
KICK
CHESTNUT

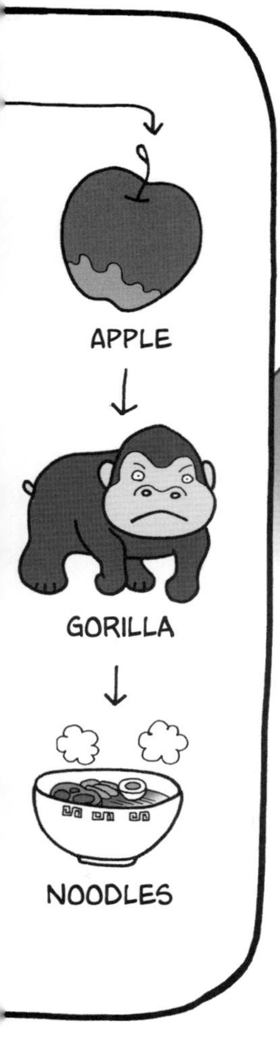
APPLE
GORILLA
NOODLES

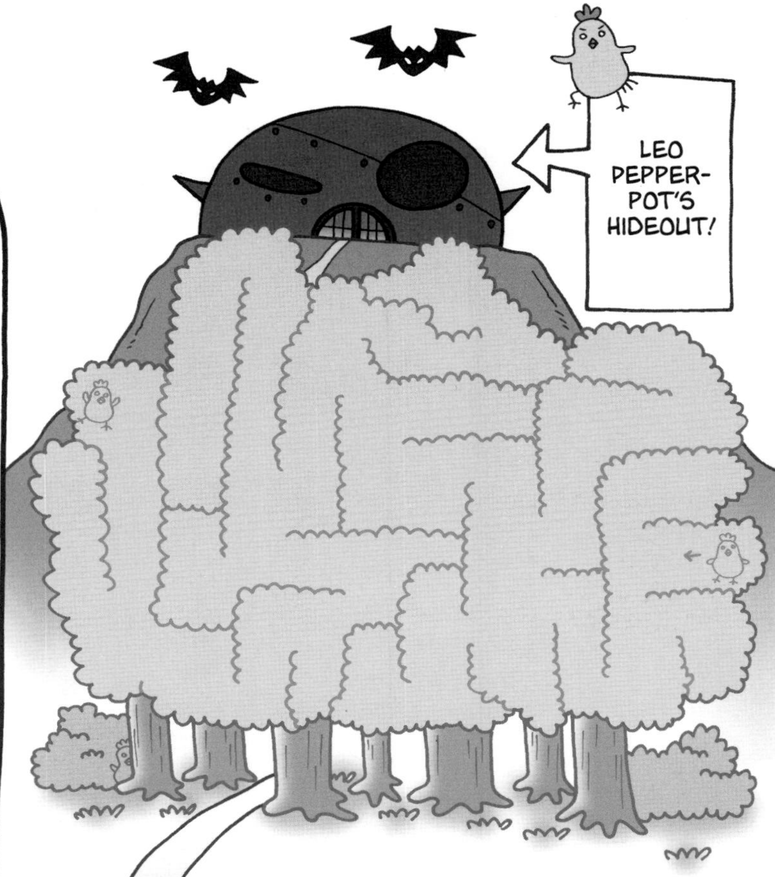
LEO PEPPER-POT'S HIDEOUT!

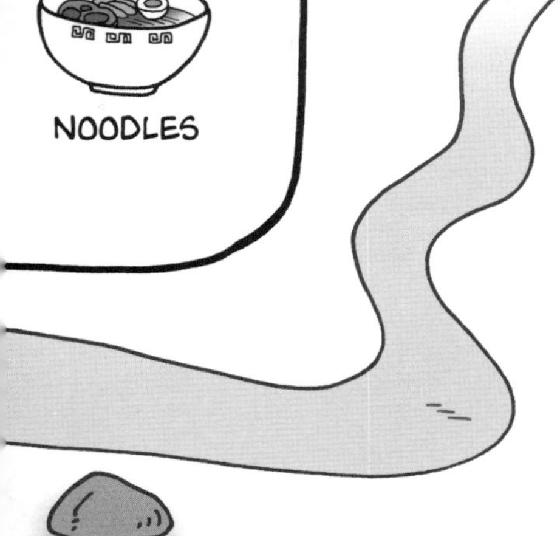

Soon Leo Pepperpot's hideout loomed in the distance.

And inside Leo Pepperpot's den, Panda Man was being watched.

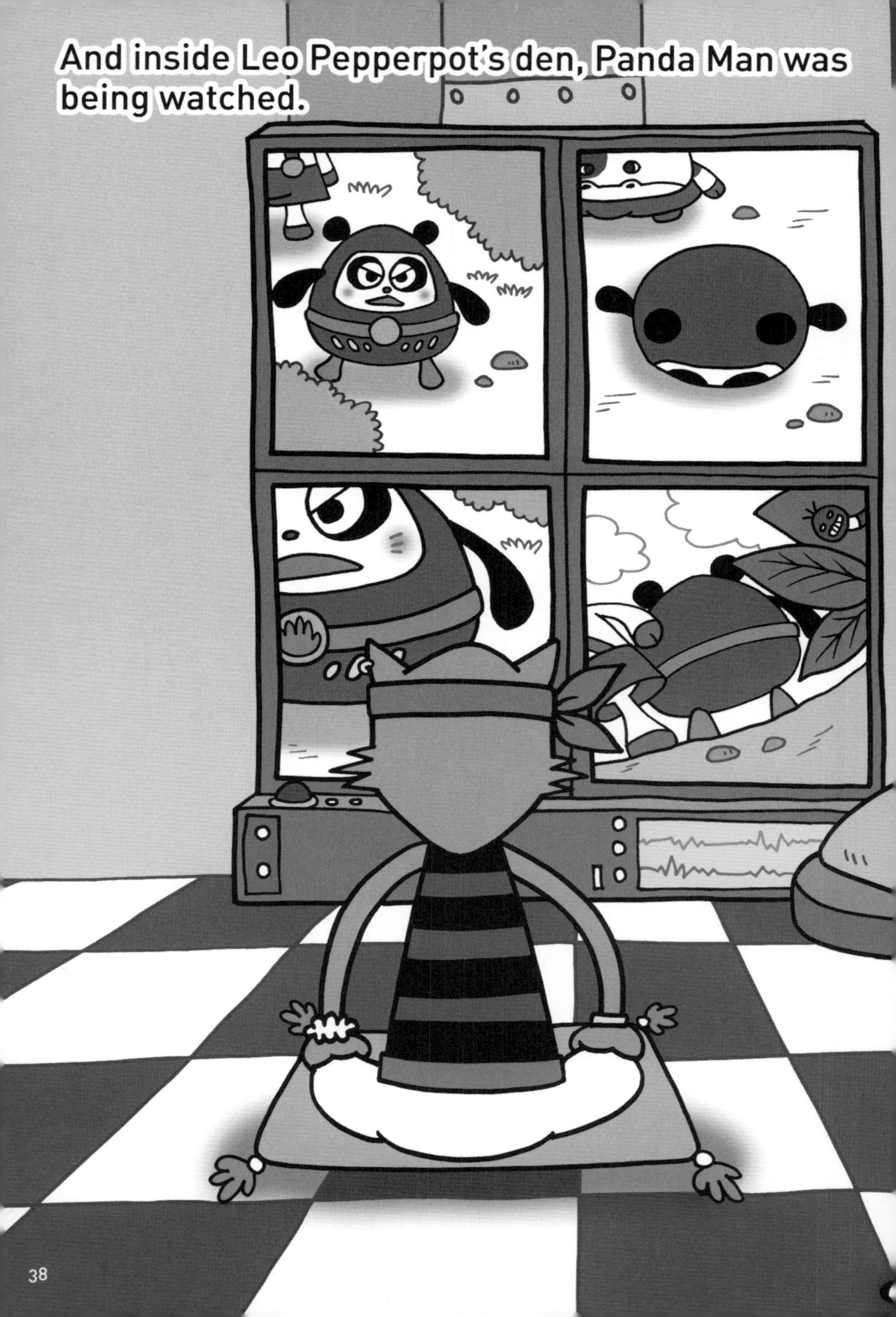

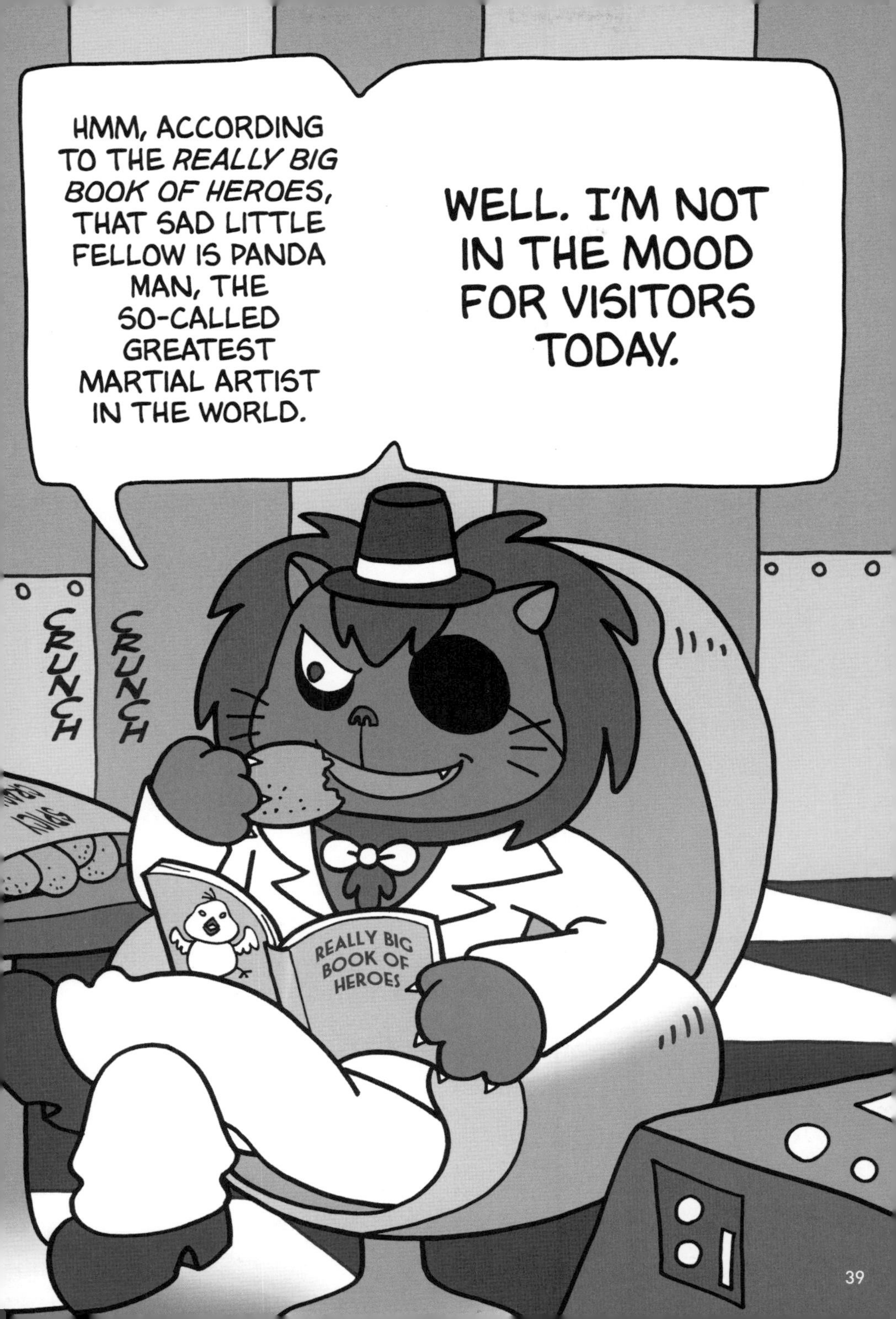
HMM, ACCORDING TO THE *REALLY BIG BOOK OF HEROES*, THAT SAD LITTLE FELLOW IS PANDA MAN, THE SO-CALLED GREATEST MARTIAL ARTIST IN THE WORLD.
WELL. I'M NOT IN THE MOOD FOR VISITORS TODAY.
CRUNCH
CRUNCH
REALLY BIG BOOK OF HEROES

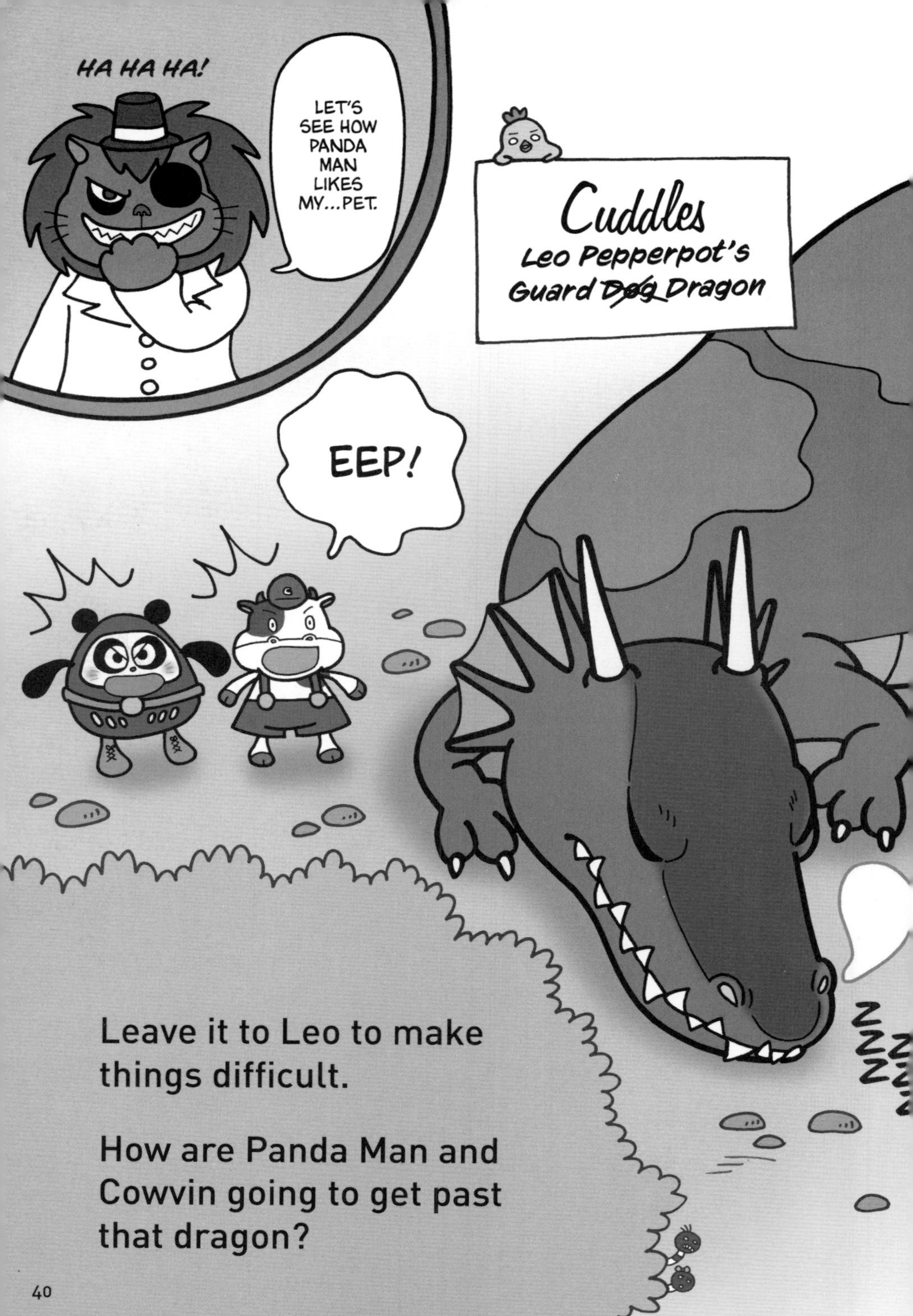
HA HA HA!
LET'S SEE HOW PANDA MAN LIKES MY...PET.
Cuddles
Leo Pepperpot's
Guard ~~Dog~~ Dragon
EEP!
ZZZZ

Leave it to Leo to make things difficult.

How are Panda Man and Cowvin going to get past that dragon?

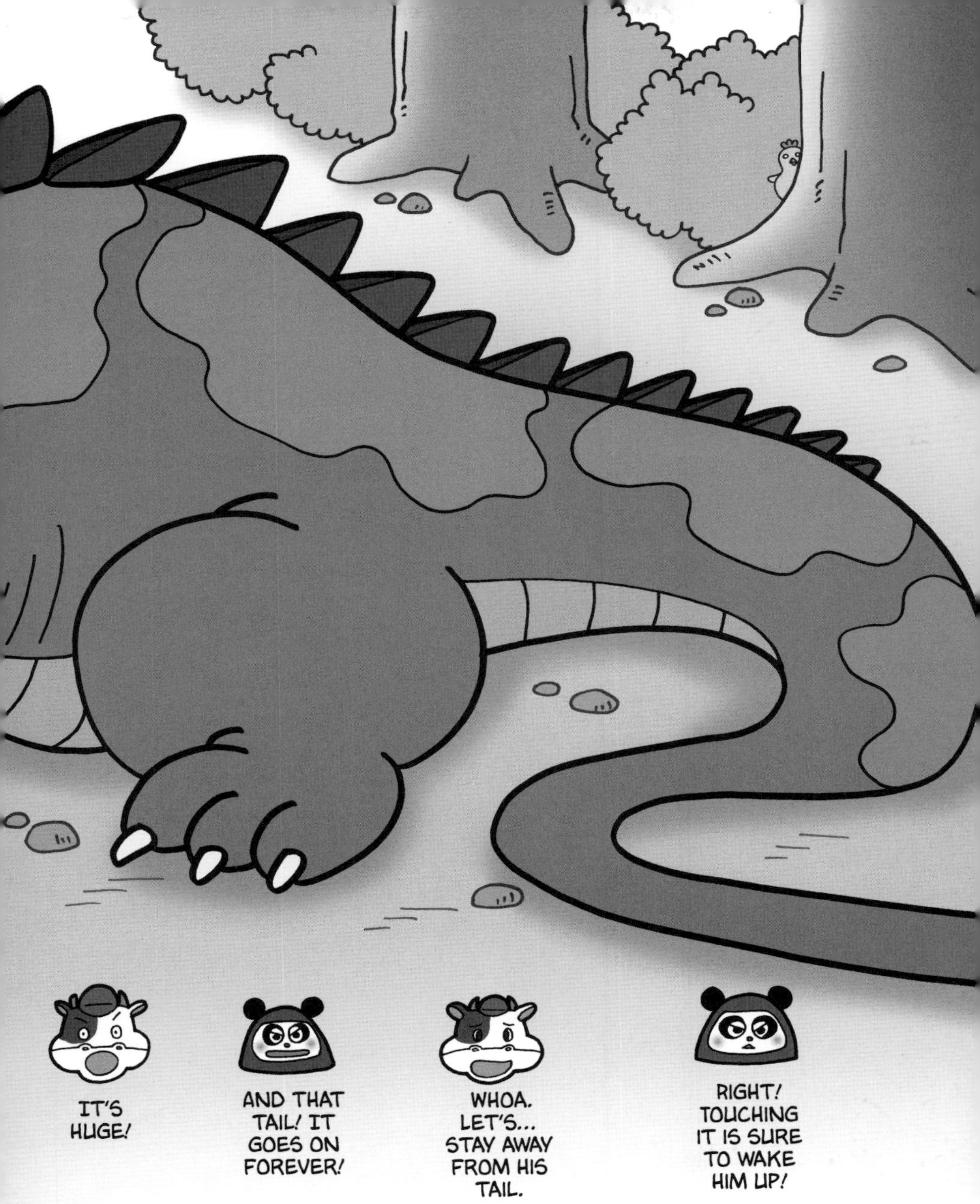
IT'S HUGE!
AND THAT TAIL! IT GOES ON FOREVER!
WHOA. LET'S... STAY AWAY FROM HIS TAIL.
RIGHT! TOUCHING IT IS SURE TO WAKE HIM UP!

It's up to you!

Help Panda Man get past Cuddles without waking him. You can go through tunnels and over bridges, but don't touch that tail!

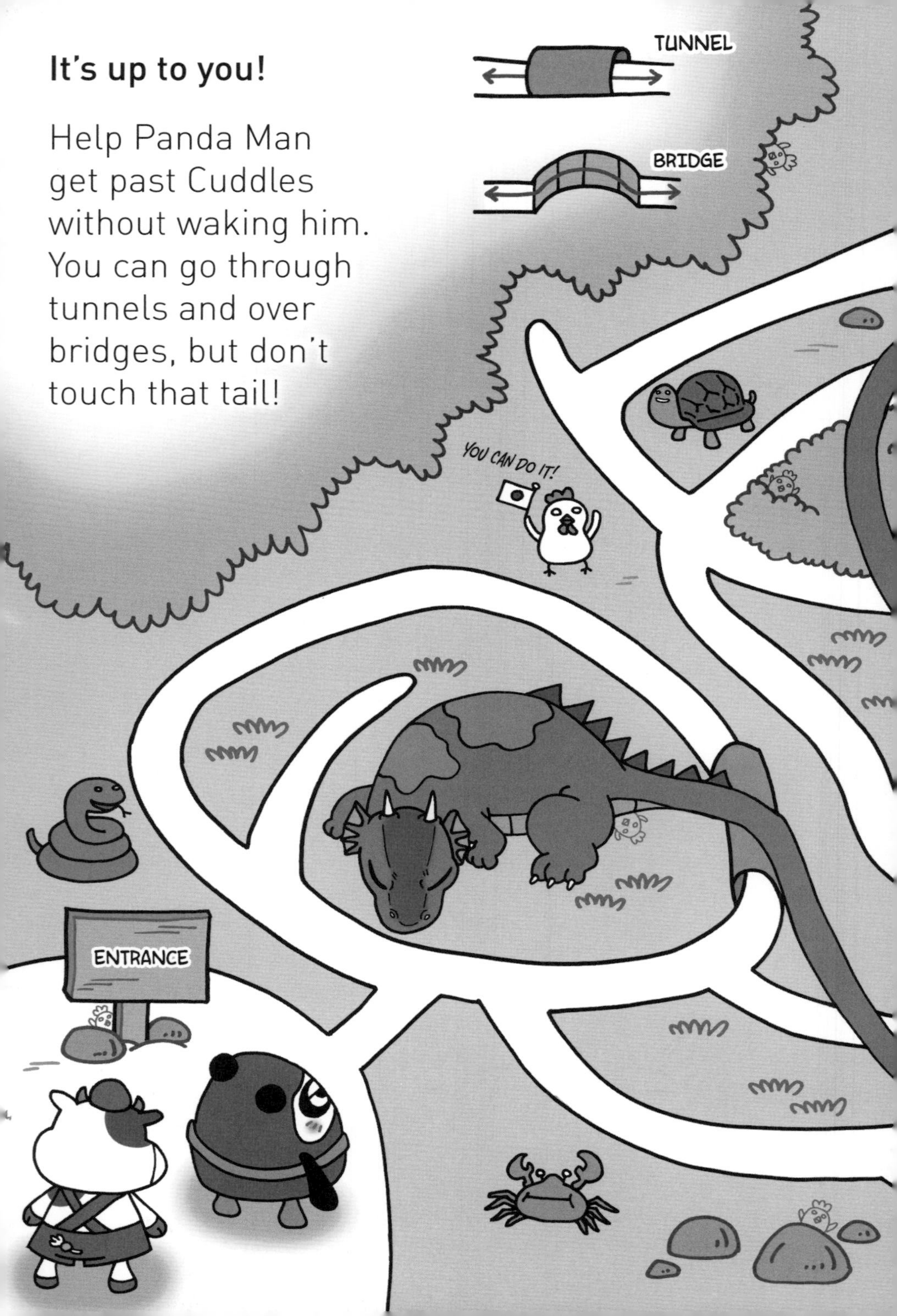
TUNNEL
BRIDGE
YOU CAN DO IT!
ENTRANCE

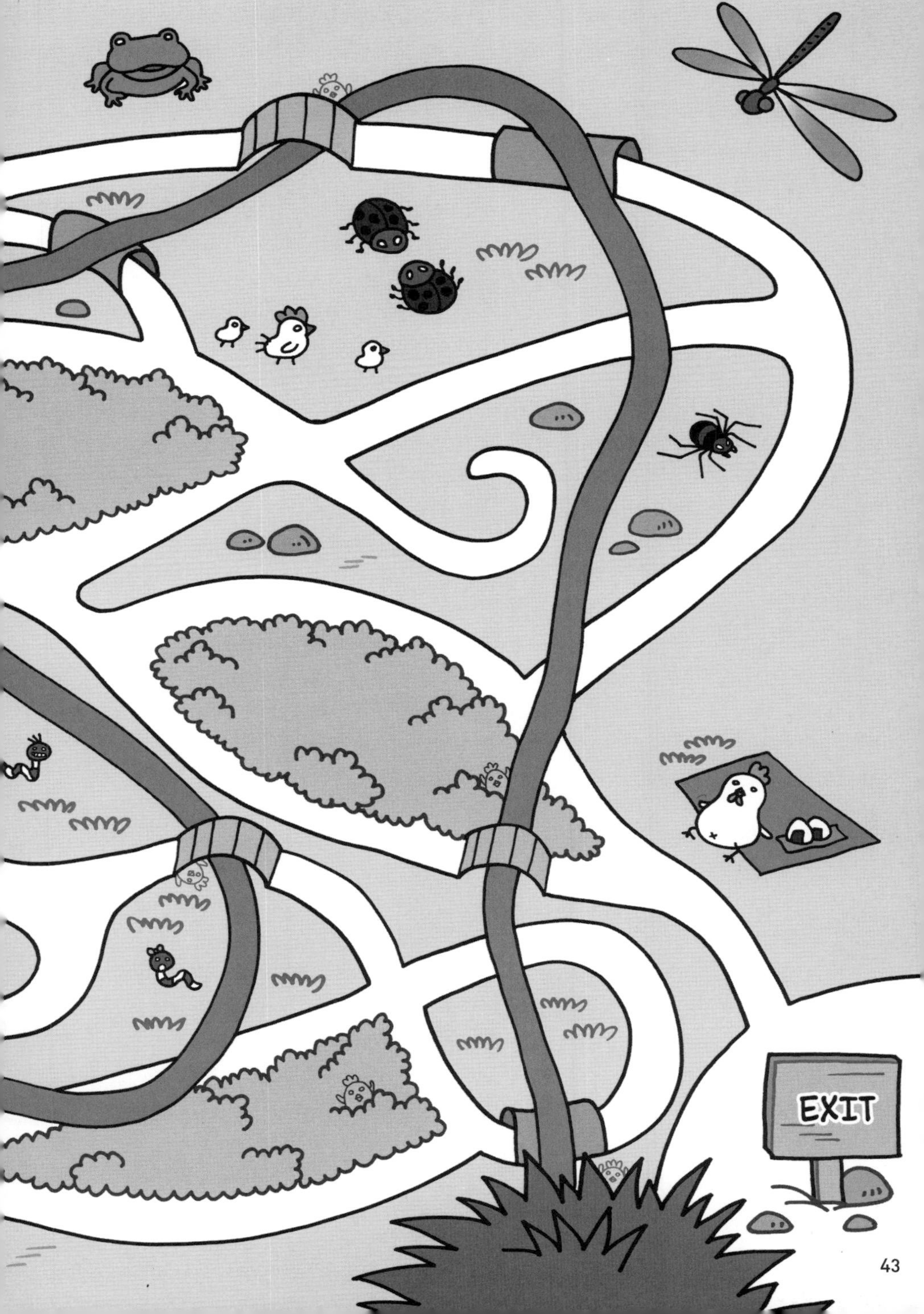
EXIT

Just when they thought they were safer, the world's most unlucky thing happened.

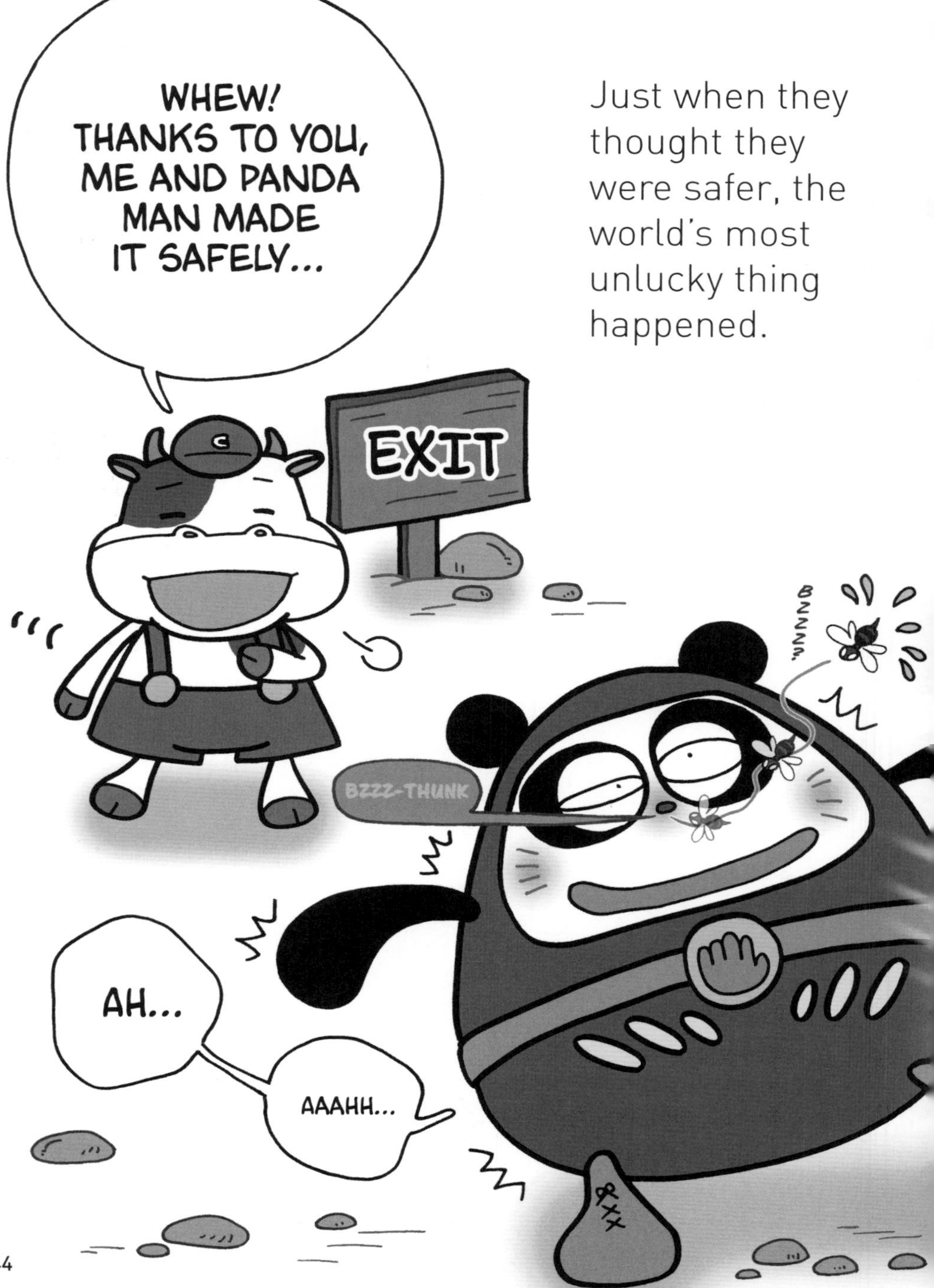
WHEW! THANKS TO YOU, ME AND PANDA MAN MADE IT SAFELY...
EXIT
BZZZ-THUNK
AH...
AAAHH...

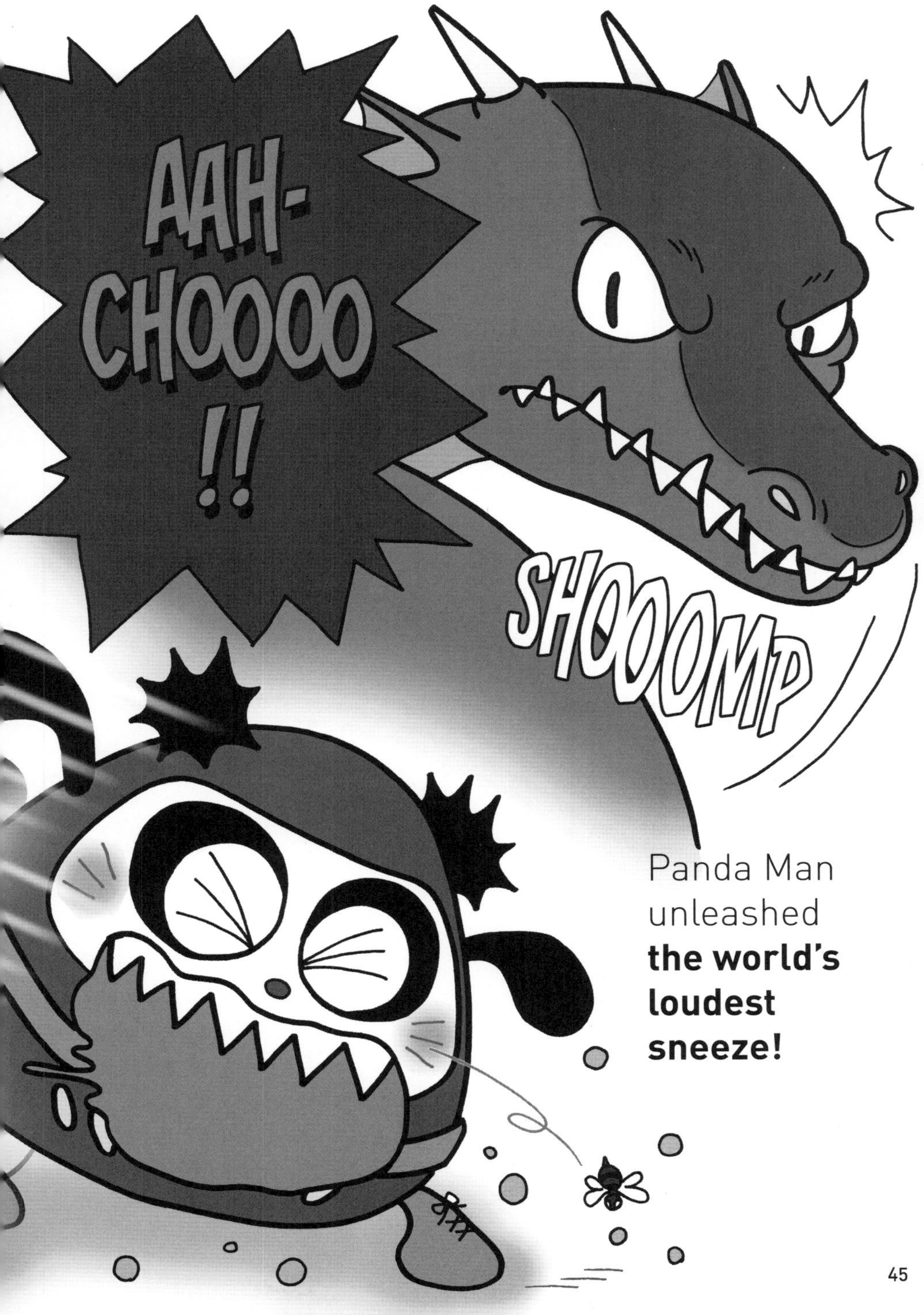
AAH-
CHOOOO
!!
SHOOOOMP

Panda Man unleashed **the world's loudest sneeze!**

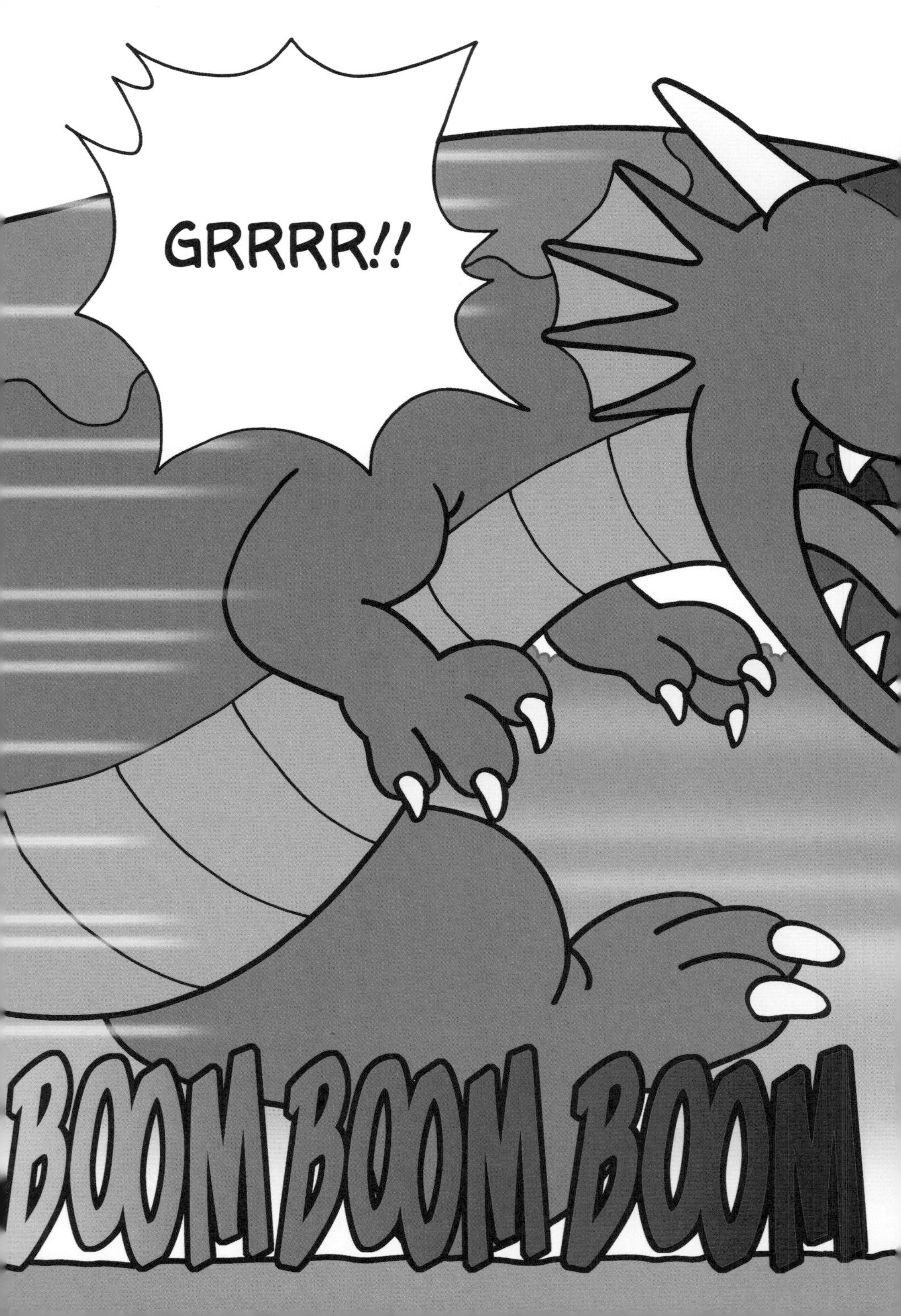
GRRRR!!
BOOM BOOM BOOM

Cuddles was awake!

And Panda Man was on the run!

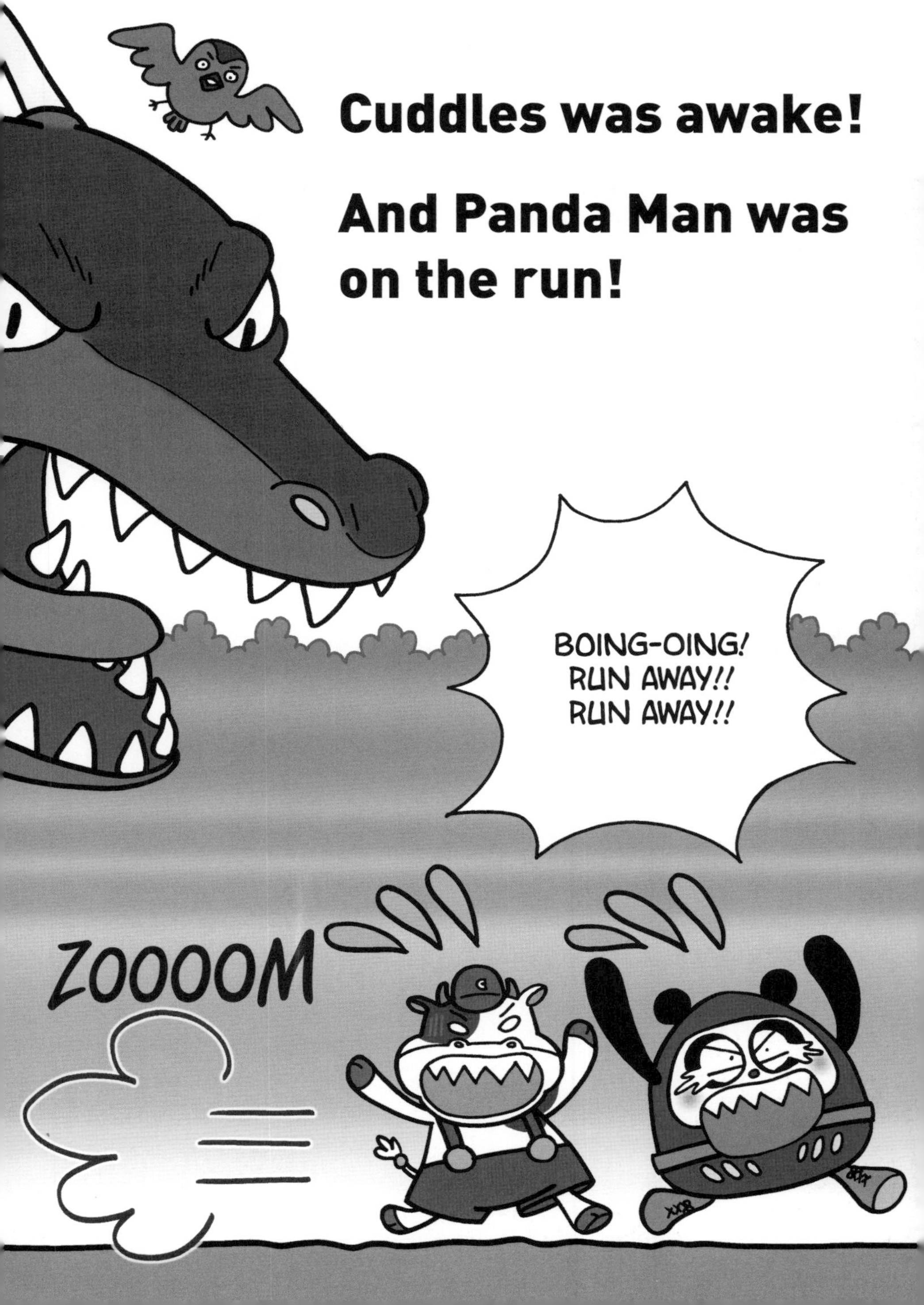
BOING-OING! RUN AWAY!! RUN AWAY!!
ZOOOOM

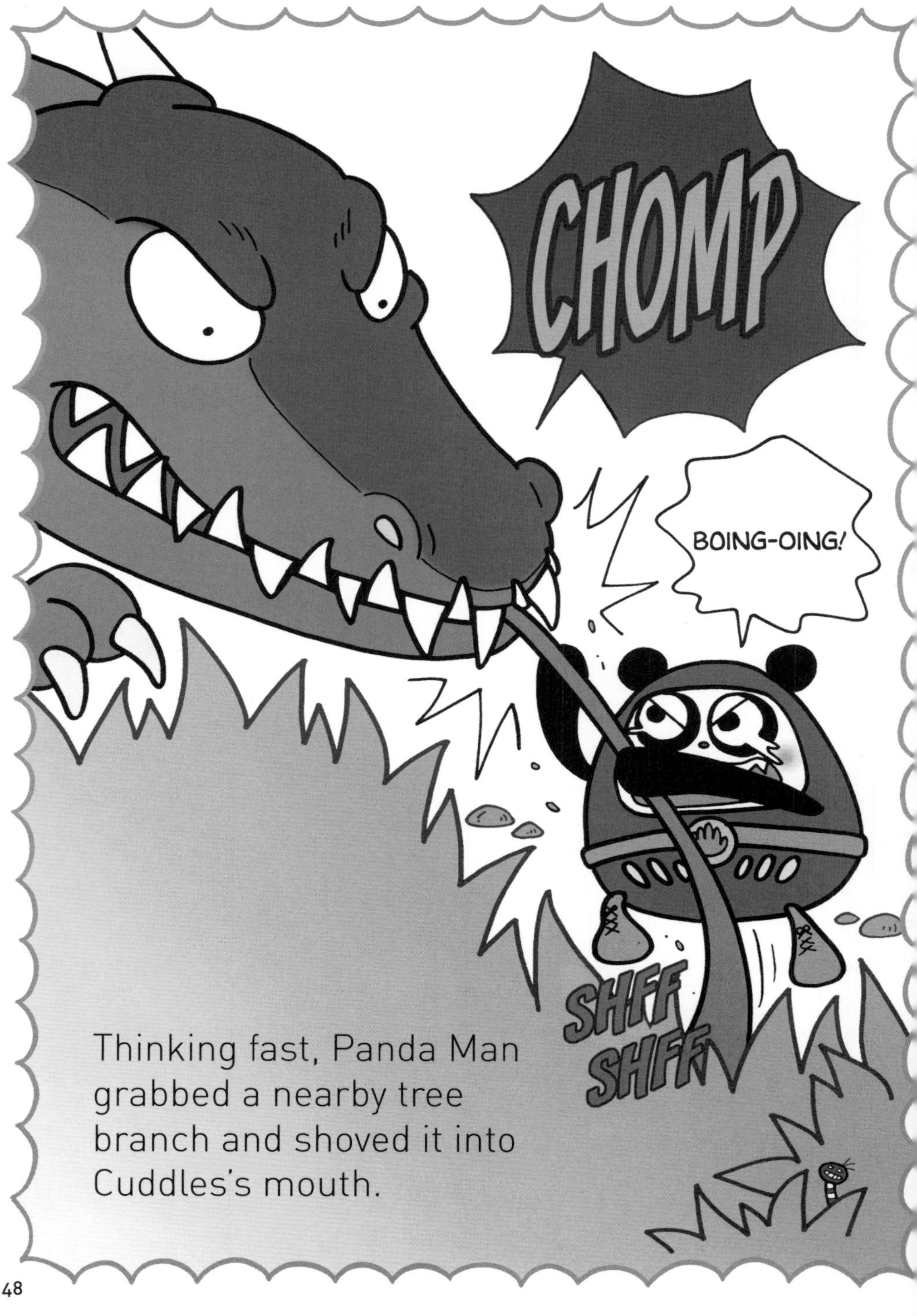
CHOMP
BOING-OING!
SHFF SHFF

Thinking fast, Panda Man grabbed a nearby tree branch and shoved it into Cuddles's mouth.

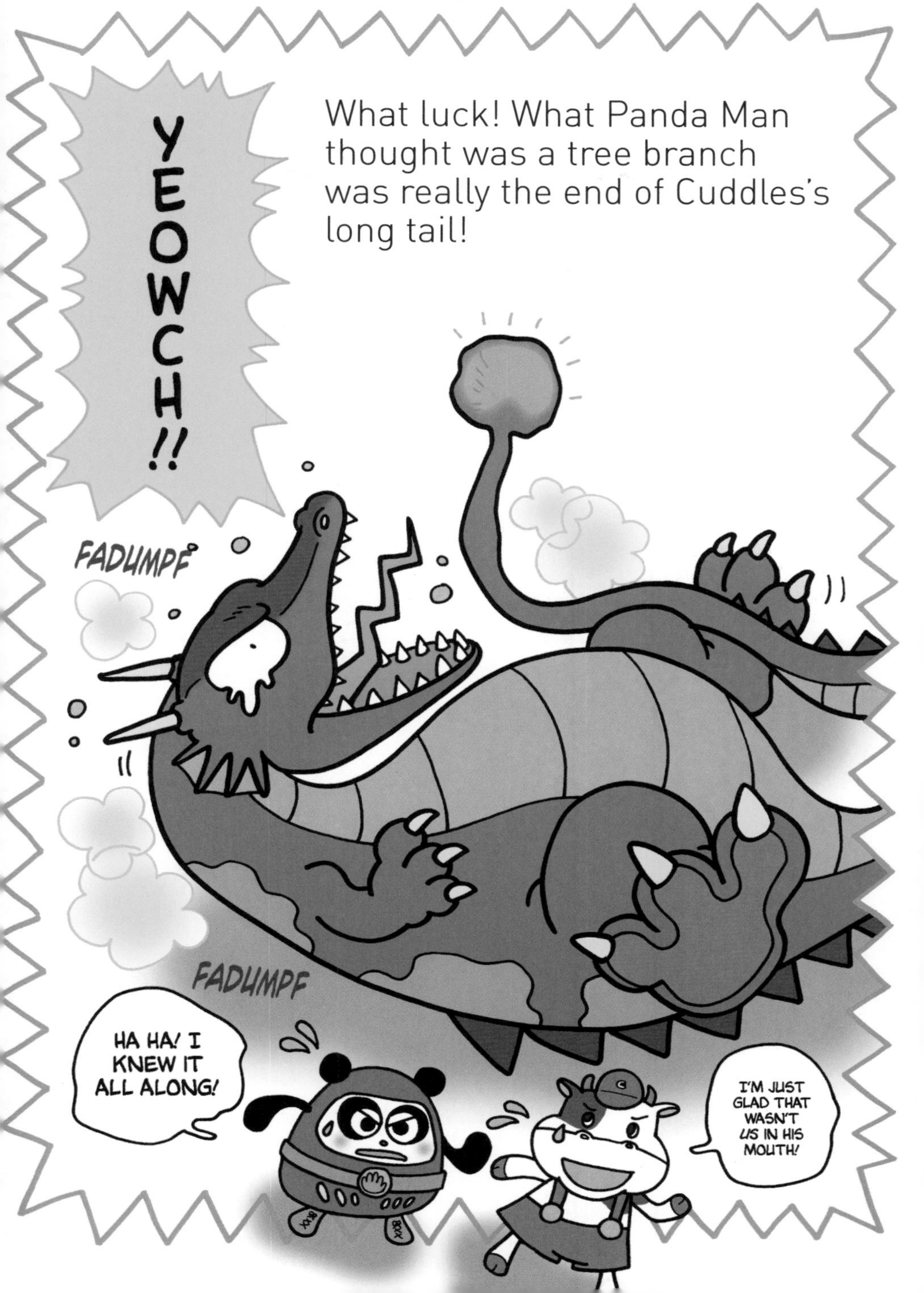
YEOWCH!!
What luck! What Panda Man thought was a tree branch was really the end of Cuddles's long tail!
FADUMPF
FADUMPF
HA HA! I KNEW IT ALL ALONG!
I'M JUST GLAD THAT WASN'T US IN HIS MOUTH!

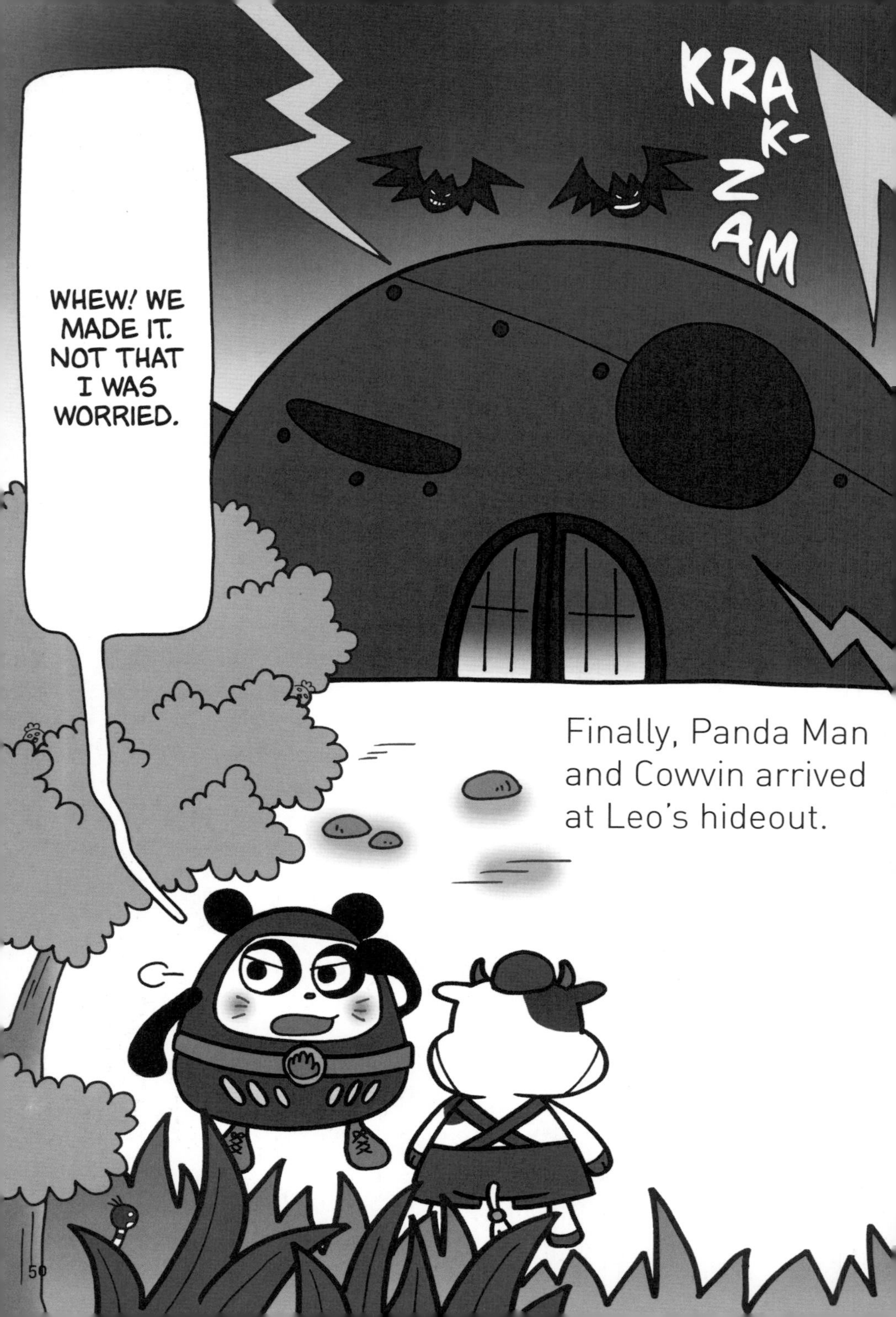
KRAK-ZAM
WHEW! WE MADE IT. NOT THAT I WAS WORRIED.
Finally, Panda Man and Cowvin arrived at Leo's hideout.

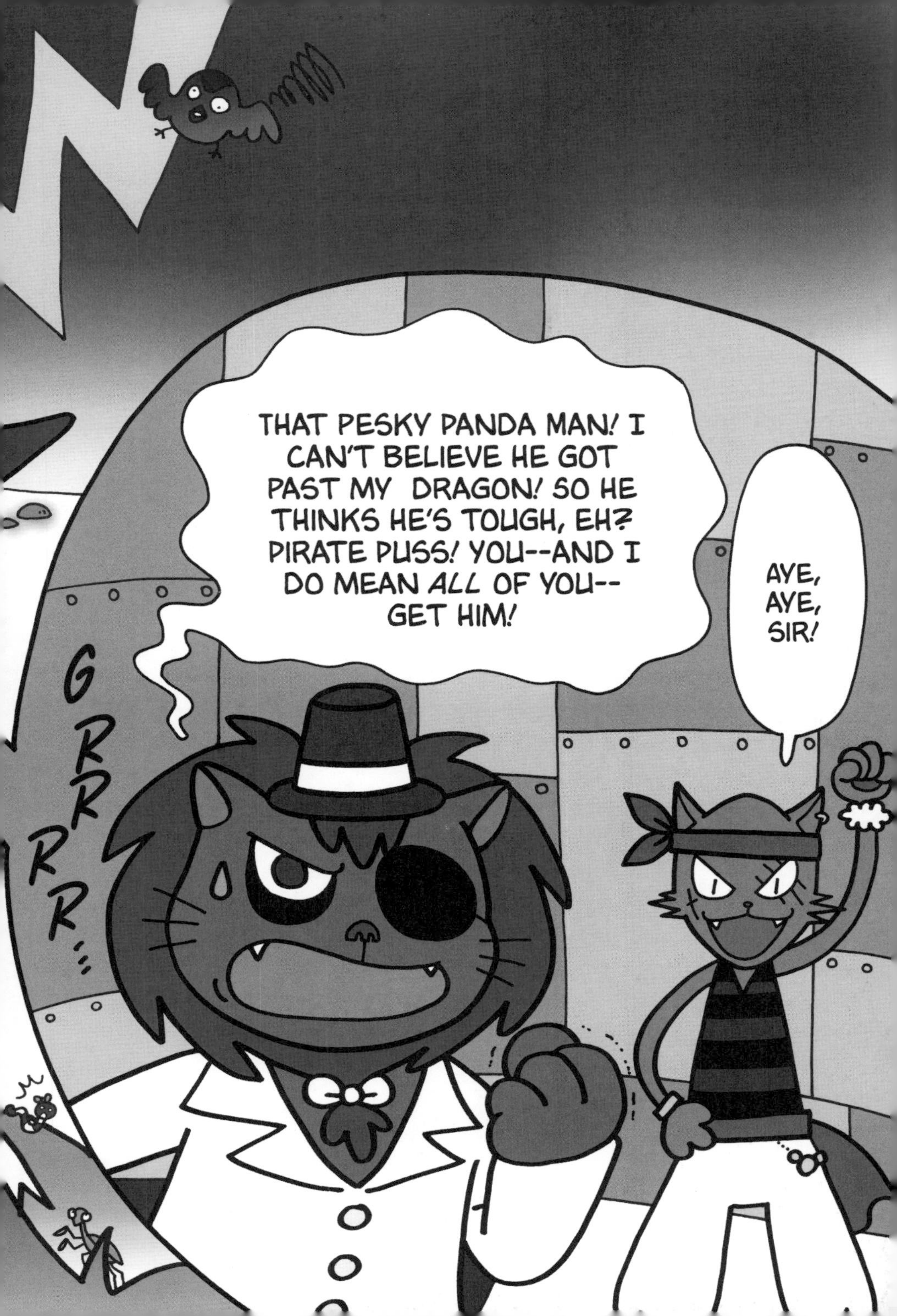
THAT PESKY PANDA MAN! I CAN'T BELIEVE HE GOT PAST MY DRAGON! SO HE THINKS HE'S TOUGH, EH? PIRATE PUSS! YOU--AND I DO MEAN *ALL* OF YOU--GET HIM!
AYE, AYE, SIR!
GRRRRR...

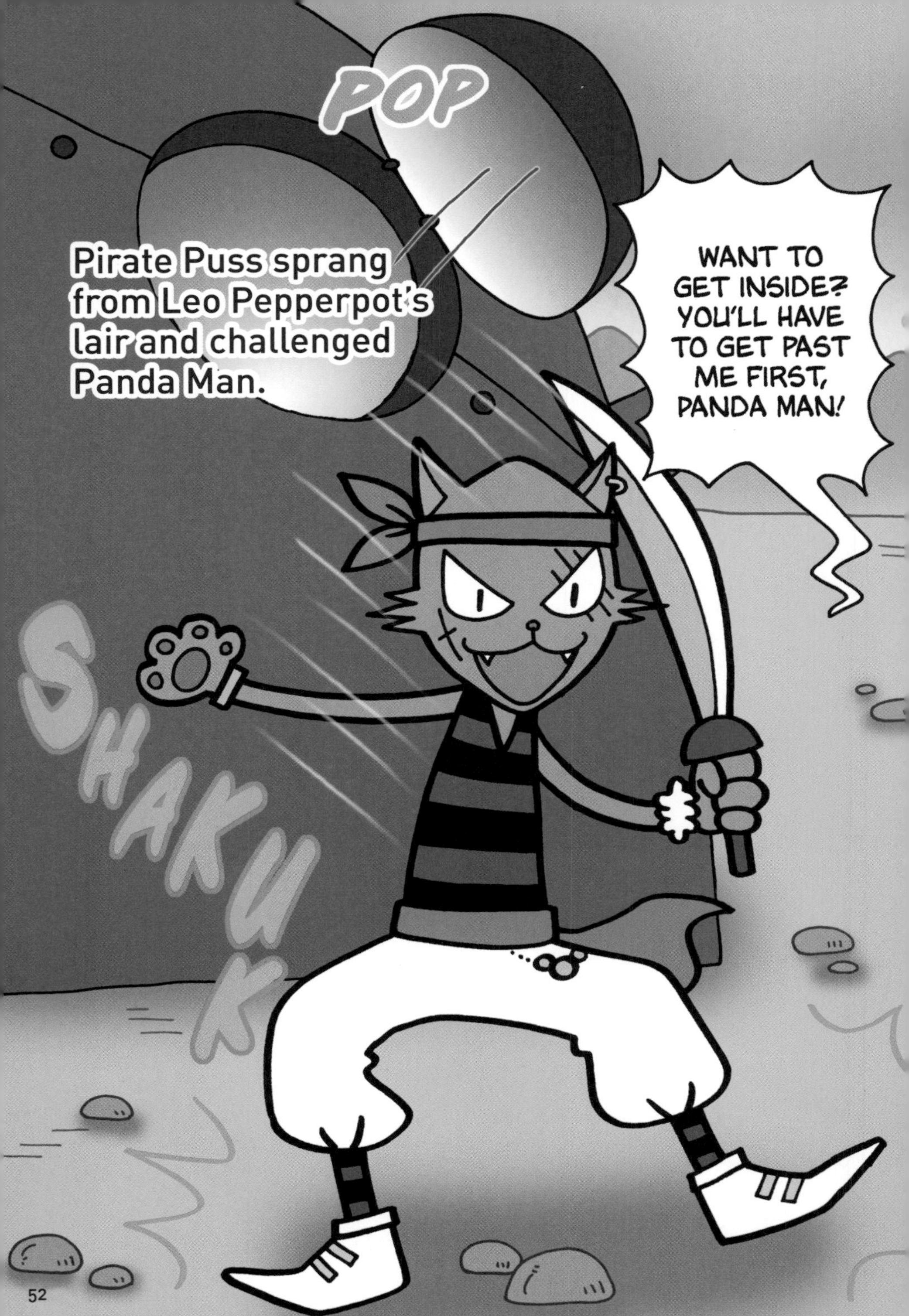
POP
Pirate Puss sprang from Leo Pepperpot's lair and challenged Panda Man.
WANT TO GET INSIDE? YOU'LL HAVE TO GET PAST ME FIRST, PANDA MAN!
SHAKUUK

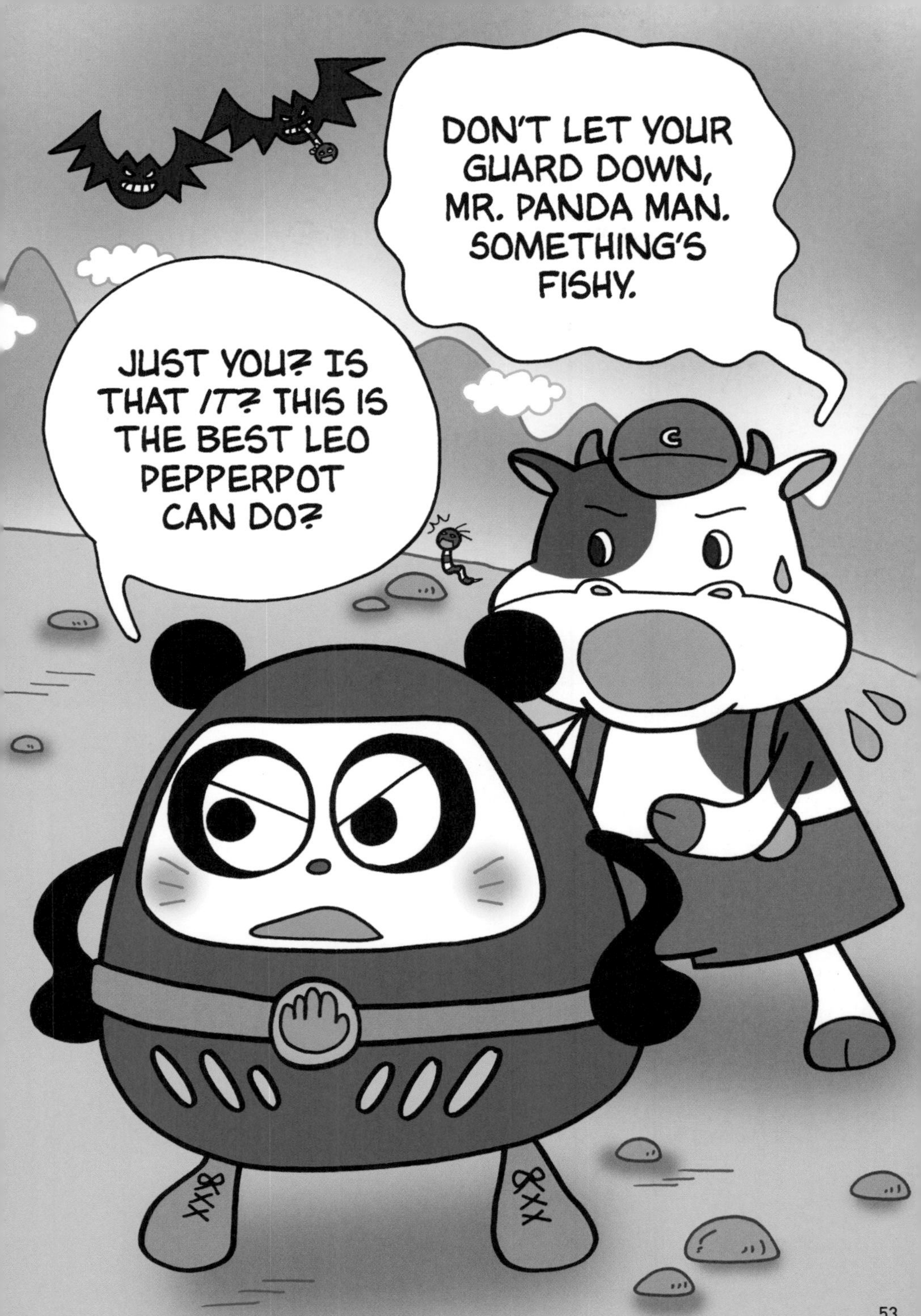
DON'T LET YOUR GUARD DOWN, MR. PANDA MAN. SOMETHING'S FISHY.
JUST YOU? IS THAT *IT*? THIS IS THE BEST LEO PEPPERPOT CAN DO?

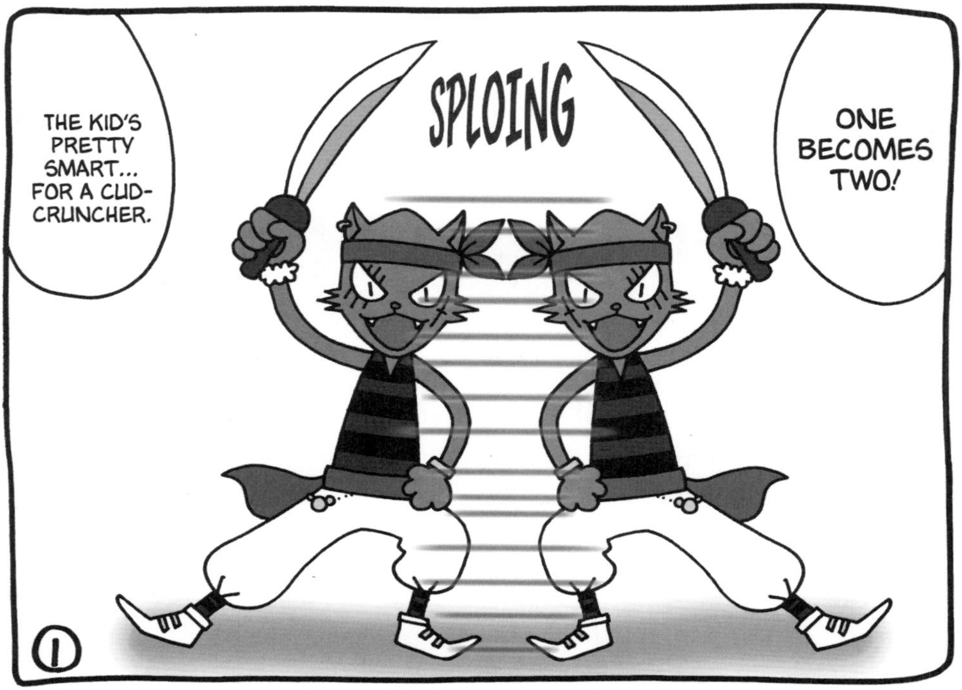
THE KID'S PRETTY SMART... FOR A CUD-CRUNCHER.
SPLOING
ONE BECOMES TWO!
1

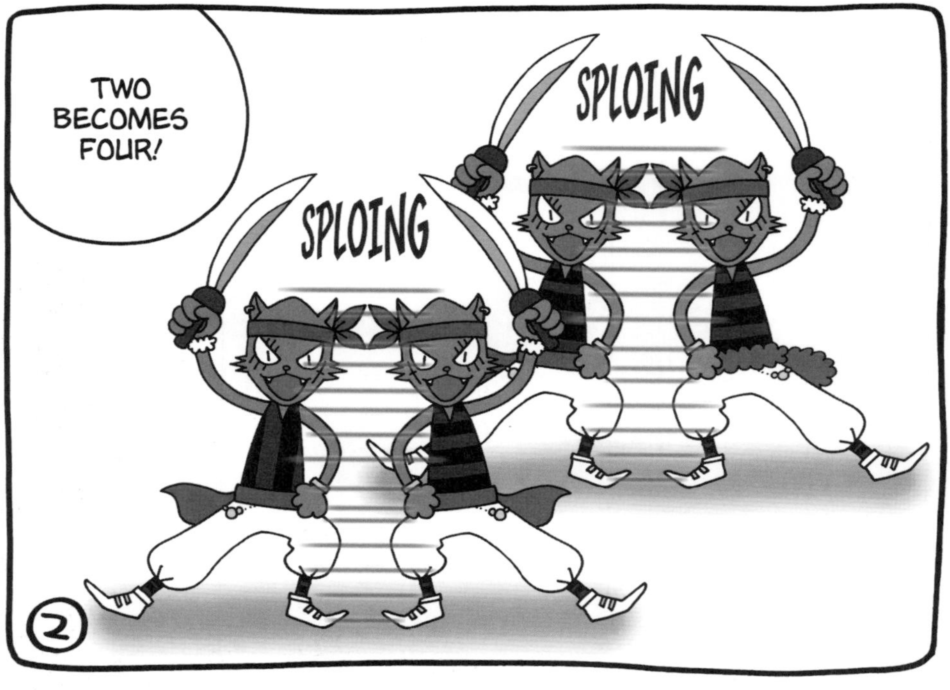
TWO BECOMES FOUR!
SPLOING
SPLOING
2

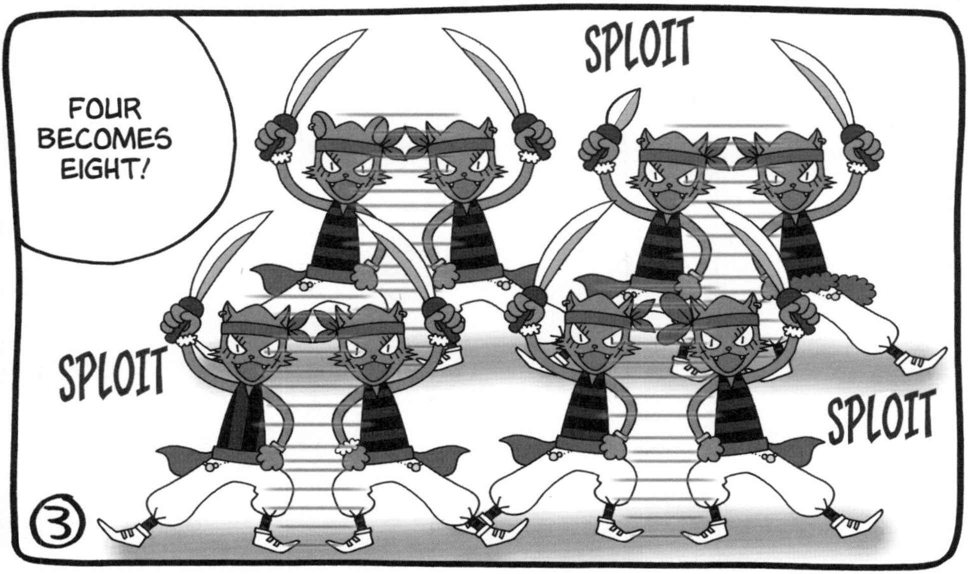
FOUR BECOMES EIGHT!
SPLOIT
SPLOIT
SPLOIT

Pirate Puss was making copies of himself!

And if Panda Man didn't do something fast, he'd soon have a **pirate platoon** on his hands!

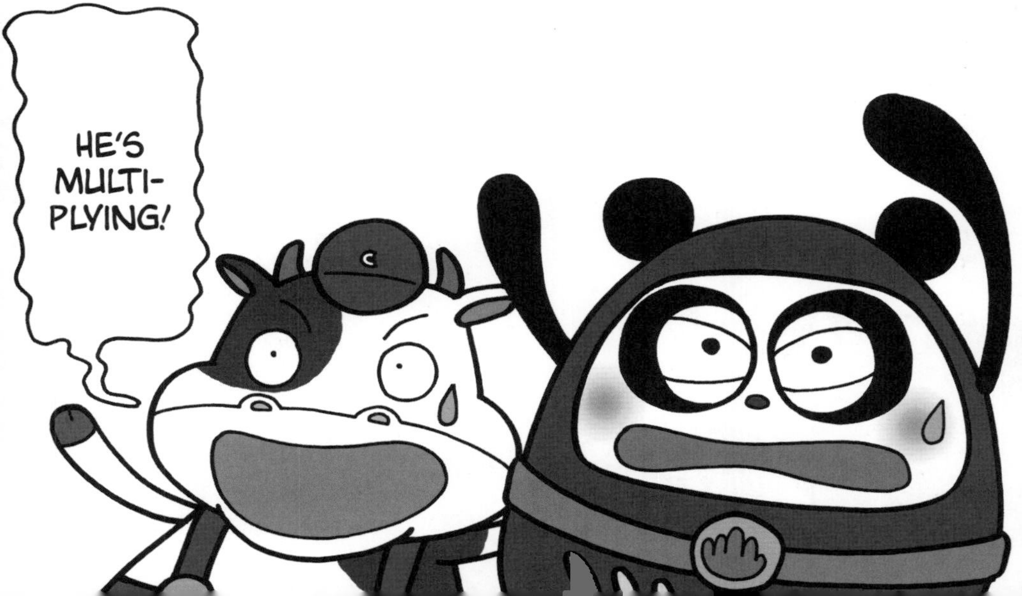
HE'S MULTI-PLYING!

"Your only hope is to find the real me! And you never will!" cackled the cat.

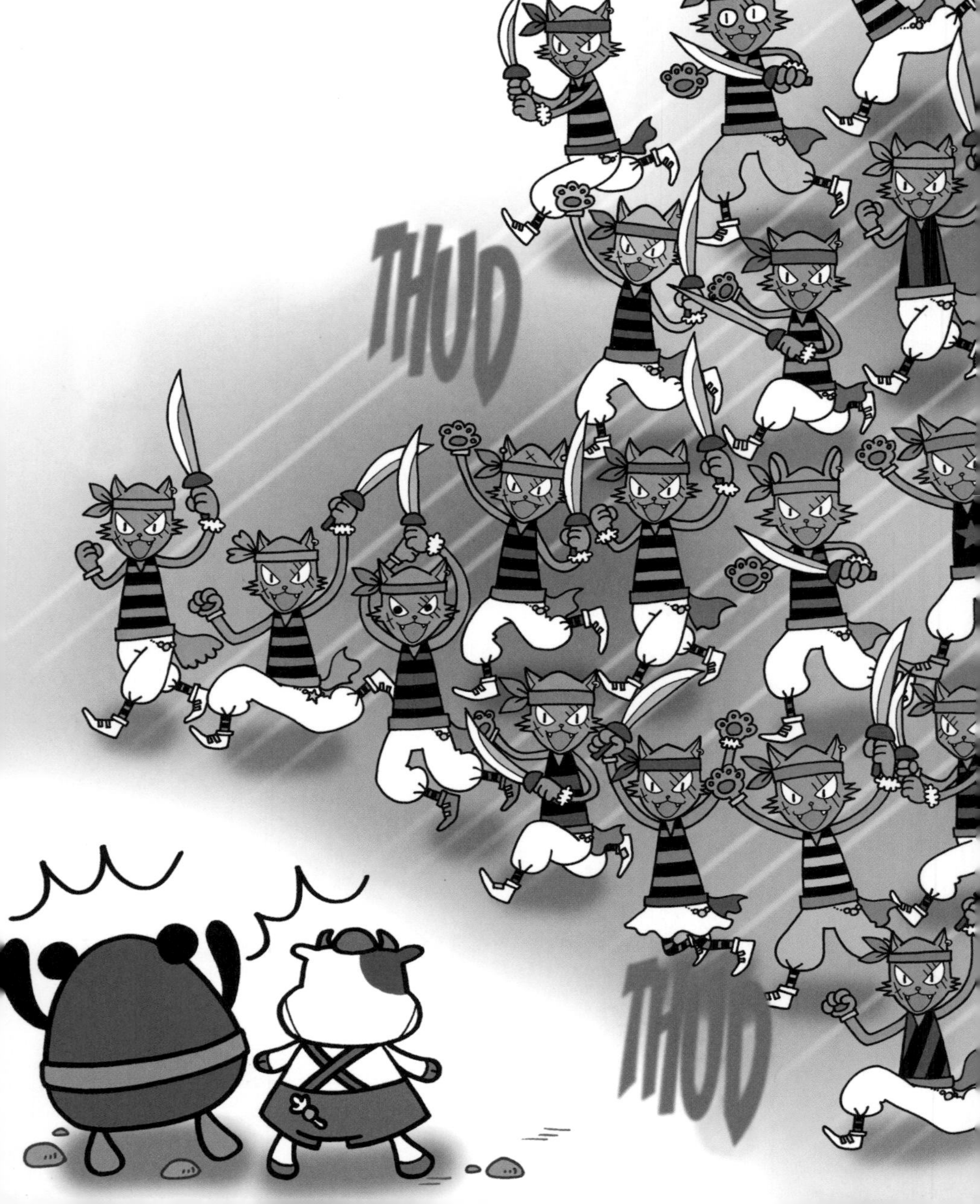
THUD
THUD

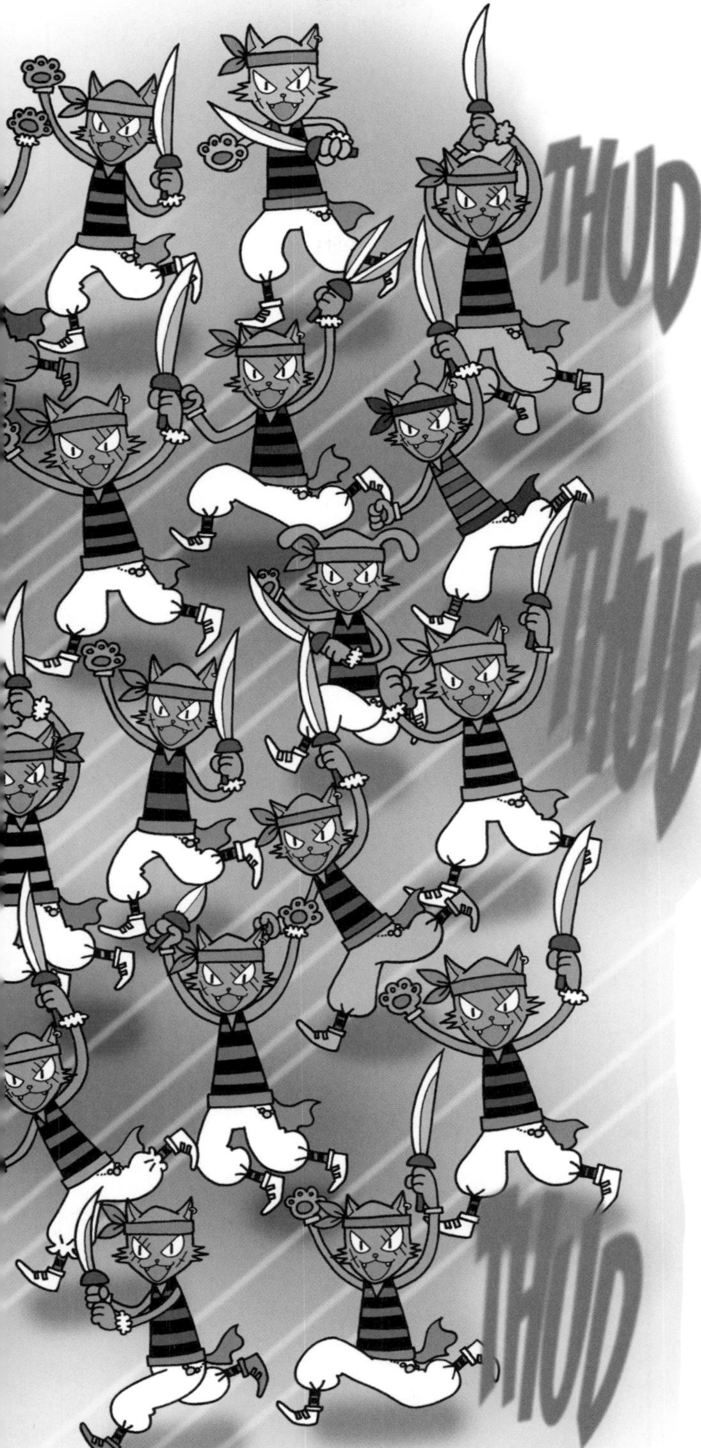
THUD
THUD
THUD

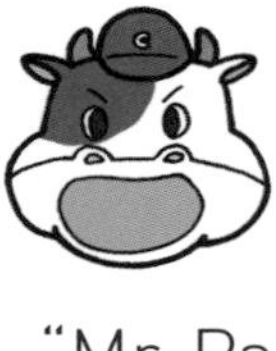

"Mr. Panda Man! We have to find the original Pirate Puss!"

Panda Man and Cowvin need your help!

Look at the drawing below and find its match!

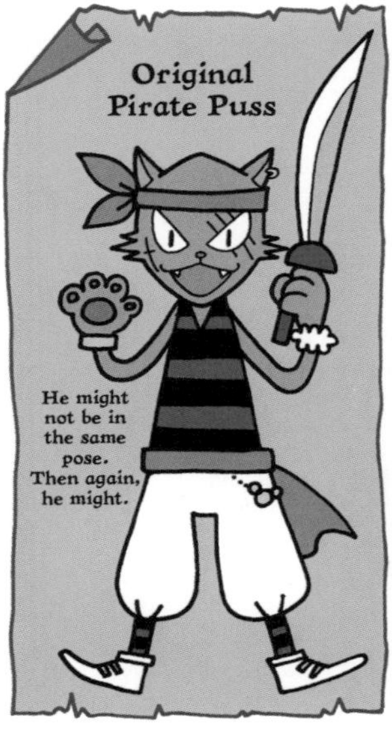
Original Pirate Puss
He might not be in the same pose. Then again, he might.

Panda Man flung himself into the center of the pirates.

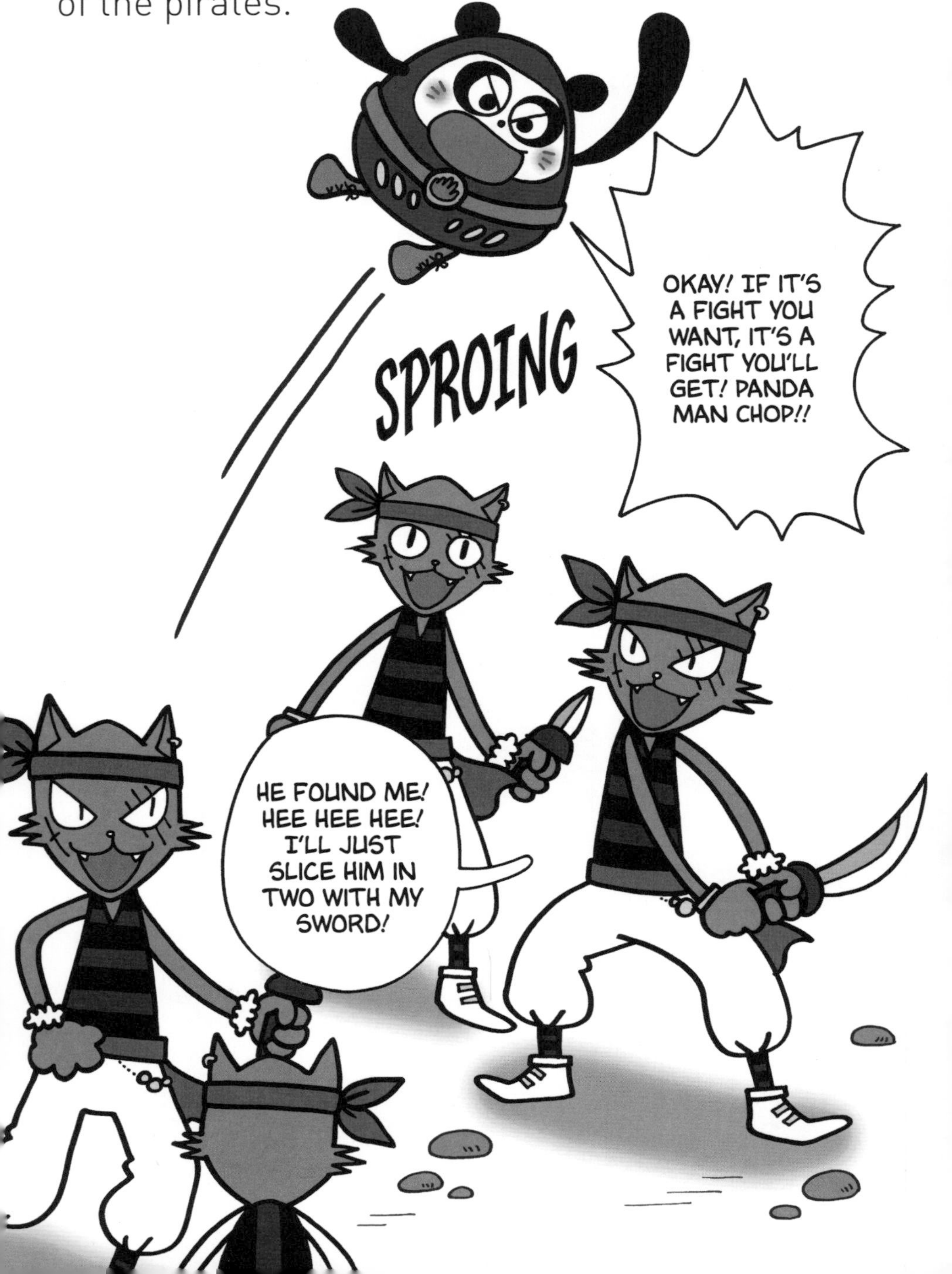
OKAY! IF IT'S A FIGHT YOU WANT, IT'S A FIGHT YOU'LL GET! PANDA MAN CHOP!!
SPROING
HE FOUND ME! HEE HEE HEE! I'LL JUST SLICE HIM IN TWO WITH MY SWORD!

Unfortunately...

He fell just short
of his goal.

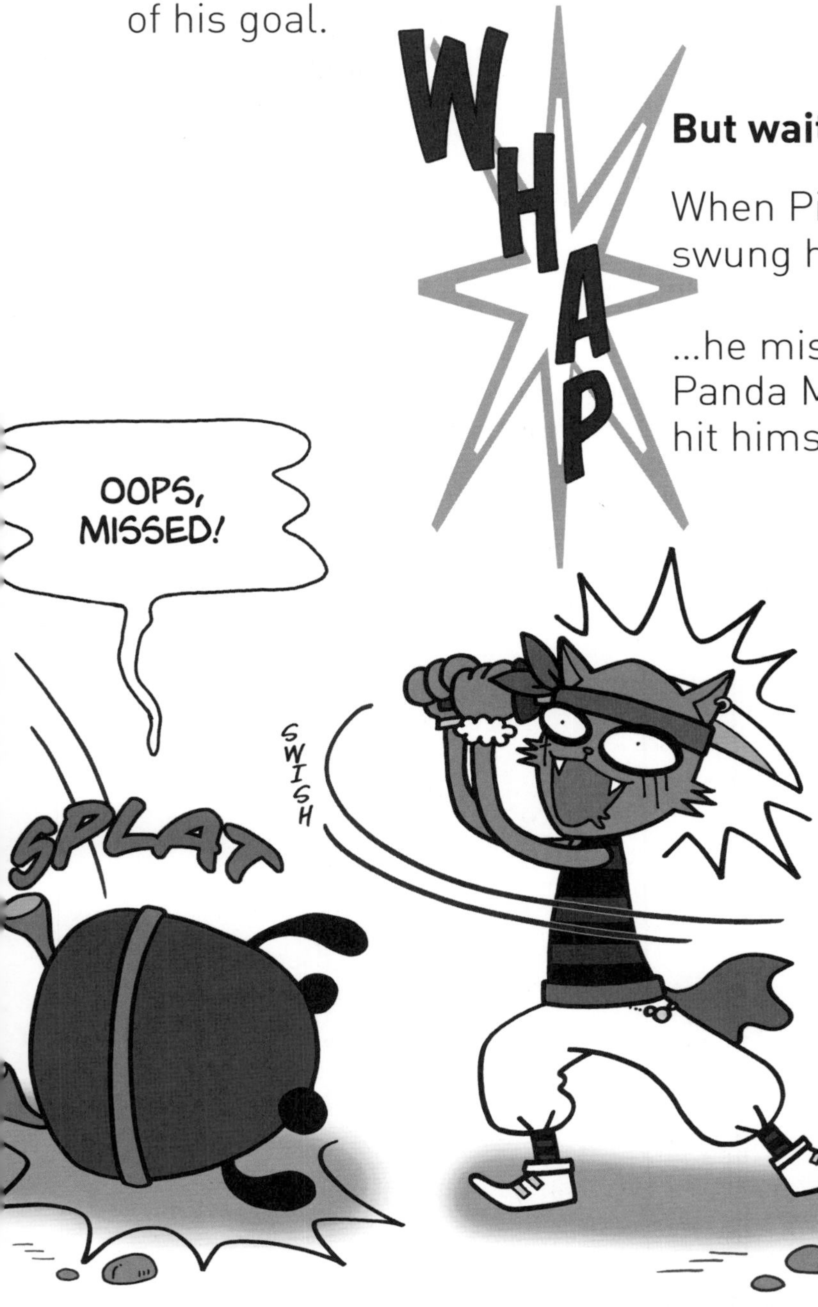
WHAP
OOPS, MISSED!
SWISH
SPLAT

But wait!

When Pirate Puss
swung his sword...

...he missed
Panda Man and
hit himself!

And so, with the real Pirate Puss down for the count, the rest of the pirates disappeared.

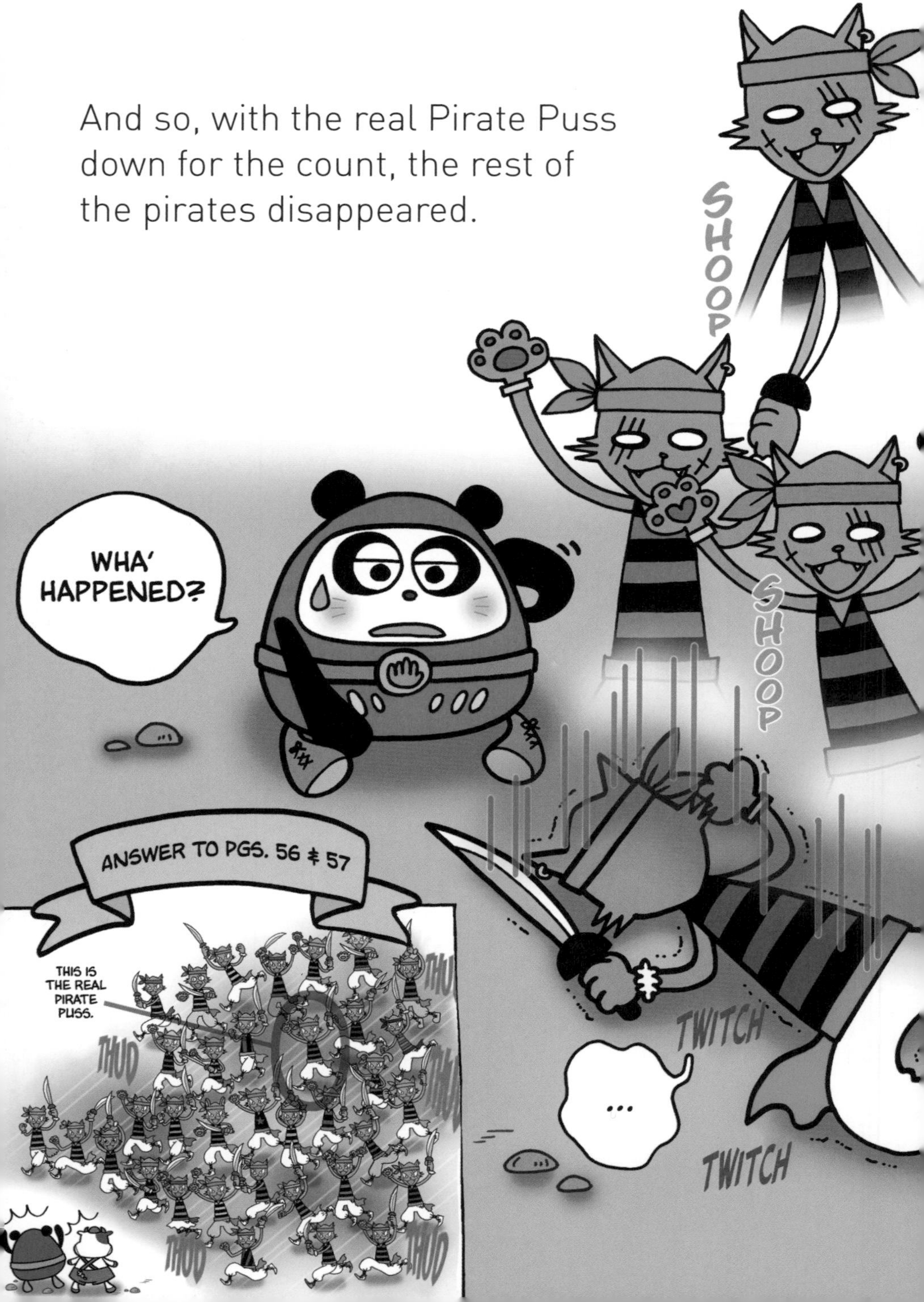
SHOOP
WHA' HAPPENED?
SHOOP
TWITCH
...
TWITCH
ANSWER TO PGS. 56 & 57
THIS IS THE REAL PIRATE PUSS.
THUD
THUD
THUD
THUD

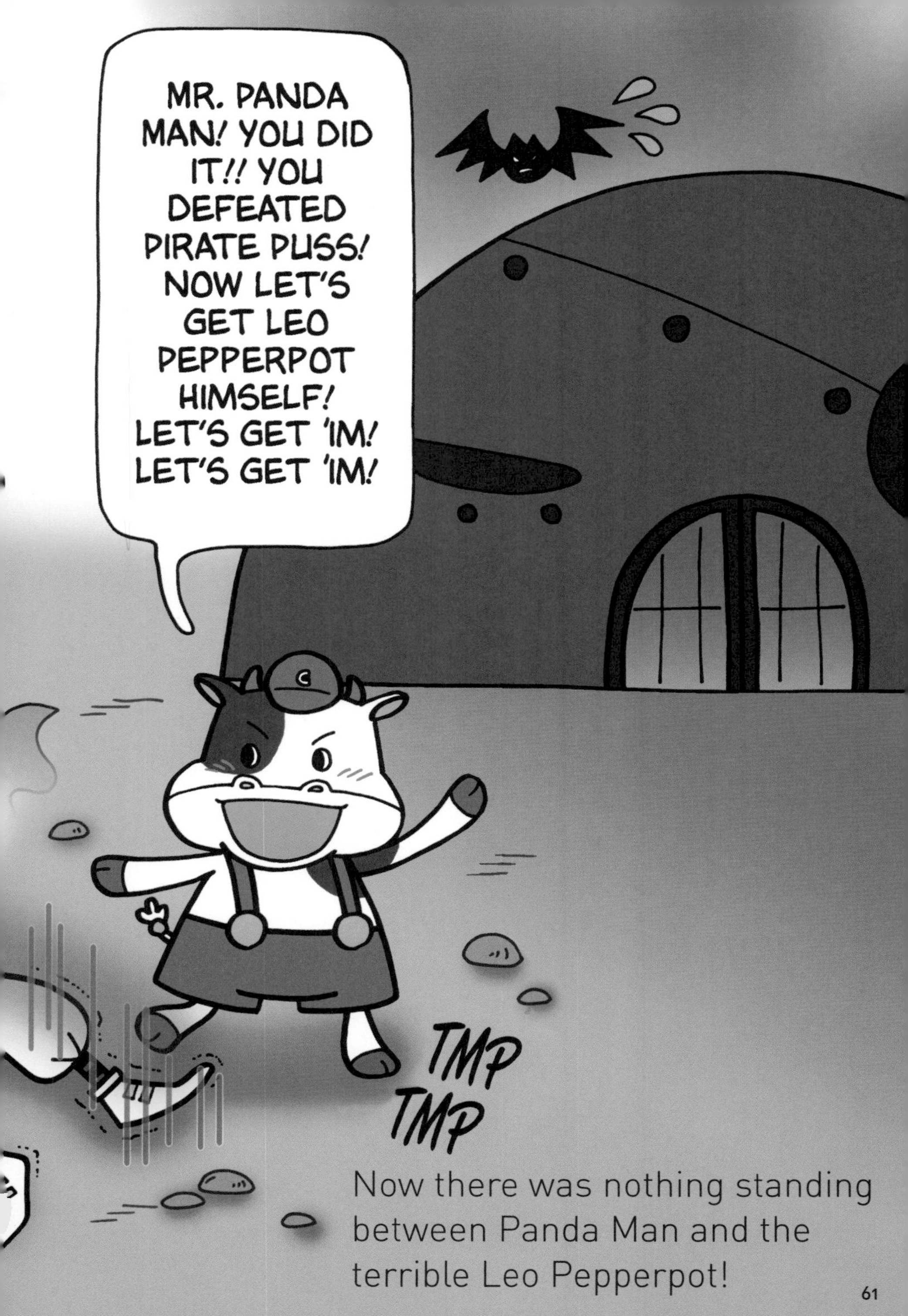
MR. PANDA MAN! YOU DID IT!! YOU DEFEATED PIRATE PUSS! NOW LET'S GET LEO PEPPERPOT HIMSELF! LET'S GET 'IM! LET'S GET 'IM!
TMP TMP

Now there was nothing standing between Panda Man and the terrible Leo Pepperpot!

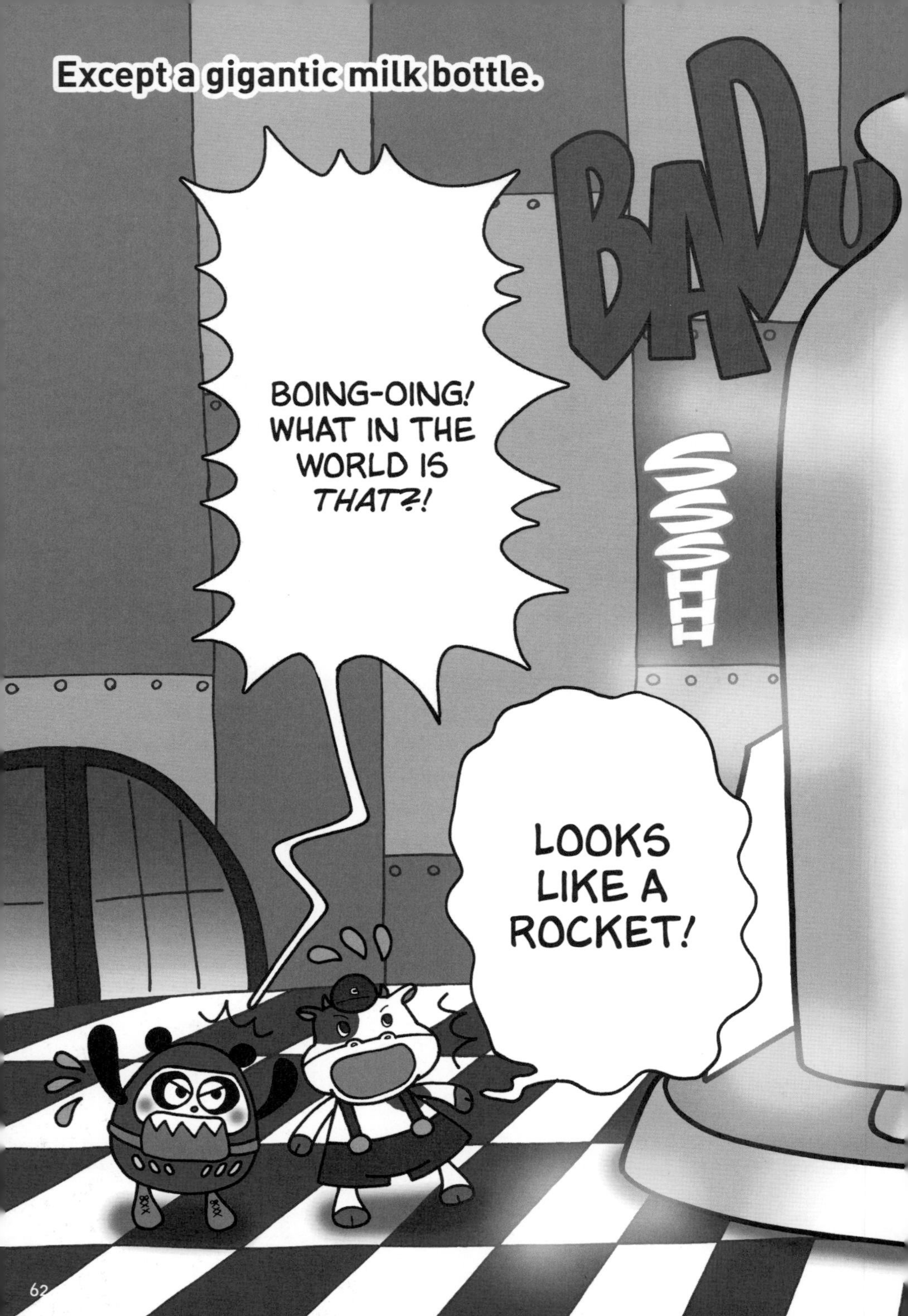
Except a gigantic milk bottle.
BADUM
BOING-OING! WHAT IN THE WORLD IS *THAT?!*
SSSHHH
LOOKS LIKE A ROCKET!

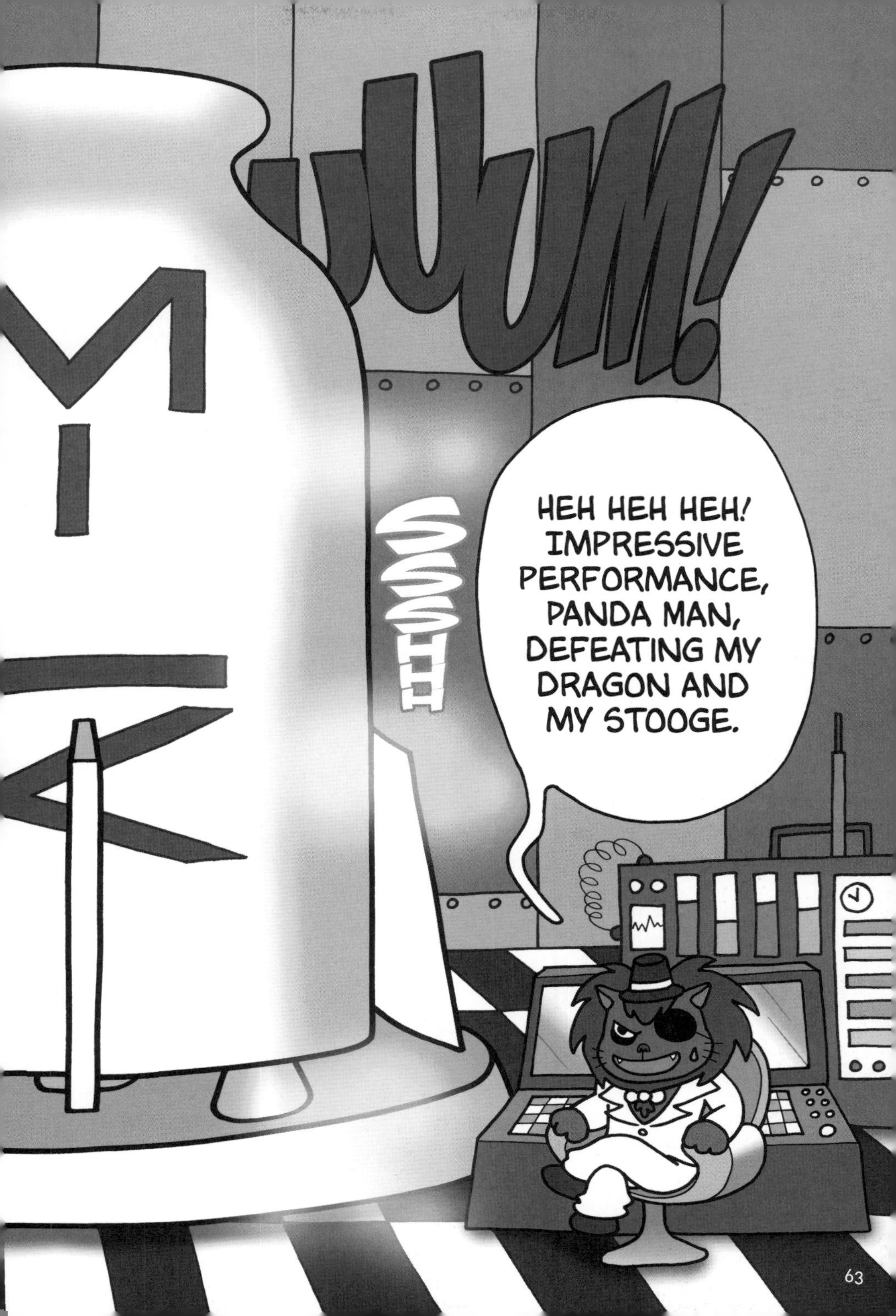
VVUUM!
HEH HEH HEH! IMPRESSIVE PERFORMANCE, PANDA MAN, DEFEATING MY DRAGON AND MY STOOGE.
SSSHHH

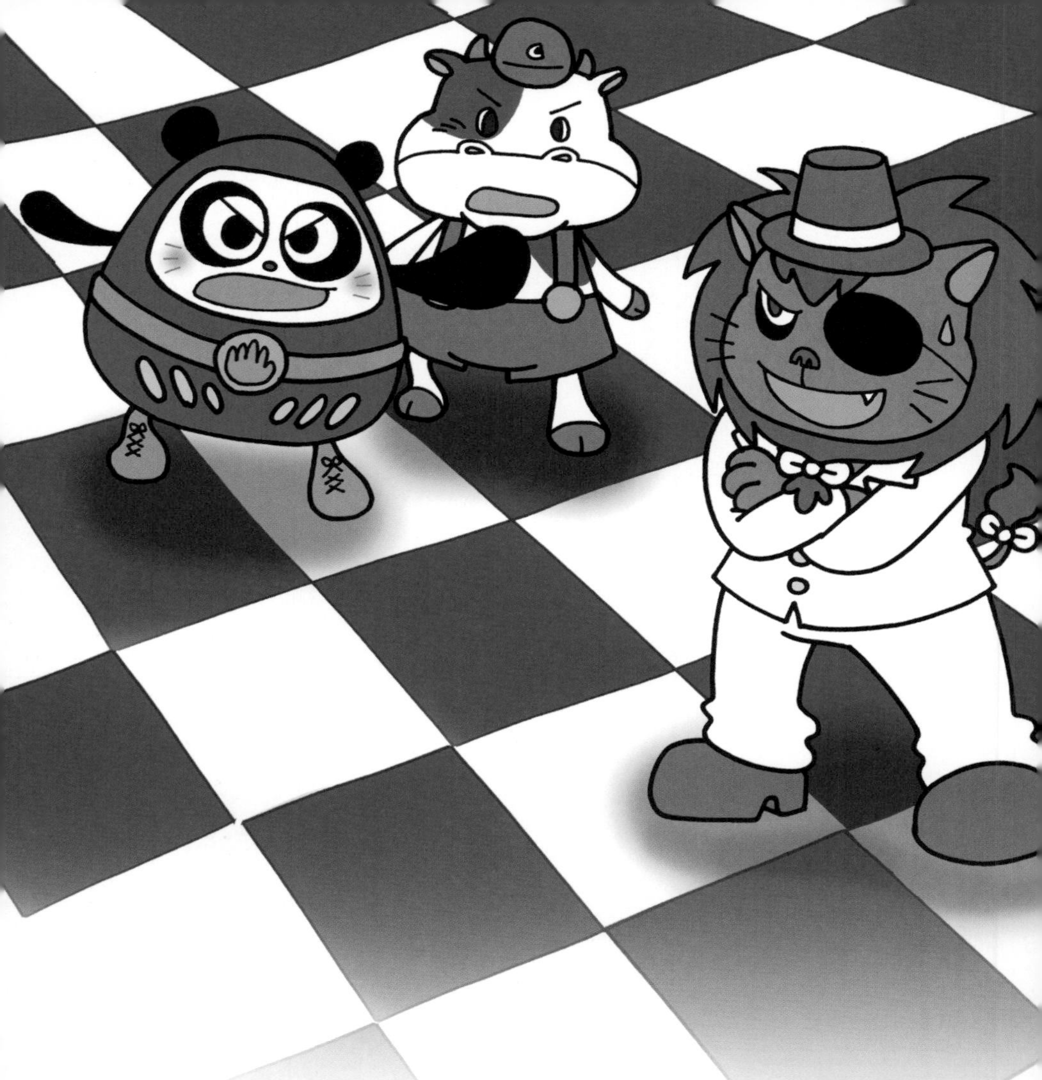

"Since you've made it this far, I'll let you in on my top secret plan," Leo smirked. "Inside this rocket is all the milk from New Milk Village."

"All of it?" Panda Man asked.

"*All* of it," Leo replied.

"What are you—"

"Stop interrupting me," Leo snapped, "and I'll tell you my plan."

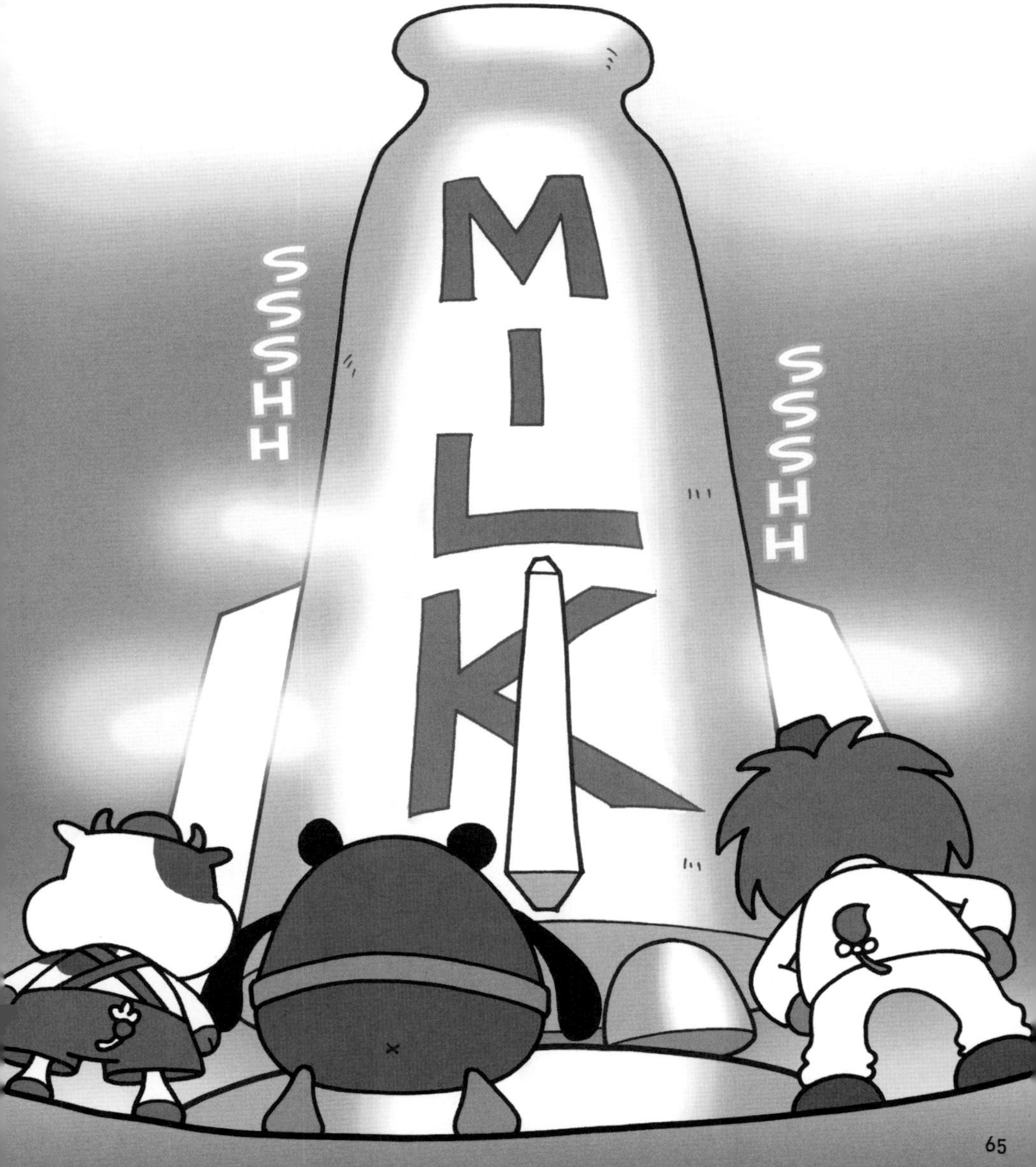
SSSHH
MILK
SSSHH

"Ever since I was a little boy, I've hated milk. No matter how I cried, my mother made me drink the stuff every day. 'But it's *good* for you,' she said. 'Good for the *bones*.' Rubbish."

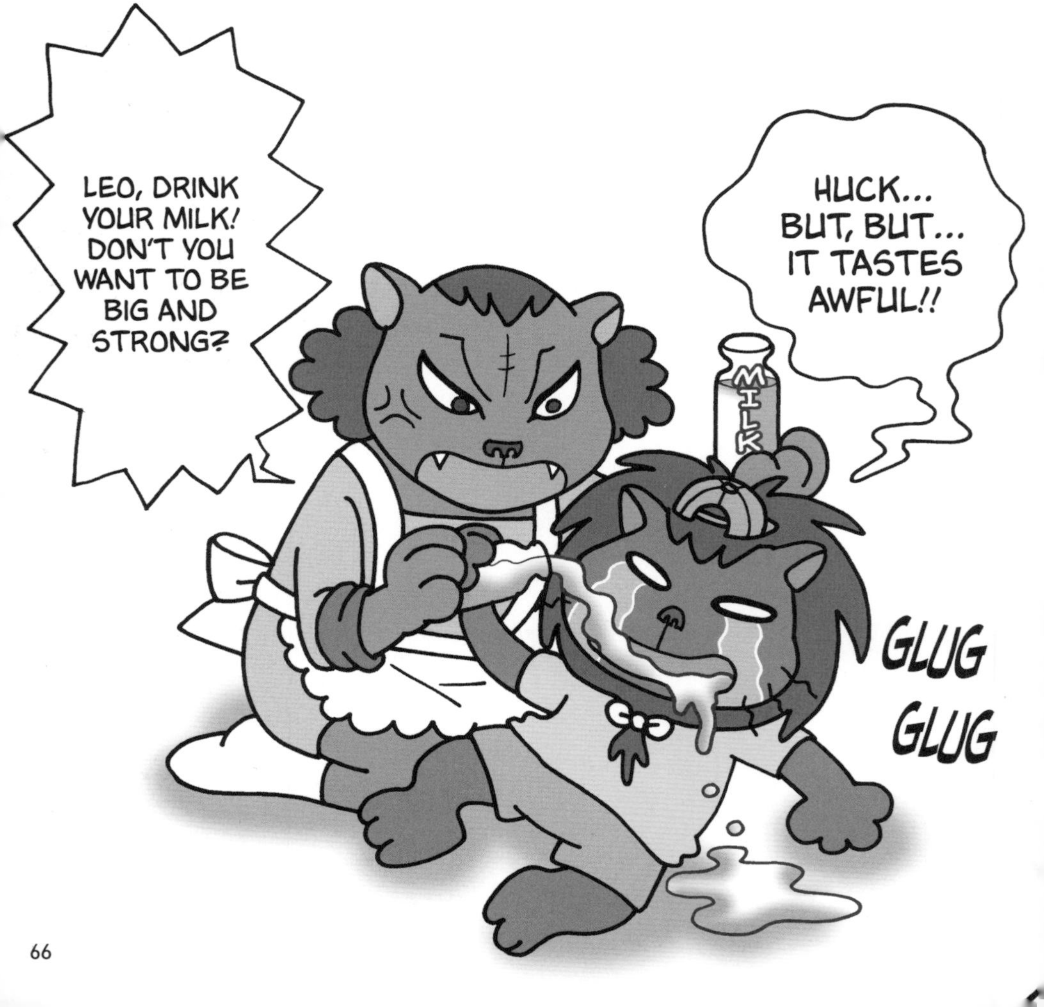

HUCK... BUT, BUT... IT TASTES AWFUL!!
LEO, DRINK YOUR MILK! DON'T YOU WANT TO BE BIG AND STRONG?
MILK
GLUG GLUG

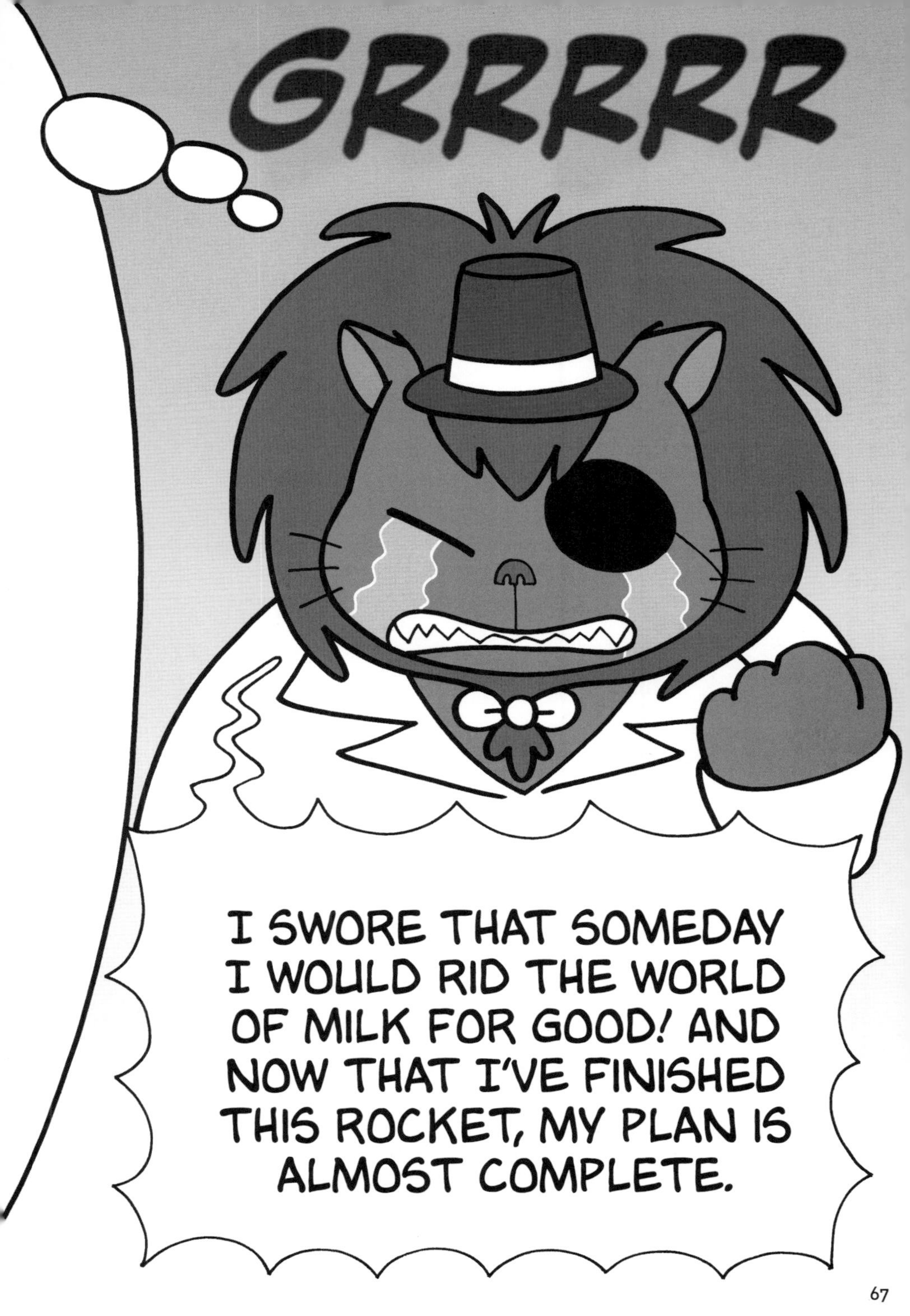
GRRRRR
I SWORE THAT SOMEDAY I WOULD RID THE WORLD OF MILK FOR GOOD! AND NOW THAT I'VE FINISHED THIS ROCKET, MY PLAN IS ALMOST COMPLETE.

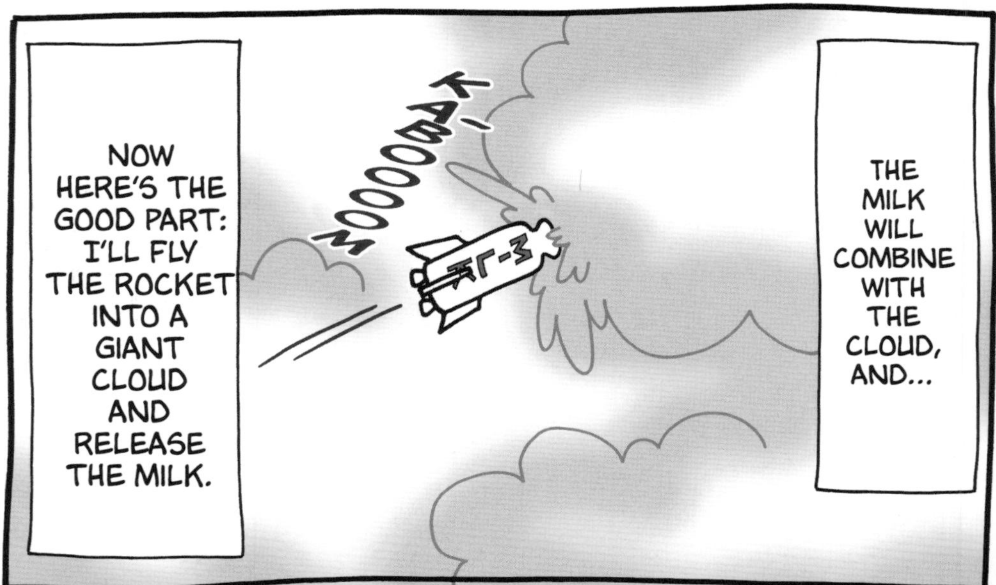
NOW HERE'S THE GOOD PART: I'LL FLY THE ROCKET INTO A GIANT CLOUD AND RELEASE THE MILK.
KABOOOOOM
THE MILK WILL COMBINE WITH THE CLOUD, AND...

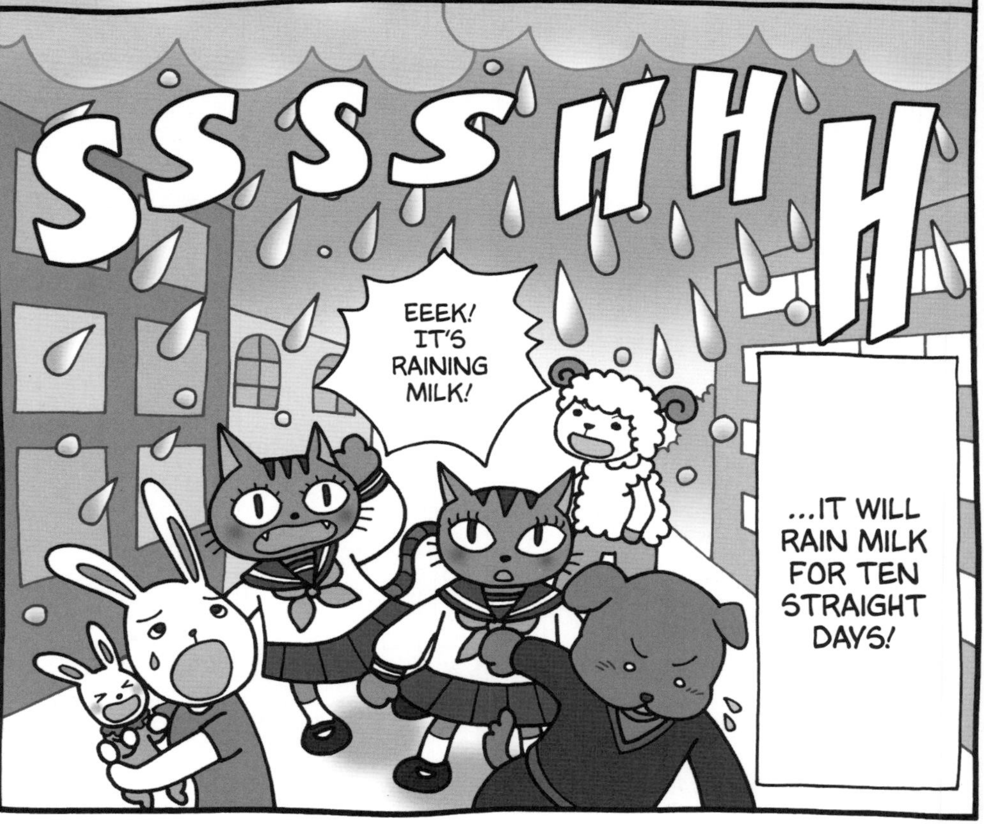
SSSSHHHH
EEEK! IT'S RAINING MILK!
...IT WILL RAIN MILK FOR TEN STRAIGHT DAYS!

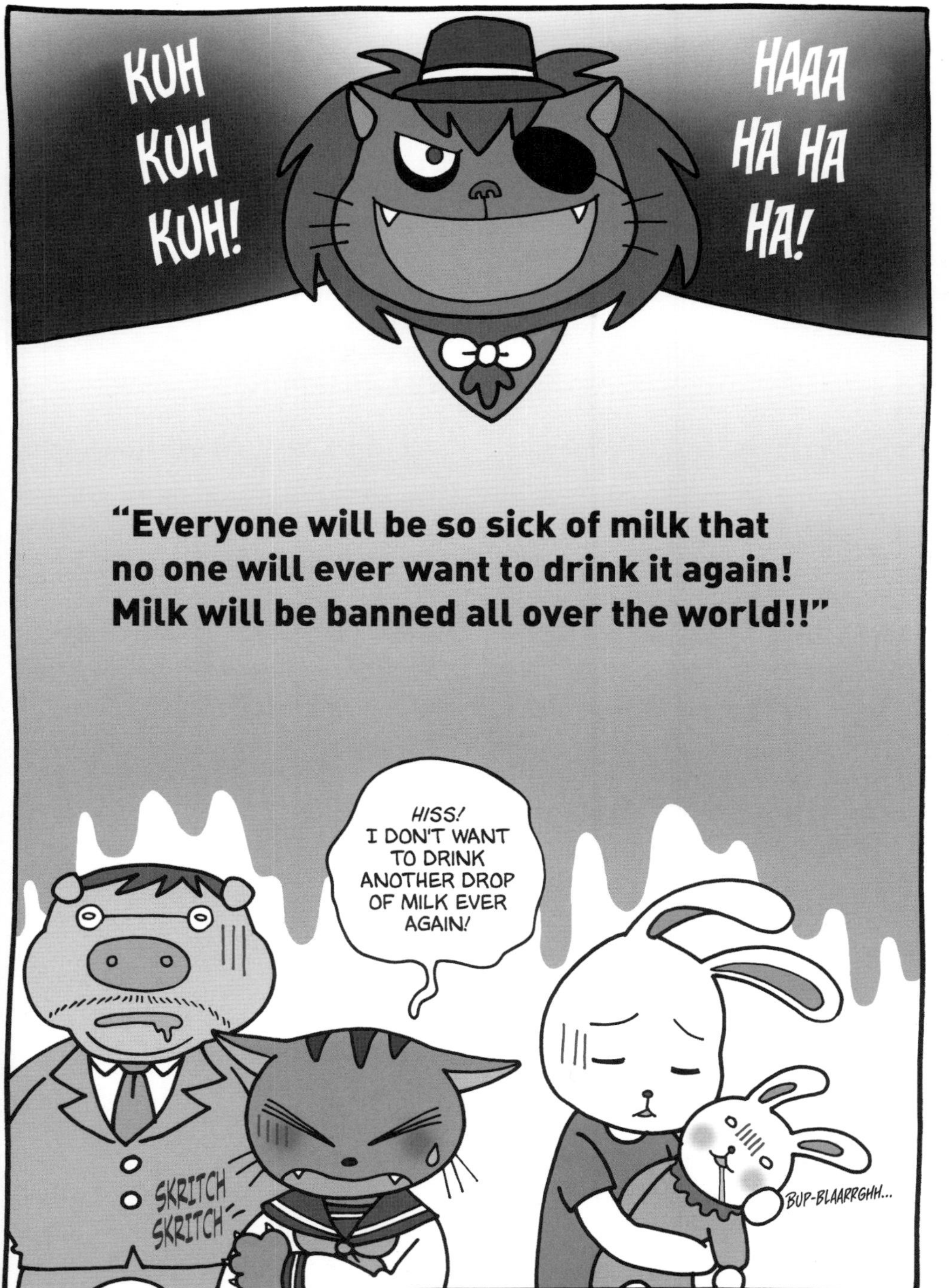
KUH KUH KUH!
HAAA HA HA HA!
"Everyone will be so sick of milk that no one will ever want to drink it again! Milk will be banned all over the world!!"
HISS! I DON'T WANT TO DRINK ANOTHER DROP OF MILK EVER AGAIN!
SKRITCH SKRITCH
BUP-BLAARRGHH...

Hearing Leo's dastardly plan made Panda Man and Cowvin piping mad!

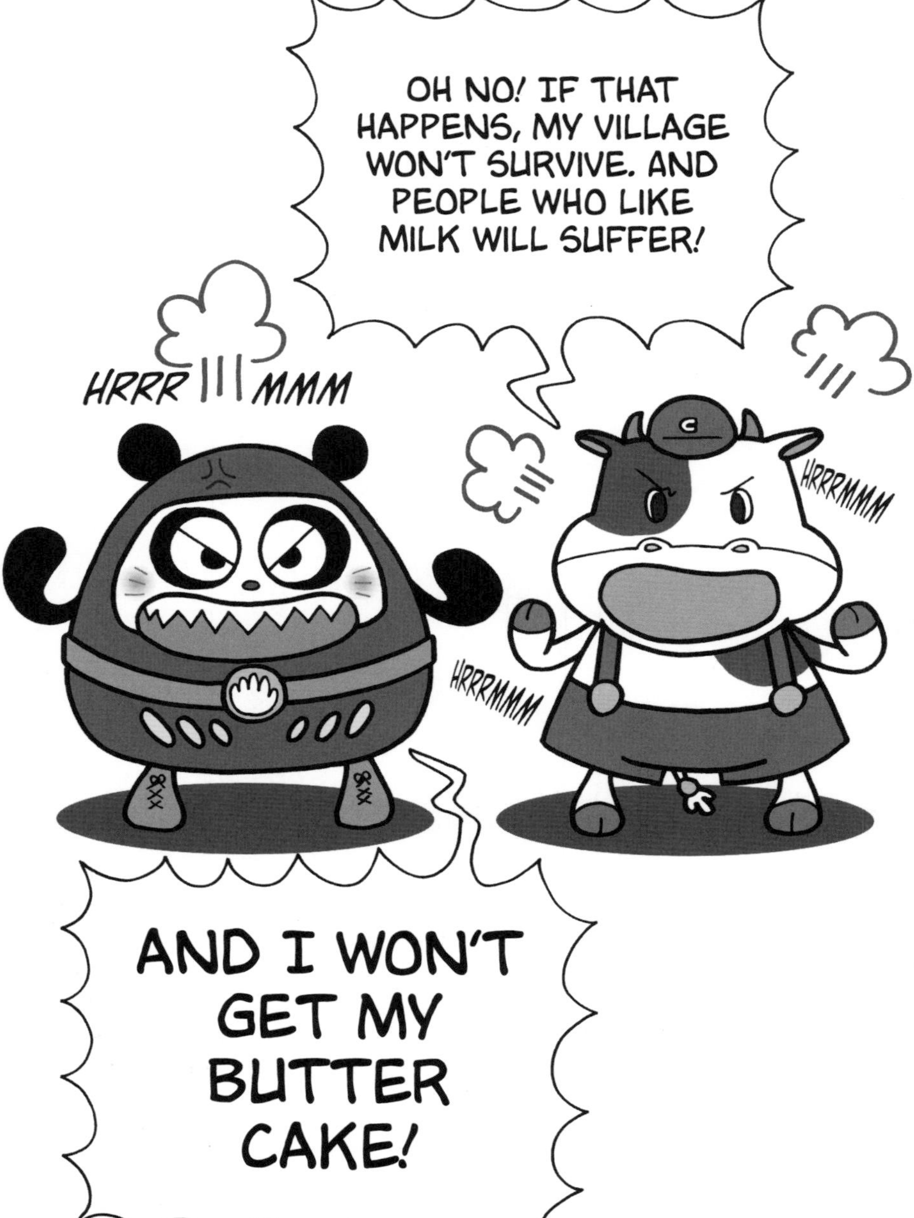
OH NO! IF THAT HAPPENS, MY VILLAGE WON'T SURVIVE. AND PEOPLE WHO LIKE MILK WILL SUFFER!
HRRR MMM
HRRRMMM
HRRRMMM
AND I WON'T GET MY BUTTER CAKE!

Without warning, Leo aimed his cannon at Panda Man and fired.

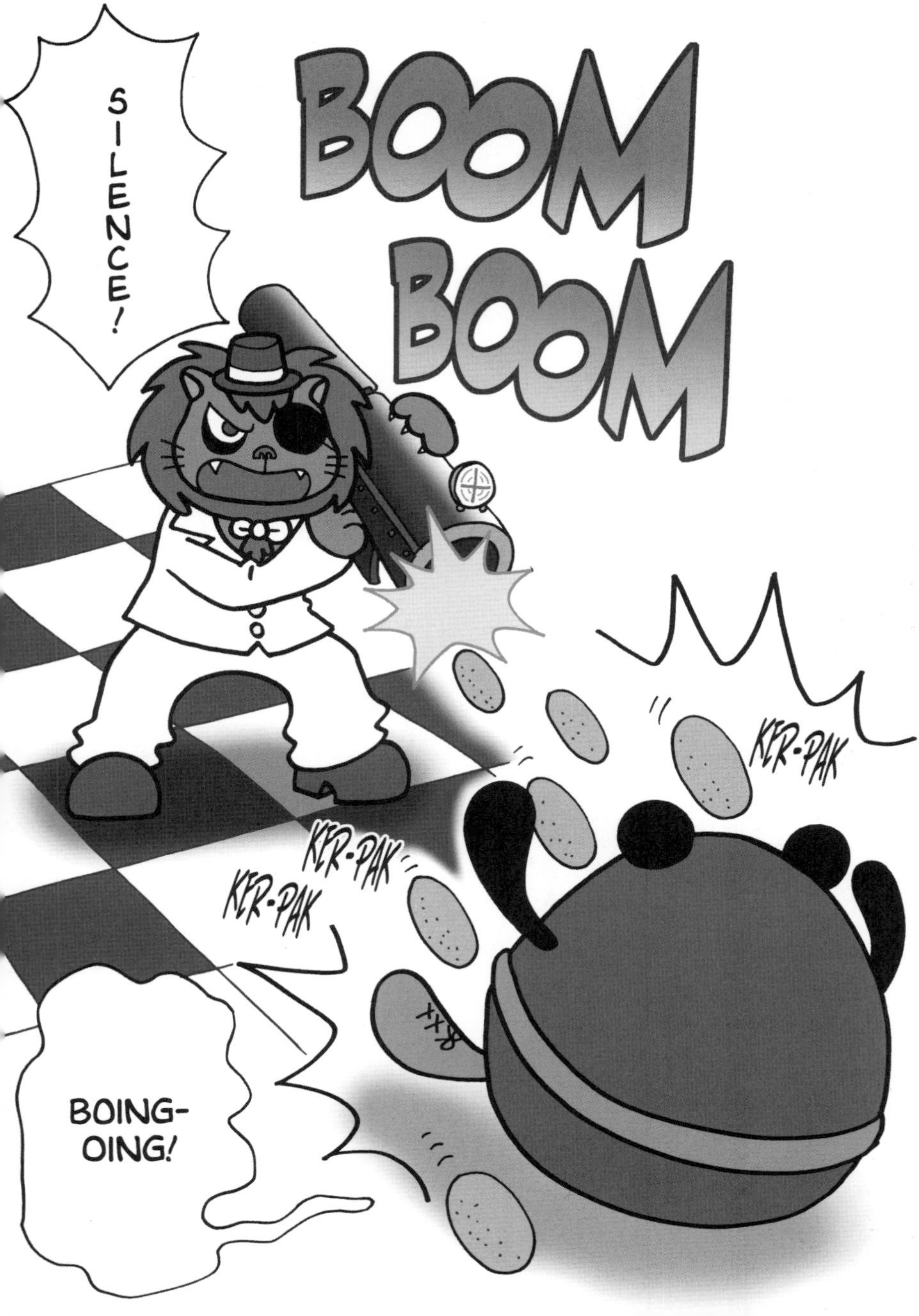
SILENCE!
BOOM BOOM
KER-PAK
KER-PAK
KER-PAK
BOING-OING!

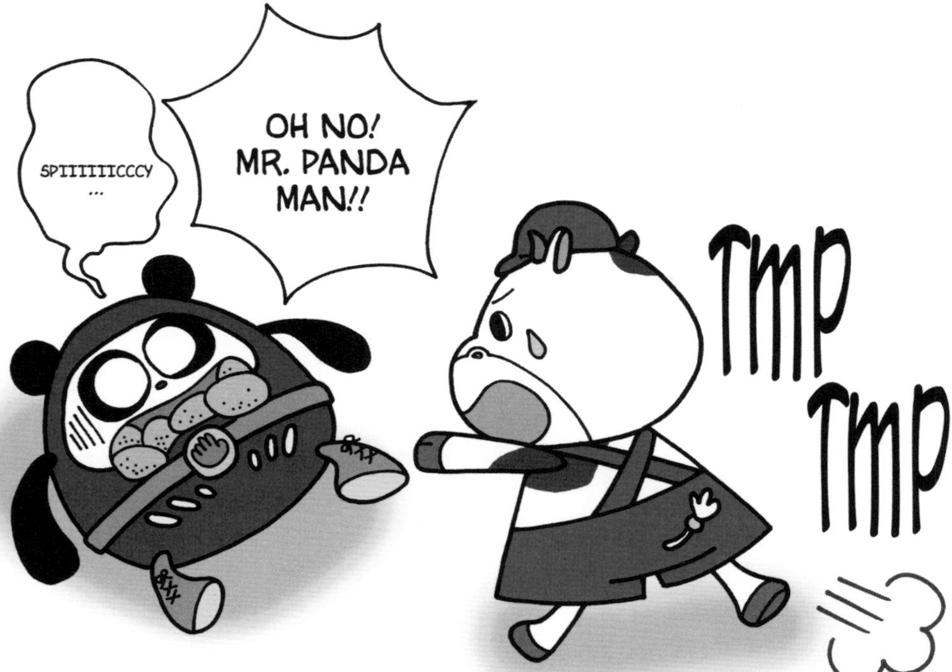
SPIIIIIICCCY ...
OH NO! MR. PANDA MAN!!
TMP
TMP

Cowvin ran to his side, but Panda Man's eyes were blank. He didn't move.

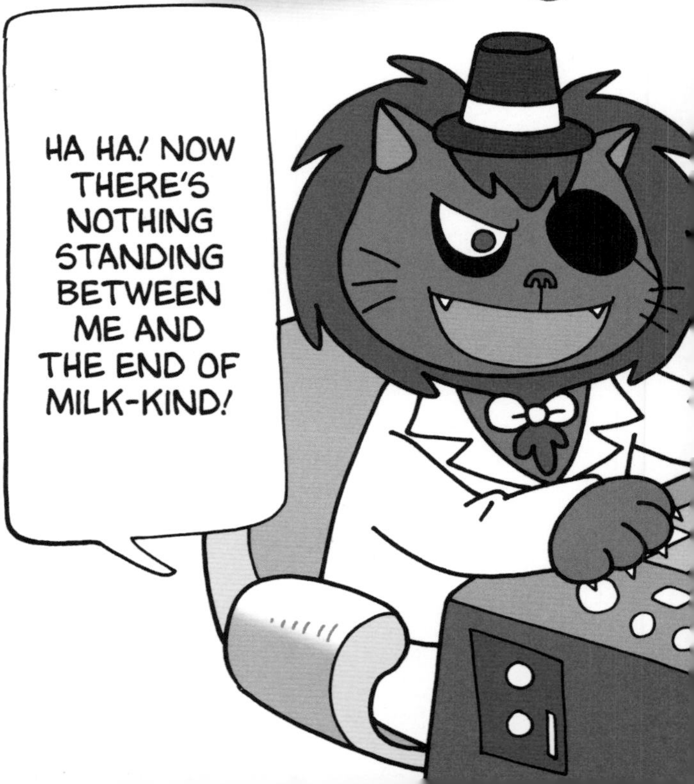
HA HA! NOW THERE'S NOTHING STANDING BETWEEN ME AND THE END OF MILK-KIND!

Leo quickly entered the launch codes for his rocket.

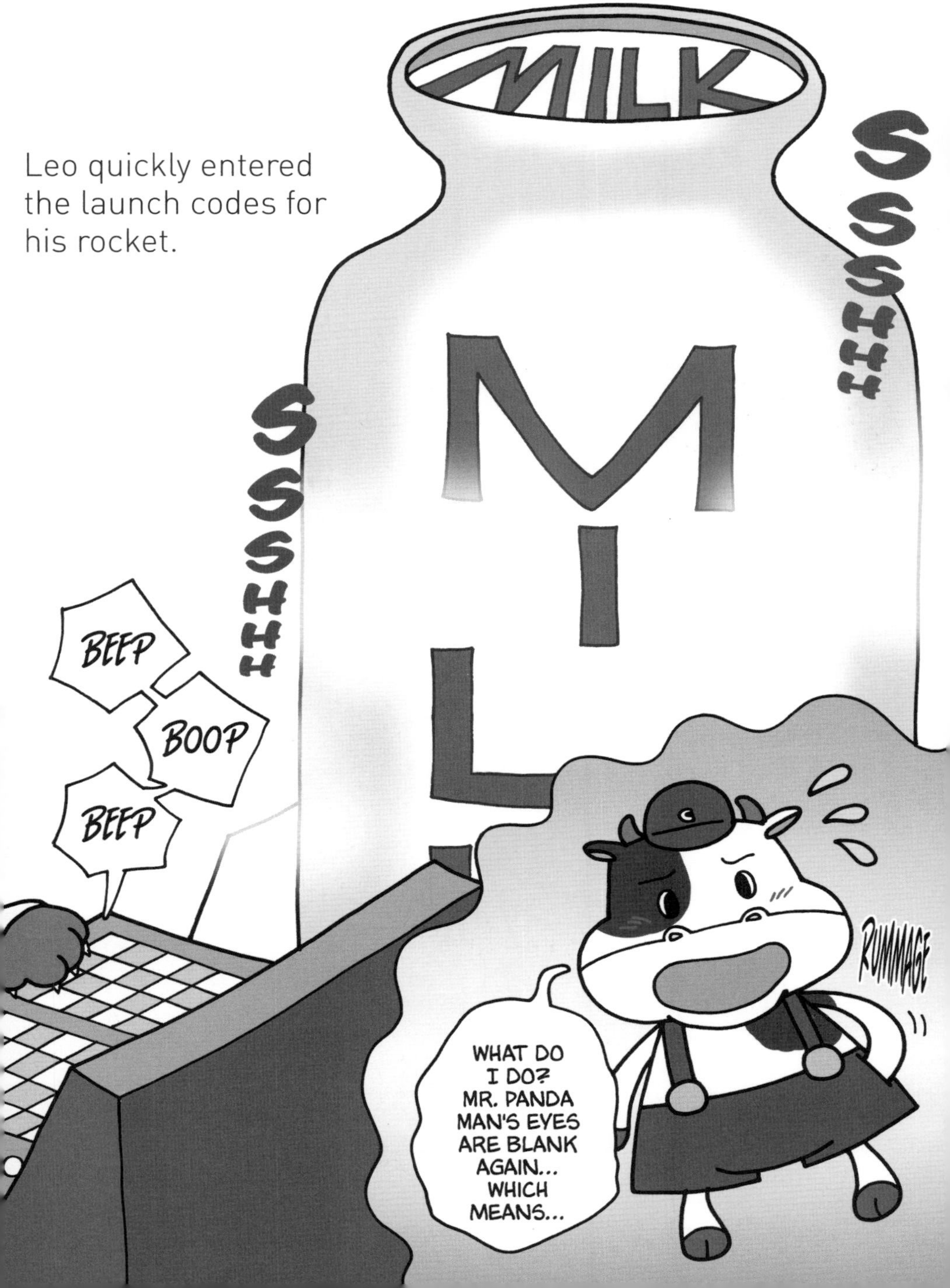
MILK
SSSSHHH
WHAT DO I DO? MR. PANDA MAN'S EYES ARE BLANK AGAIN... WHICH MEANS...
RUMMAGE
SSSSHHH
BEEP
BOOP
BEEP

Cowvin took a pencil from his pocket and...

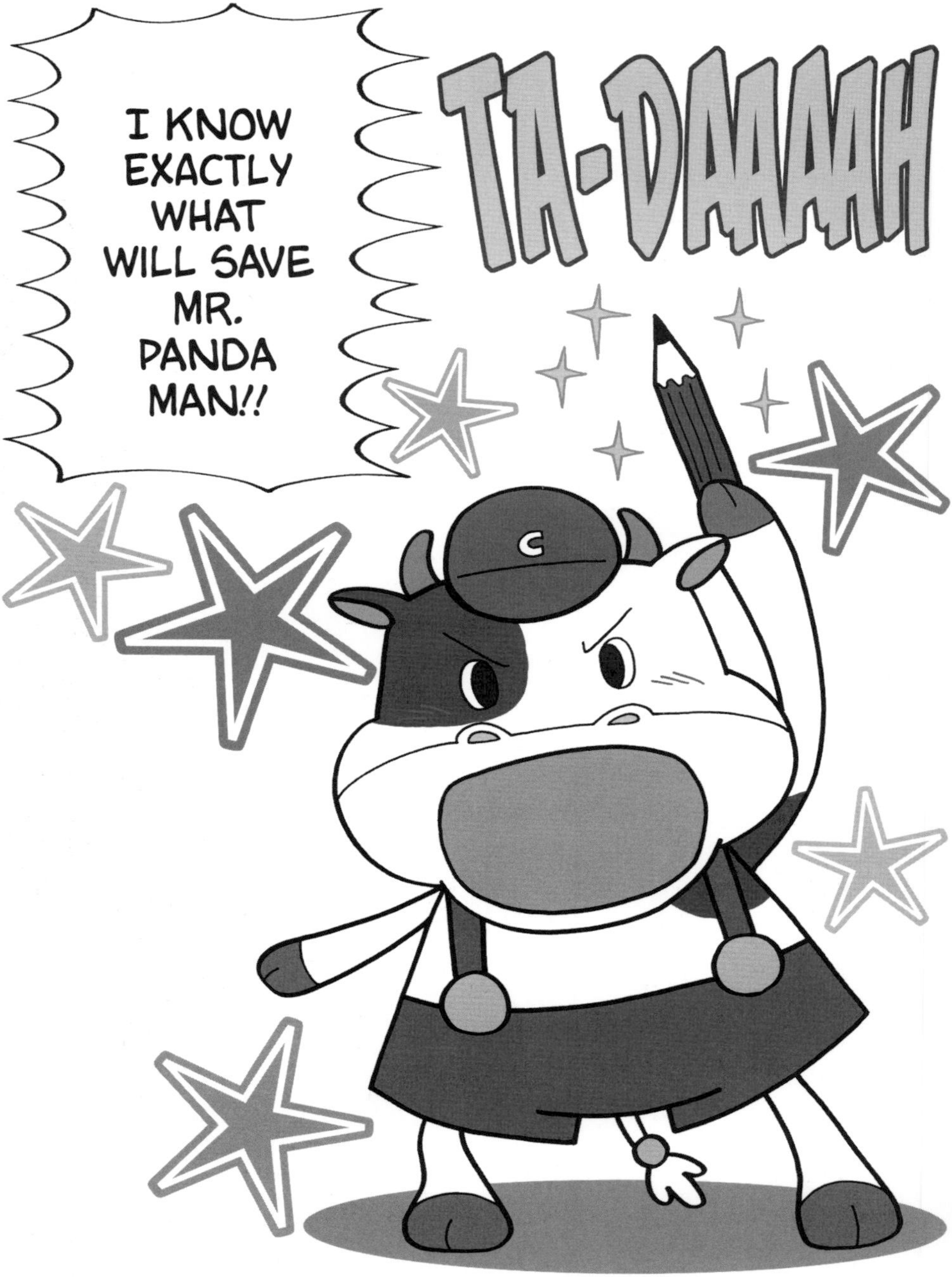
I KNOW EXACTLY WHAT WILL SAVE MR. PANDA MAN!!
TA-DAAAAH

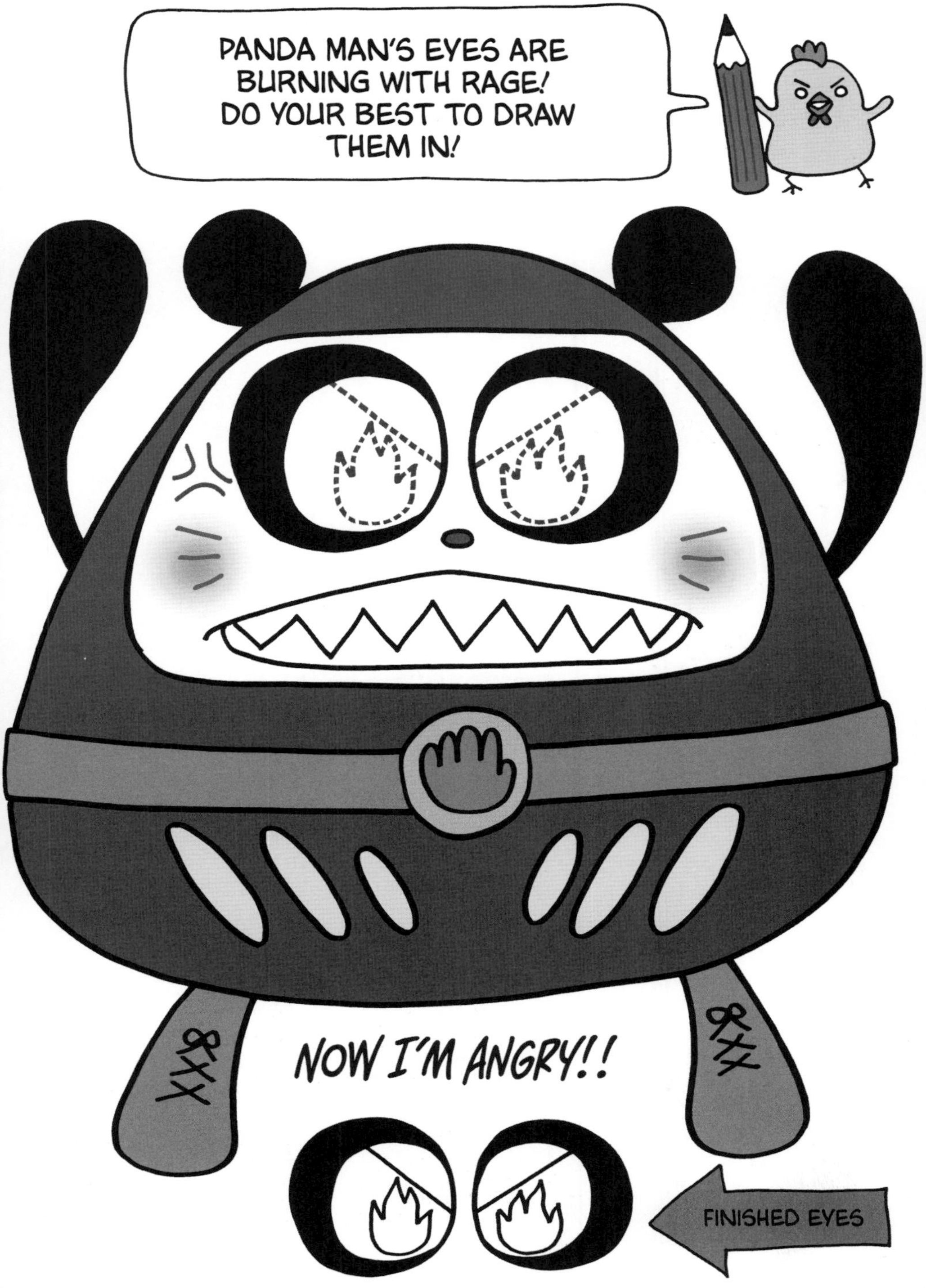
PANDA MAN'S EYES ARE BURNING WITH RAGE! DO YOUR BEST TO DRAW THEM IN!
NOW I'M ANGRY!!
FINISHED EYES

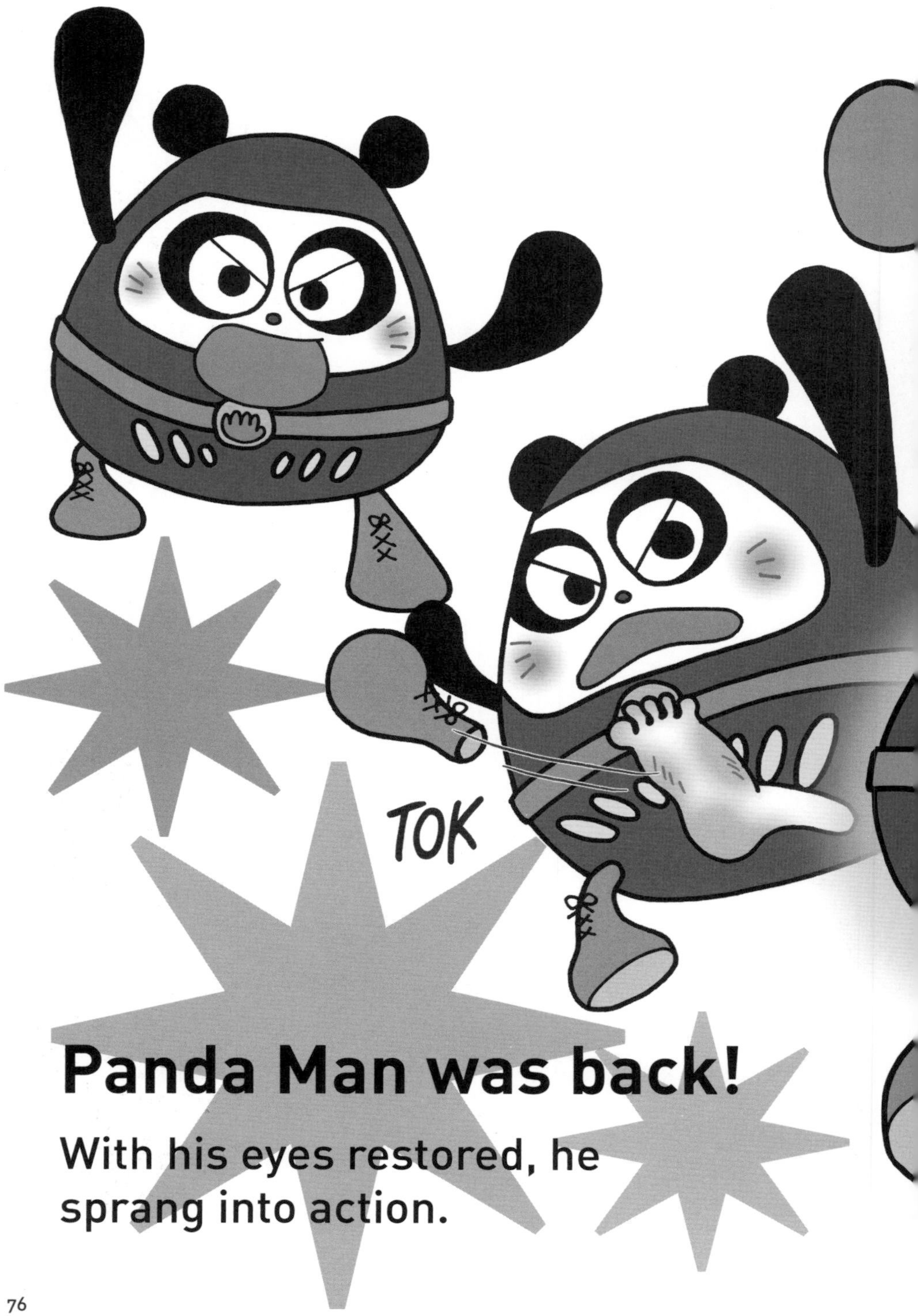
TOK

Panda Man was back!

With his eyes restored, he sprang into action.

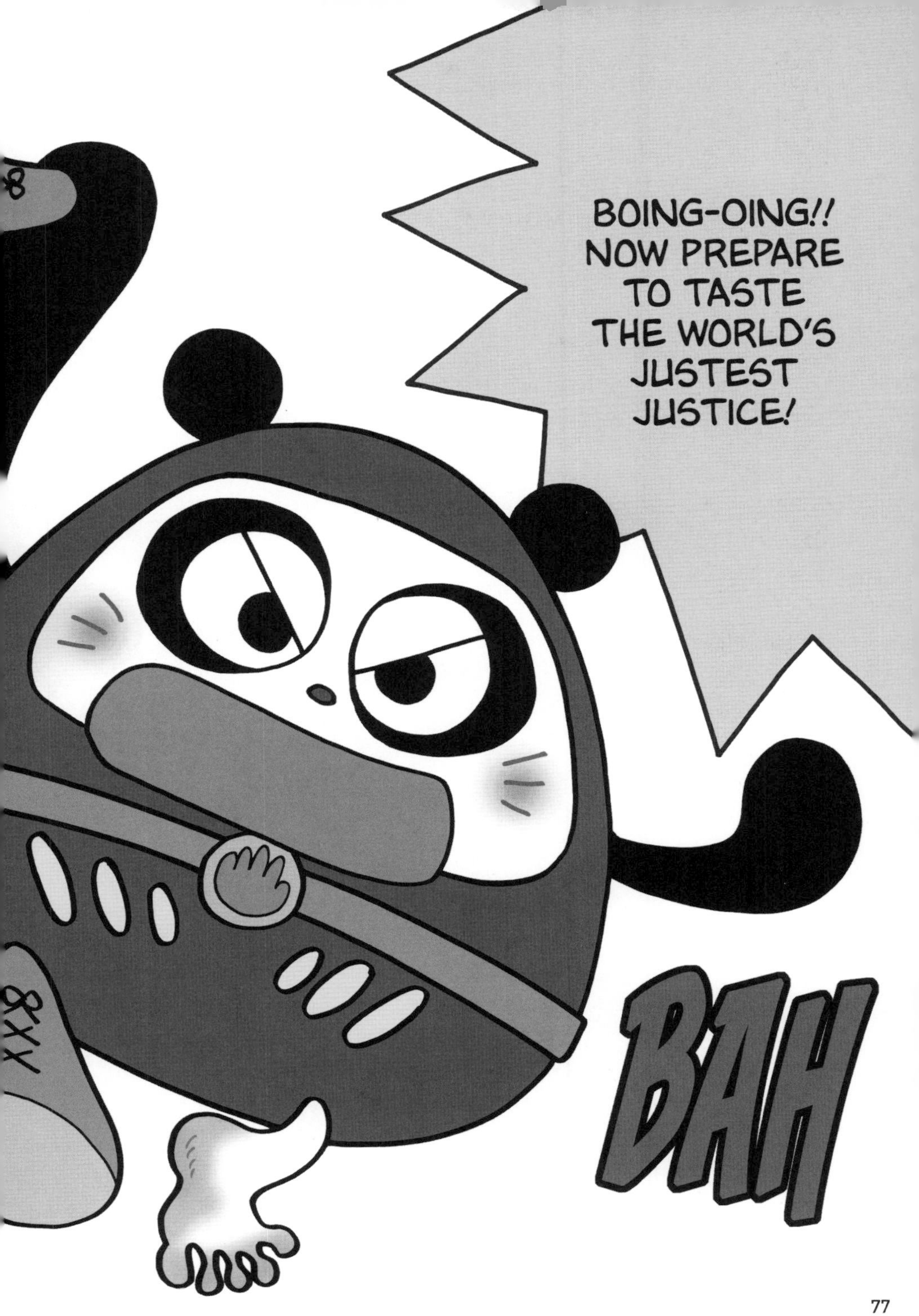
BOING-OING!! NOW PREPARE TO TASTE THE WORLD'S JUSTEST JUSTICE!
BAH

He flung off his shoe and attacked.

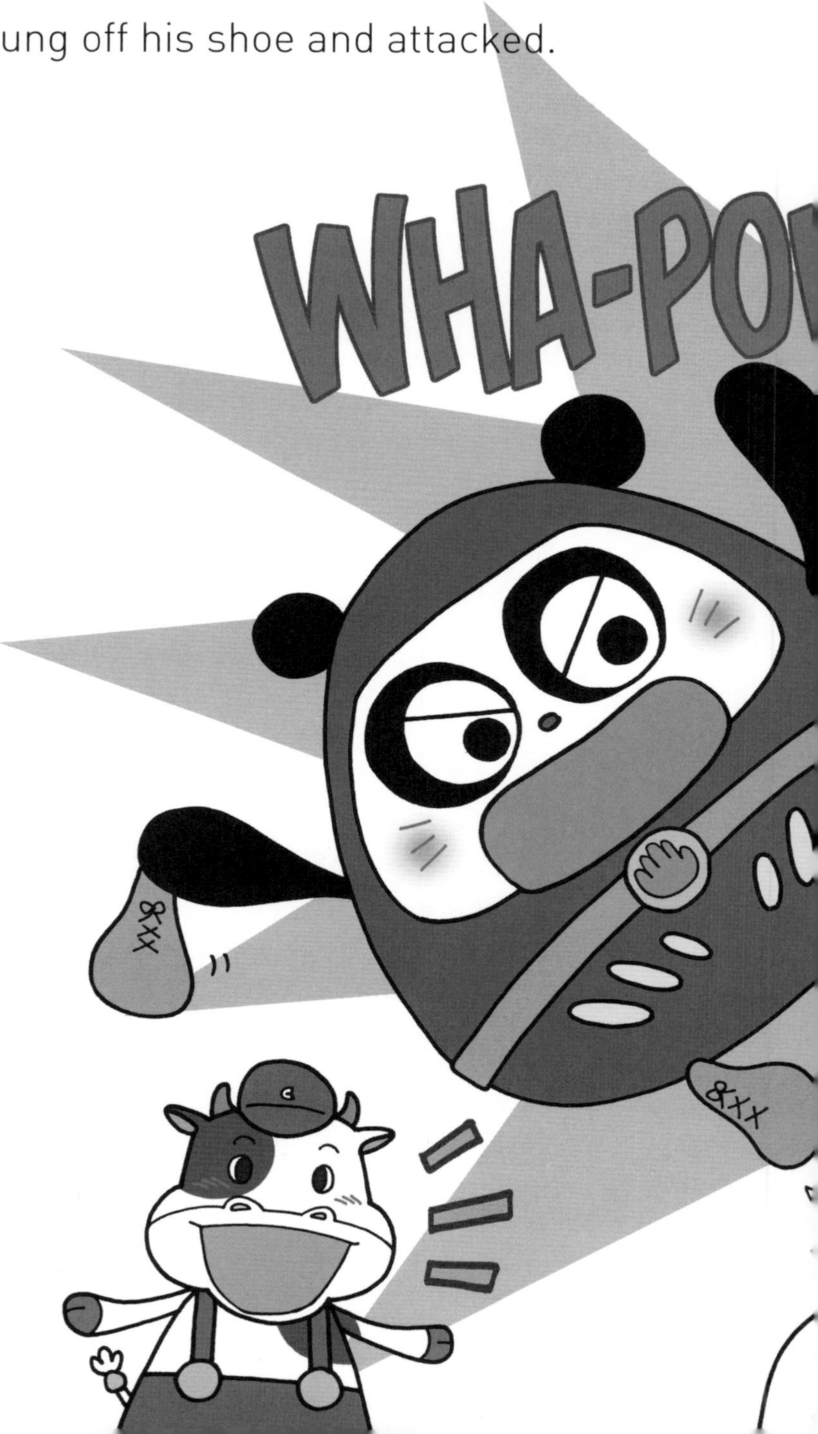
WHA-PO

Well, how about that! Panda Man might just be the world's greatest martial artist after all.

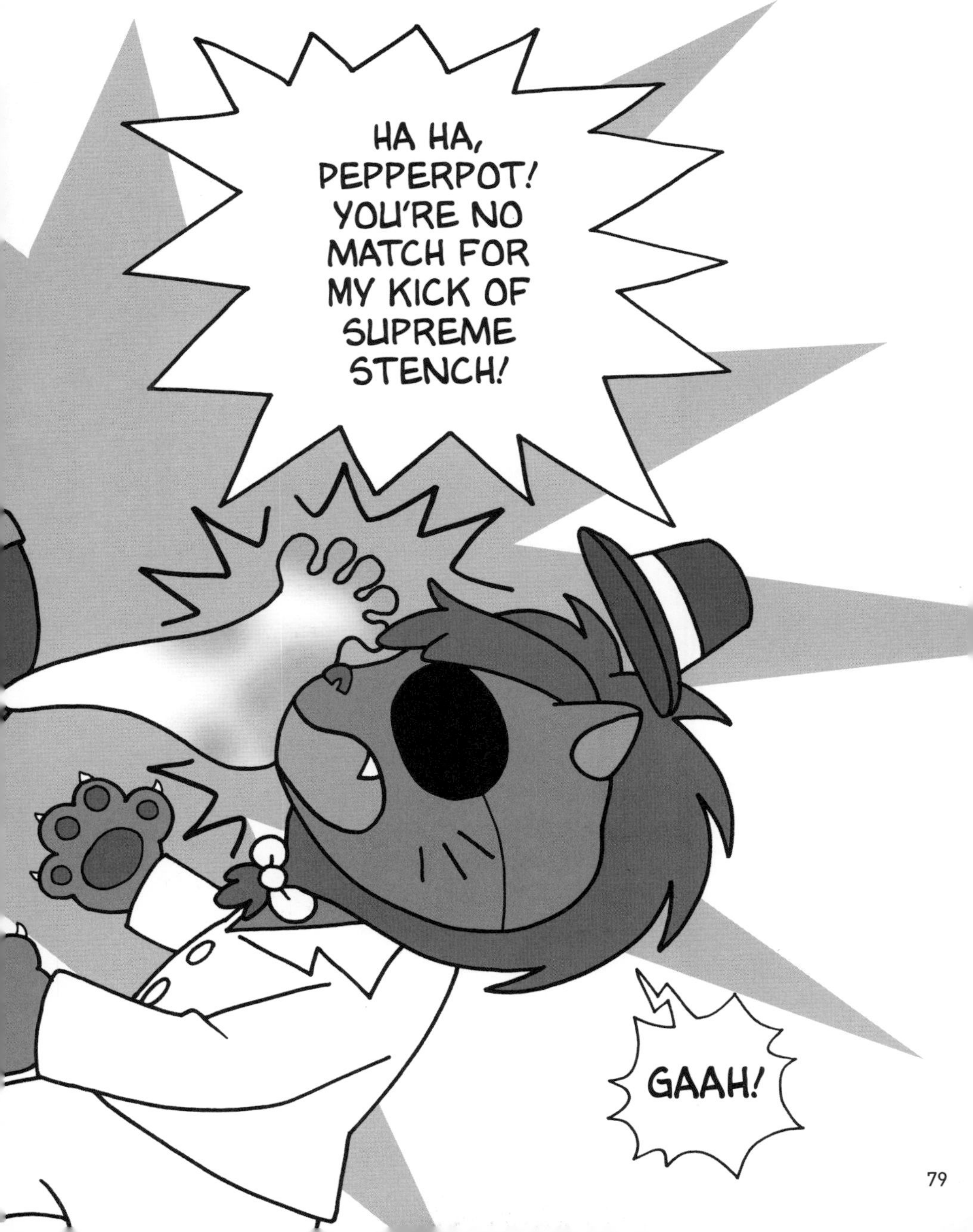
HA HA, PEPPERPOT! YOU'RE NO MATCH FOR MY KICK OF SUPREME STENCH!
GAAH!

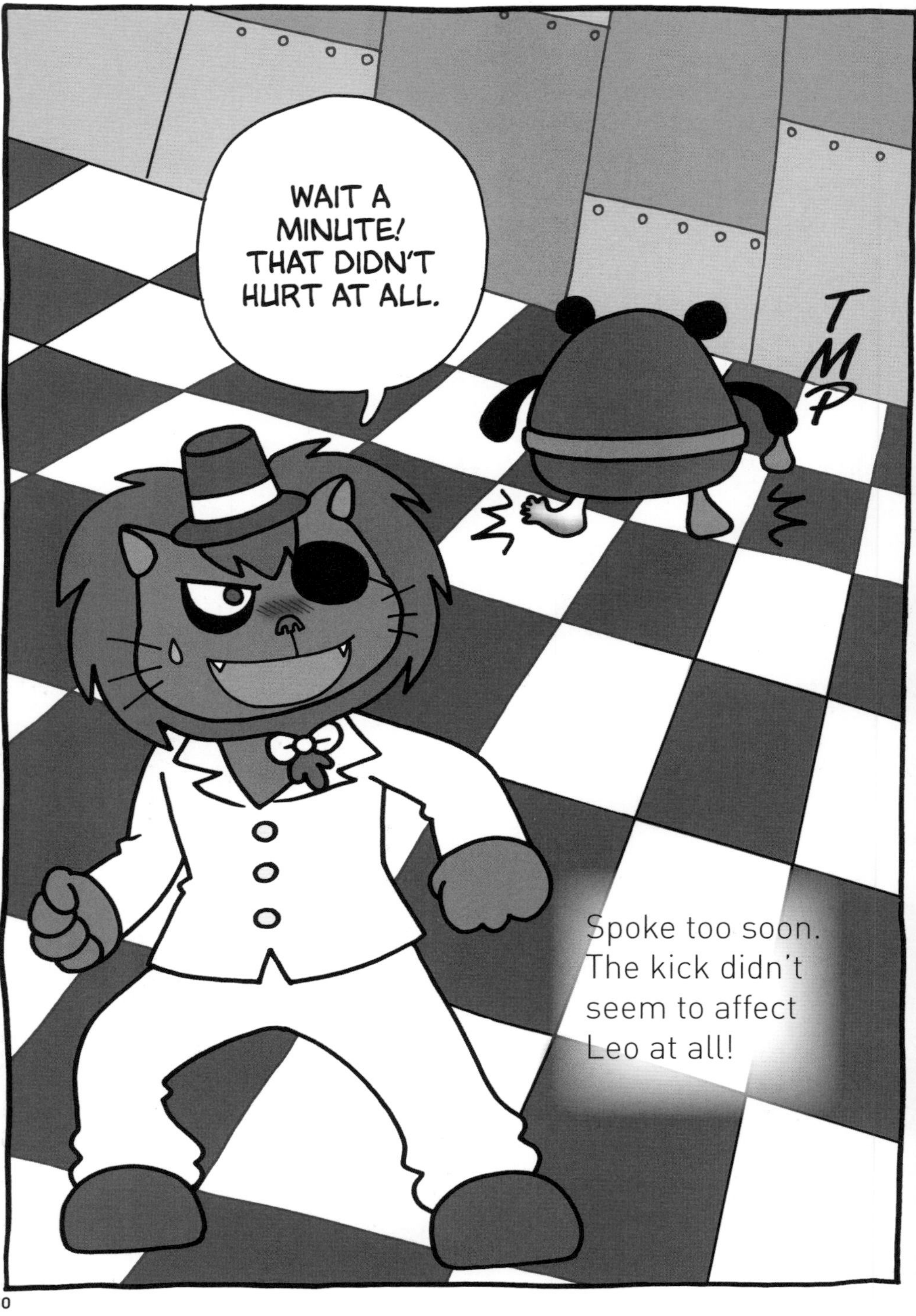
WAIT A MINUTE! THAT DIDN'T HURT AT ALL.
TMP
Spoke too soon. The kick didn't seem to affect Leo at all!

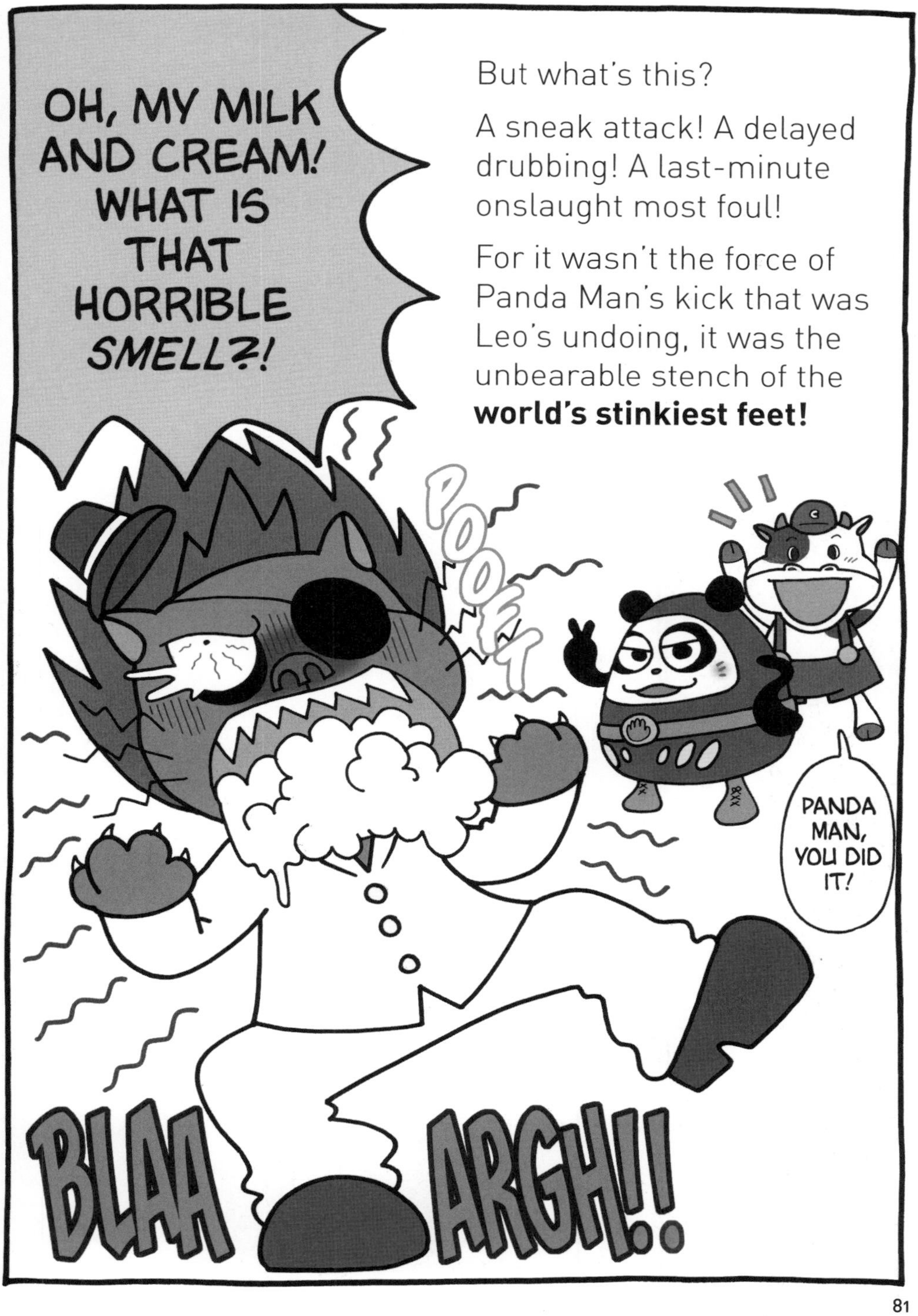
But what's this?
A sneak attack! A delayed drubbing! A last-minute onslaught most foul!
For it wasn't the force of Panda Man's kick that was Leo's undoing, it was the unbearable stench of the **world's stinkiest feet!**
OH, MY MILK AND CREAM! WHAT IS THAT HORRIBLE *SMELL?!*
POOF!
PANDA MAN, YOU DID IT!
BLAAARGH!!

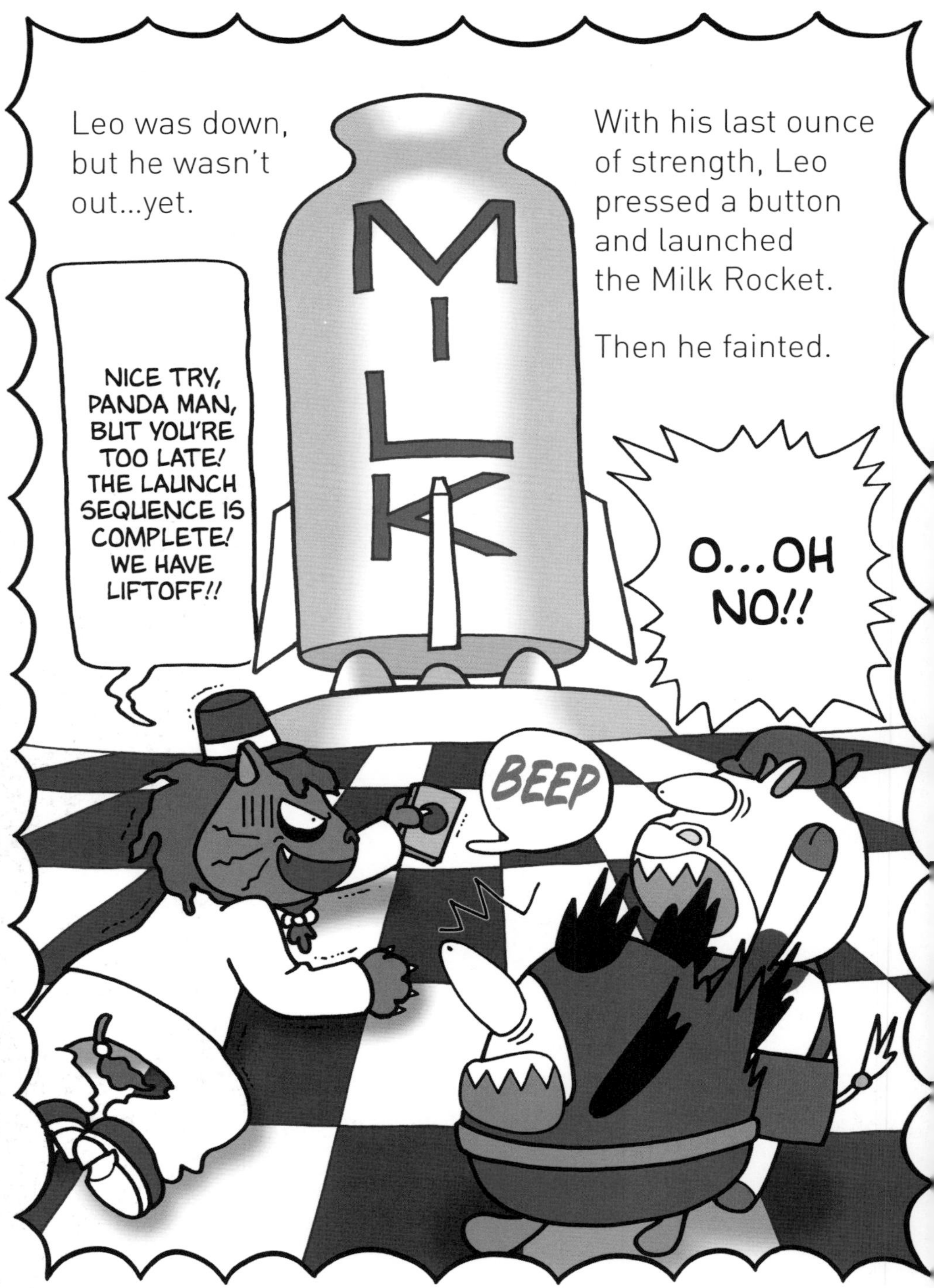
Leo was down, but he wasn't out...yet.
With his last ounce of strength, Leo pressed a button and launched the Milk Rocket.
Then he fainted.
MILK
NICE TRY, PANDA MAN, BUT YOU'RE TOO LATE! THE LAUNCH SEQUENCE IS COMPLETE! WE HAVE LIFTOFF!!
O...OH NO!!
BEEP

The rocket rumbled to life.

And without another thought, Panda Man hopped on.

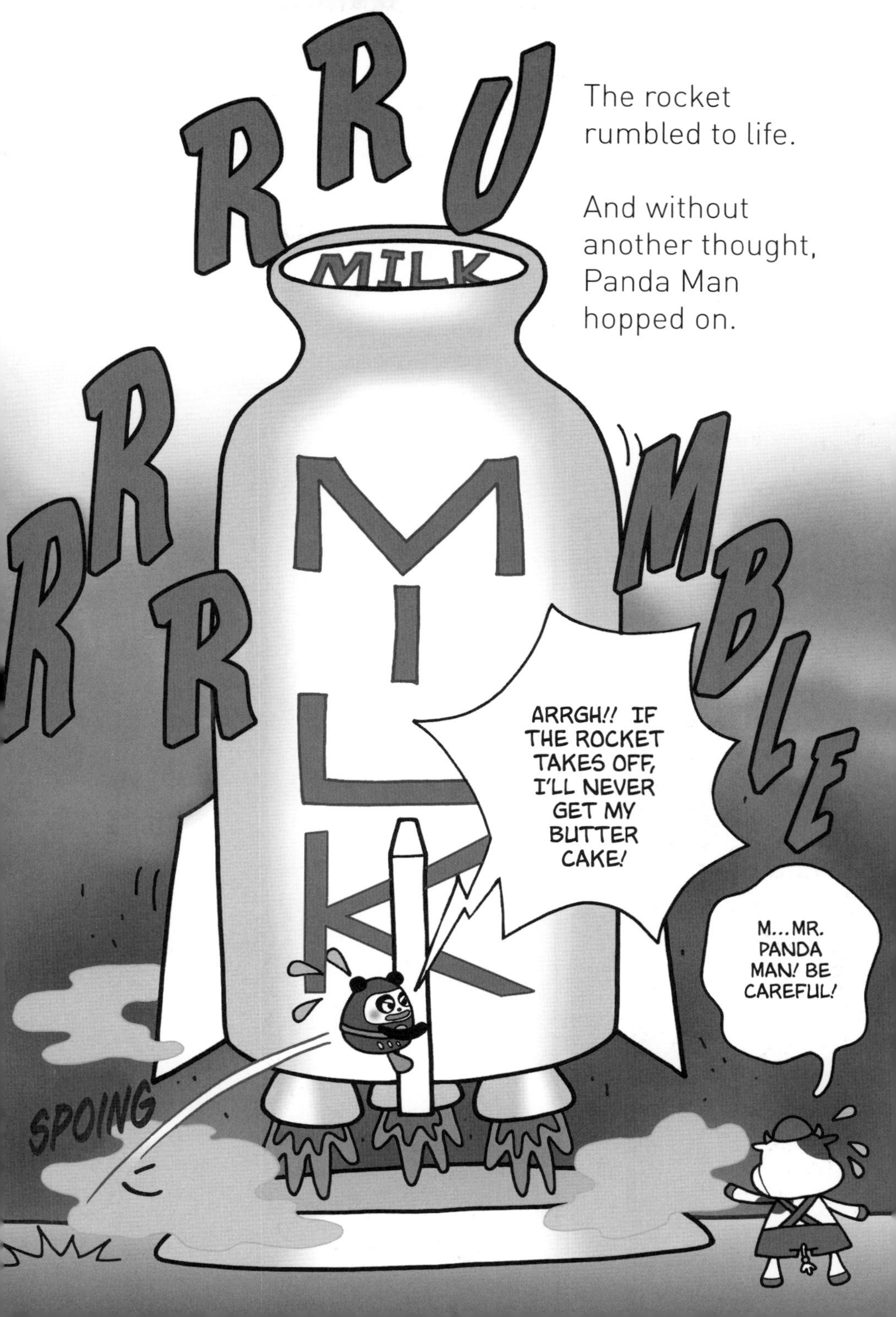
RRRU
MILK
RRRR
MBLE
MILK
ARRGH!! IF THE ROCKET TAKES OFF, I'LL NEVER GET MY BUTTER CAKE!
M...MR. PANDA MAN! BE CAREFUL!
SPOING

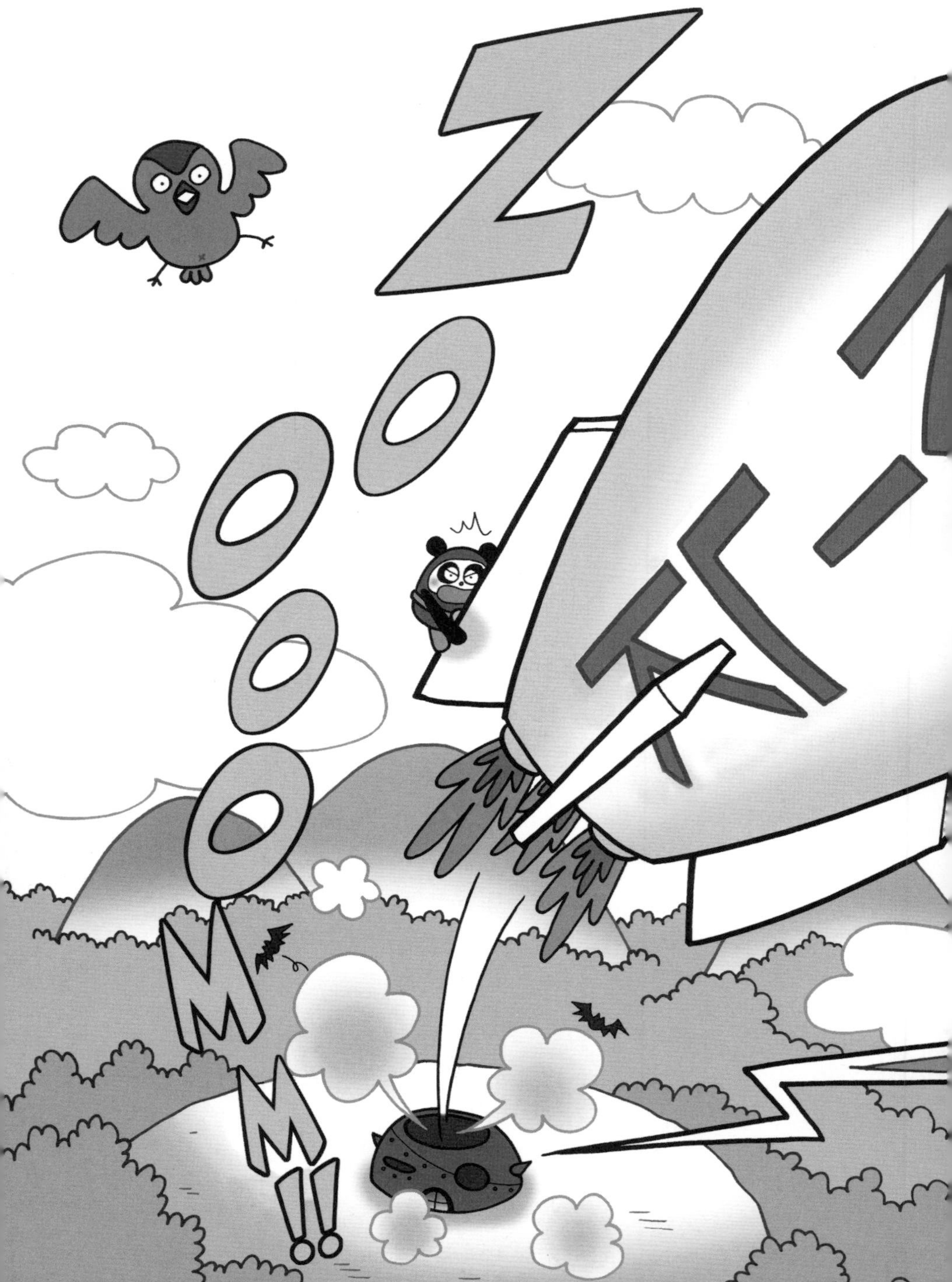
ZOOOOMM!!

The Milk Rocket raced skyward with Panda Man holding on for dear life. There wasn't much else he could do.

Did Leo win this fight?
Was this the end of milk?!

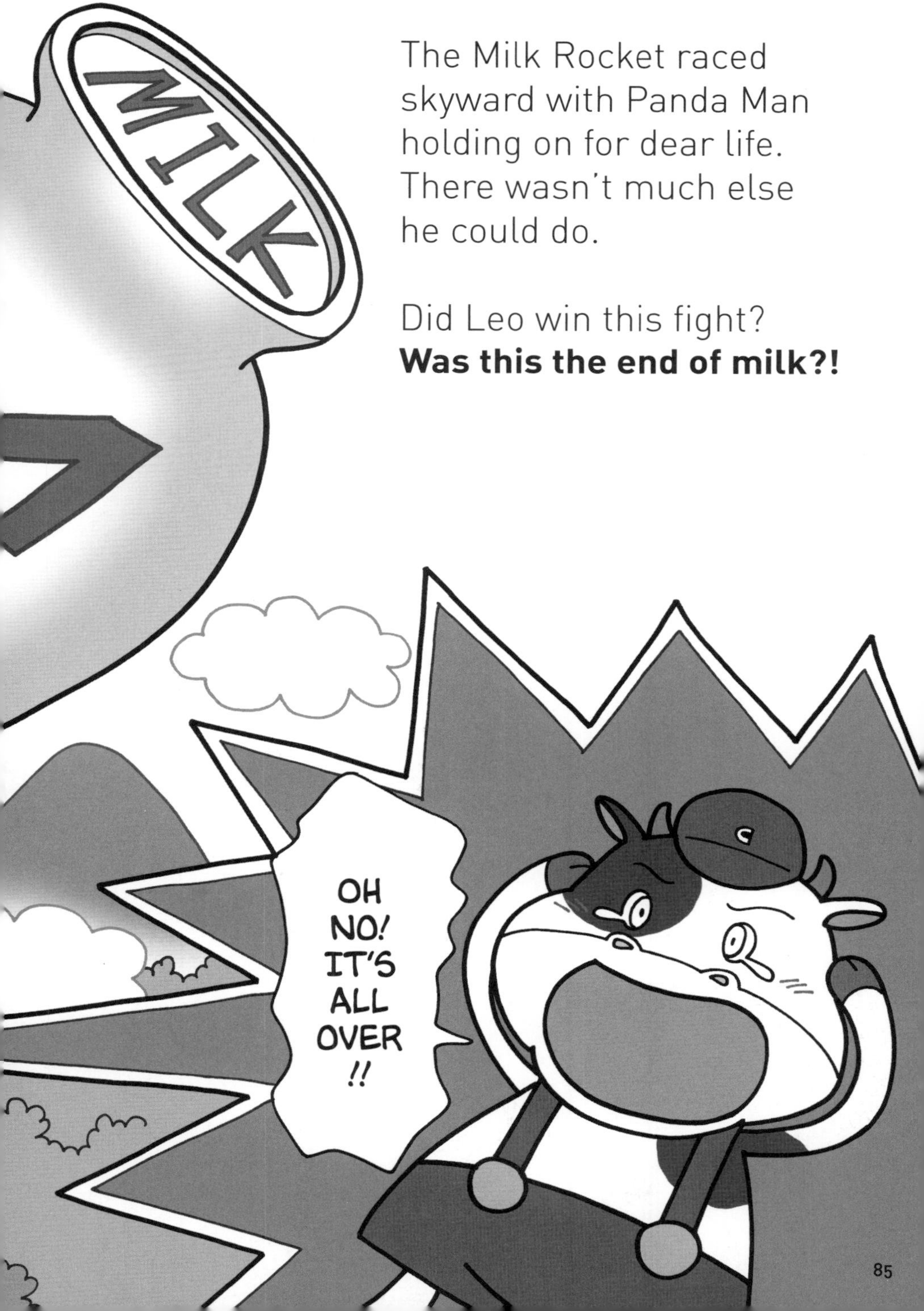
MILK
OH NO! IT'S ALL OVER!!

PPFFFTTT
VROOM
VROOM
VROOM

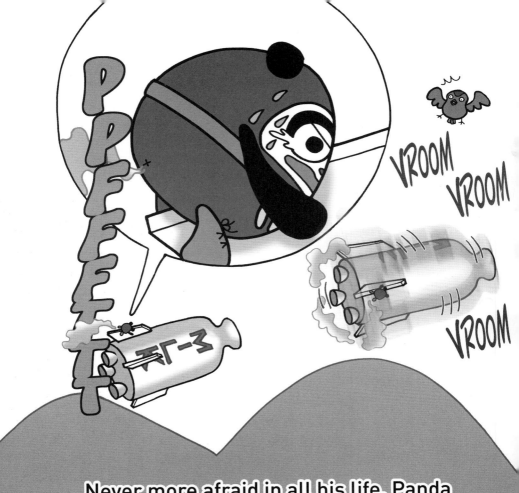

Never more afraid in all his life, Panda Man farted.

Not just any fart. The world's longest, strongest, most fartiest fart.

The sheer force of Panda Man's personal wind sent the Milk Rocket spinning.

It whipped round and round until...

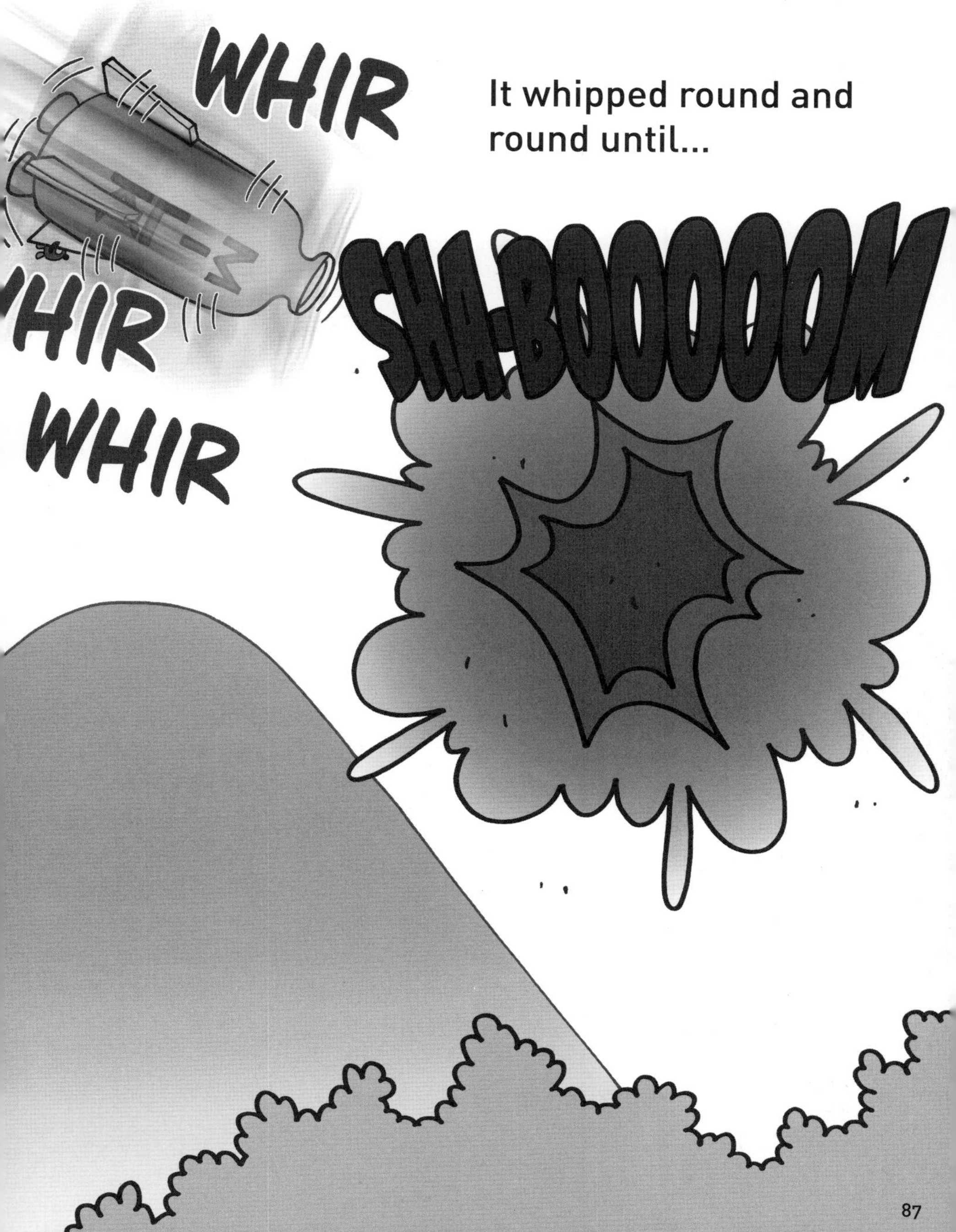
WHIR
HIR
WHIR
SHA-BOOOOOM

The Milk Rocket's spinning turned the milk into a great glob of butter. The rocket exploded right over New Milk Village, dropping the butter smack-dab in the middle of town.

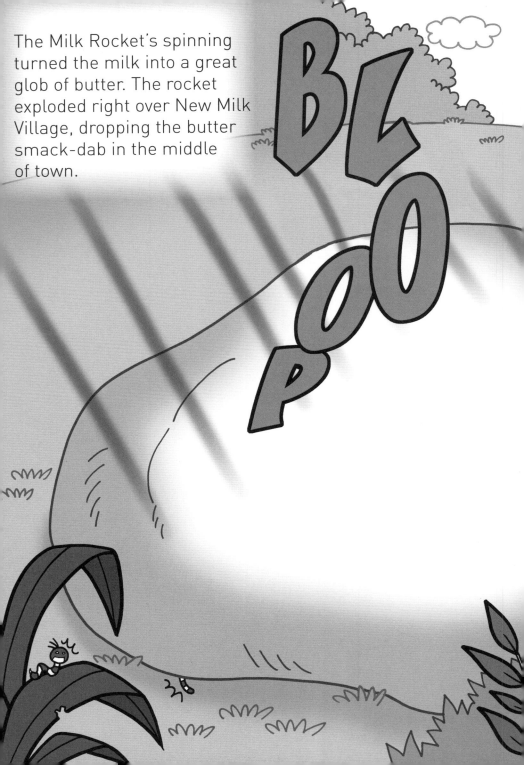

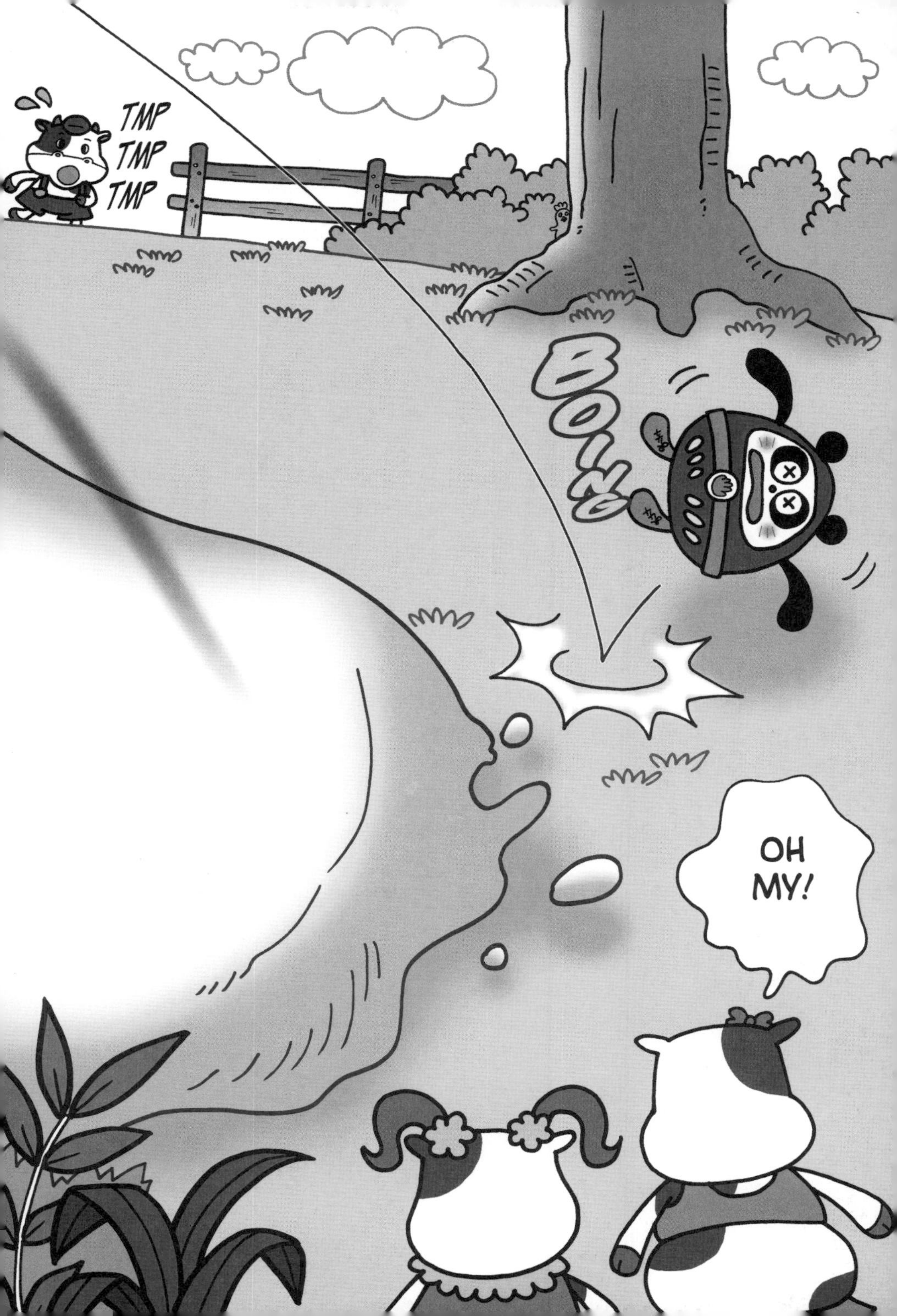
TMP
TMP
TMP
BOING
OH MY!

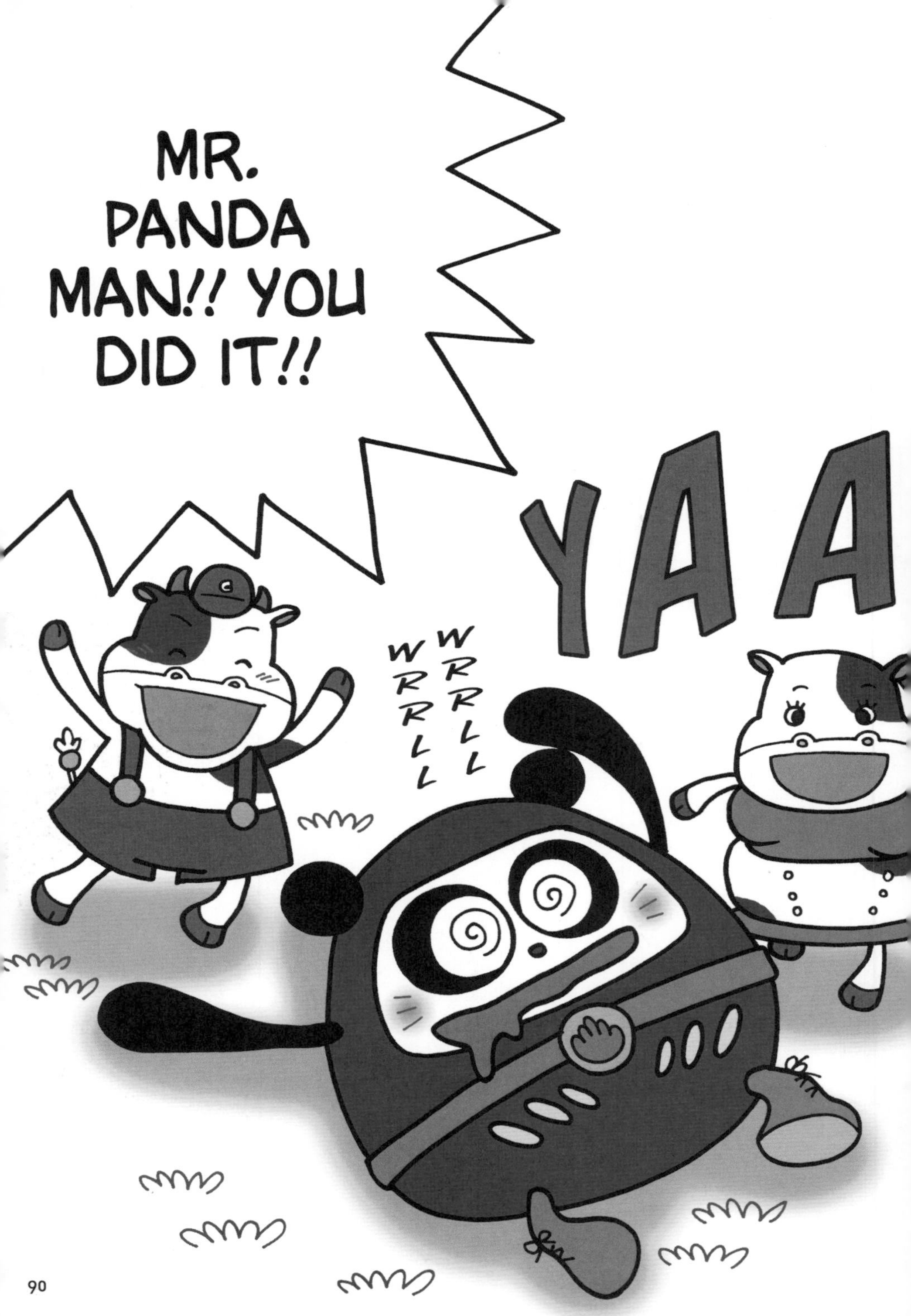
MR. PANDA MAN!! YOU DID IT!!
YAAA
WRRLL
WRRLL

Cowvin and the villagers ran to their fallen hero.

And what a hero he was. He had defeated Leo Pepperpot and saved New Milk Village, assuring milk lovers everywhere that they would never be without their milk!

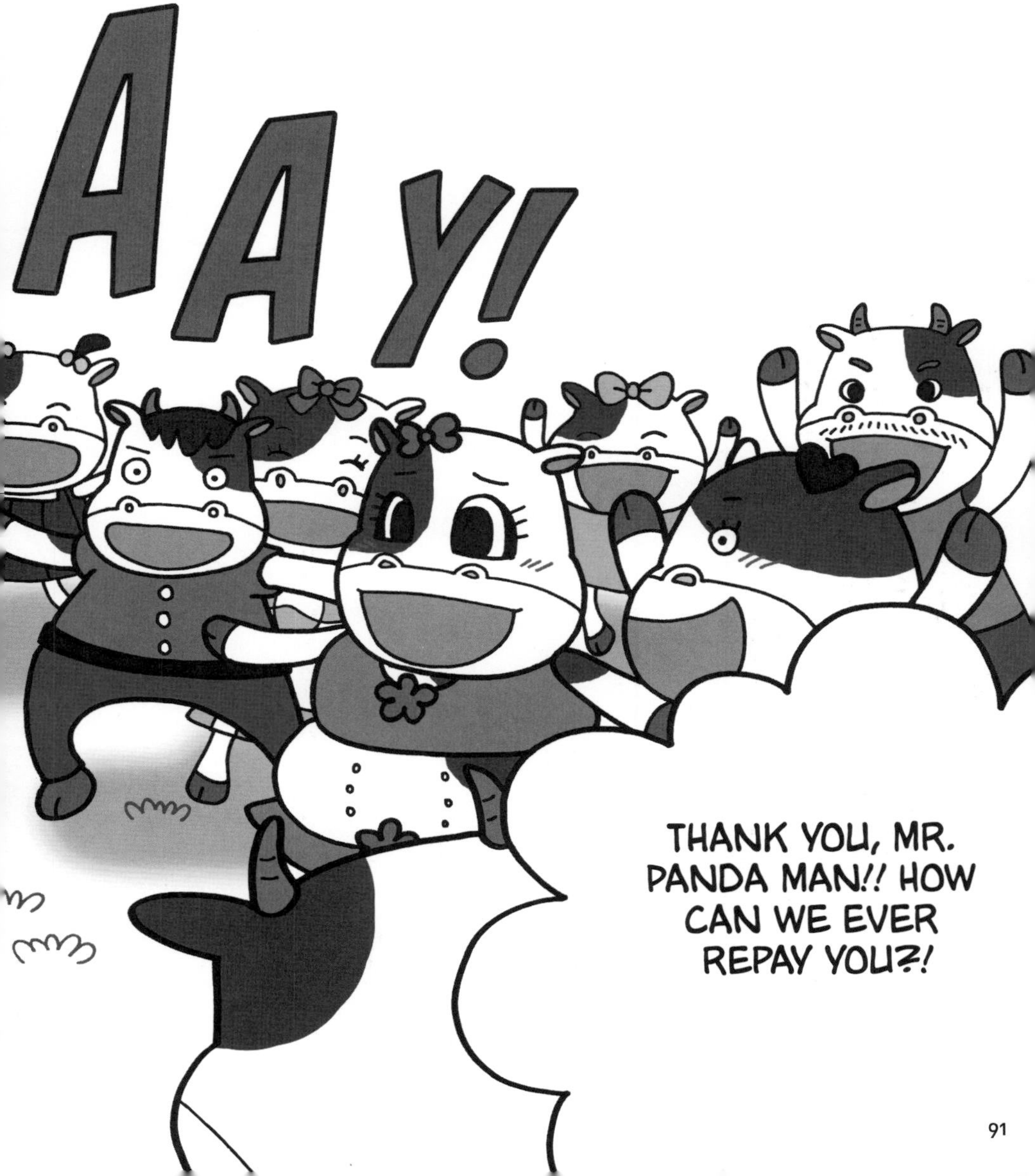
AAY!
THANK YOU, MR. PANDA MAN!! HOW CAN WE EVER REPAY YOU?!

There was only one way for the villagers to repay Panda Man. With the giant glob of butter they made the world's largest and yummiest butter cake!

Panda Man opened his mouth wide—wider than anyone in the world—and...

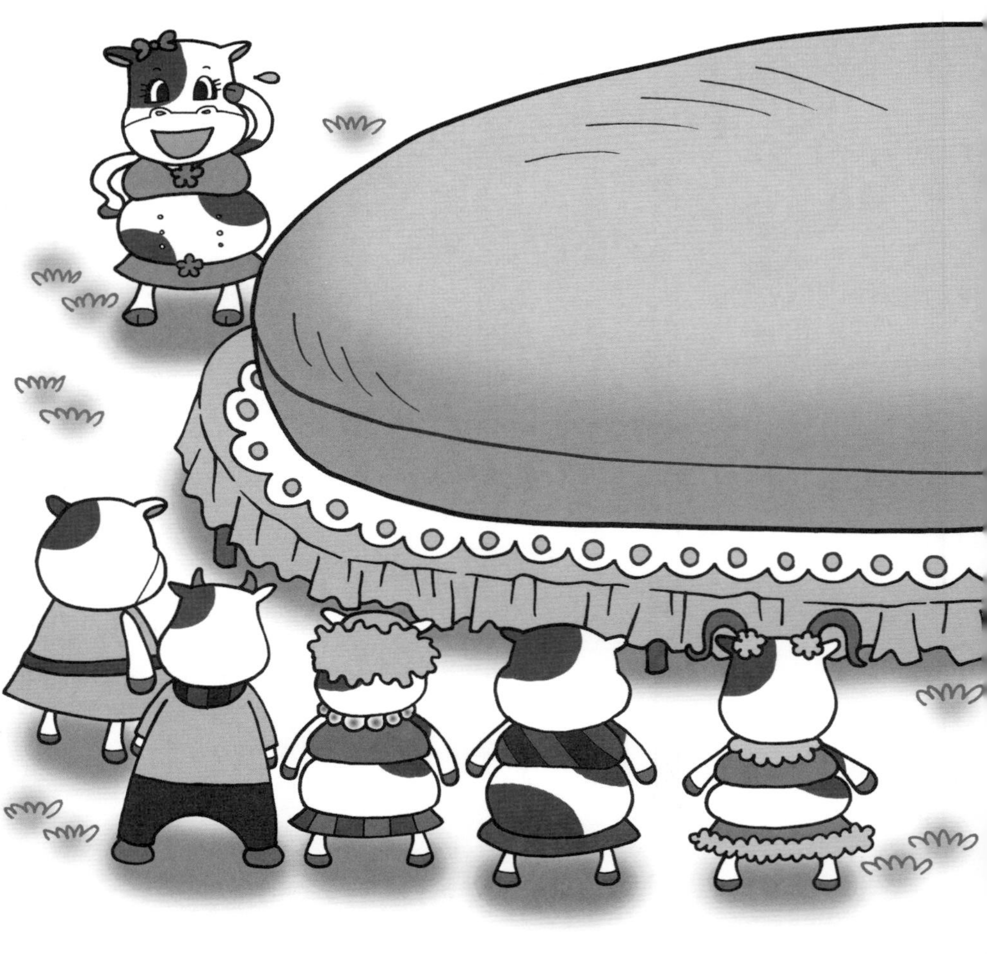

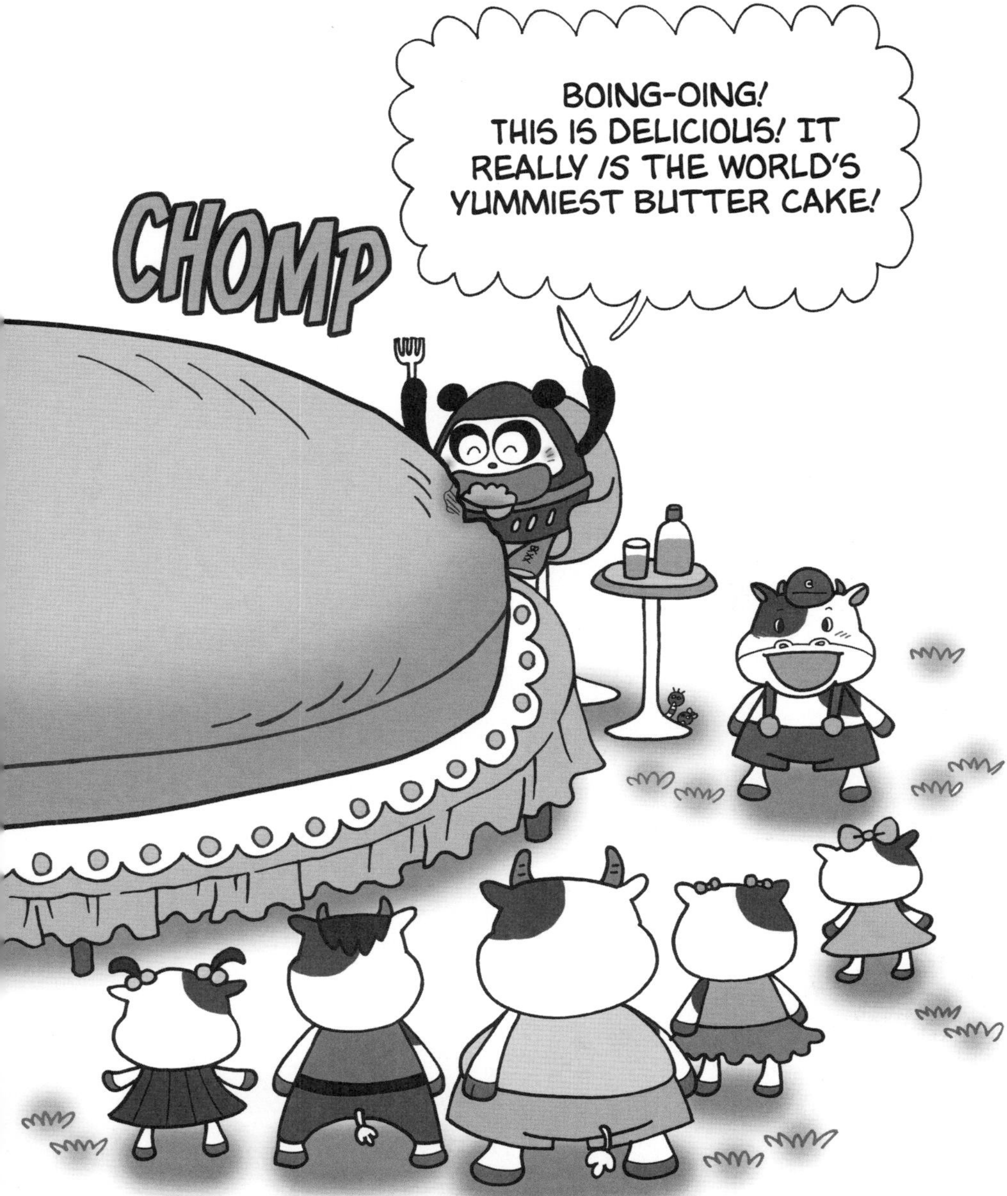
CHOMP
BOING-OING! THIS IS DELICIOUS! IT REALLY IS THE WORLD'S YUMMIEST BUTTER CAKE!

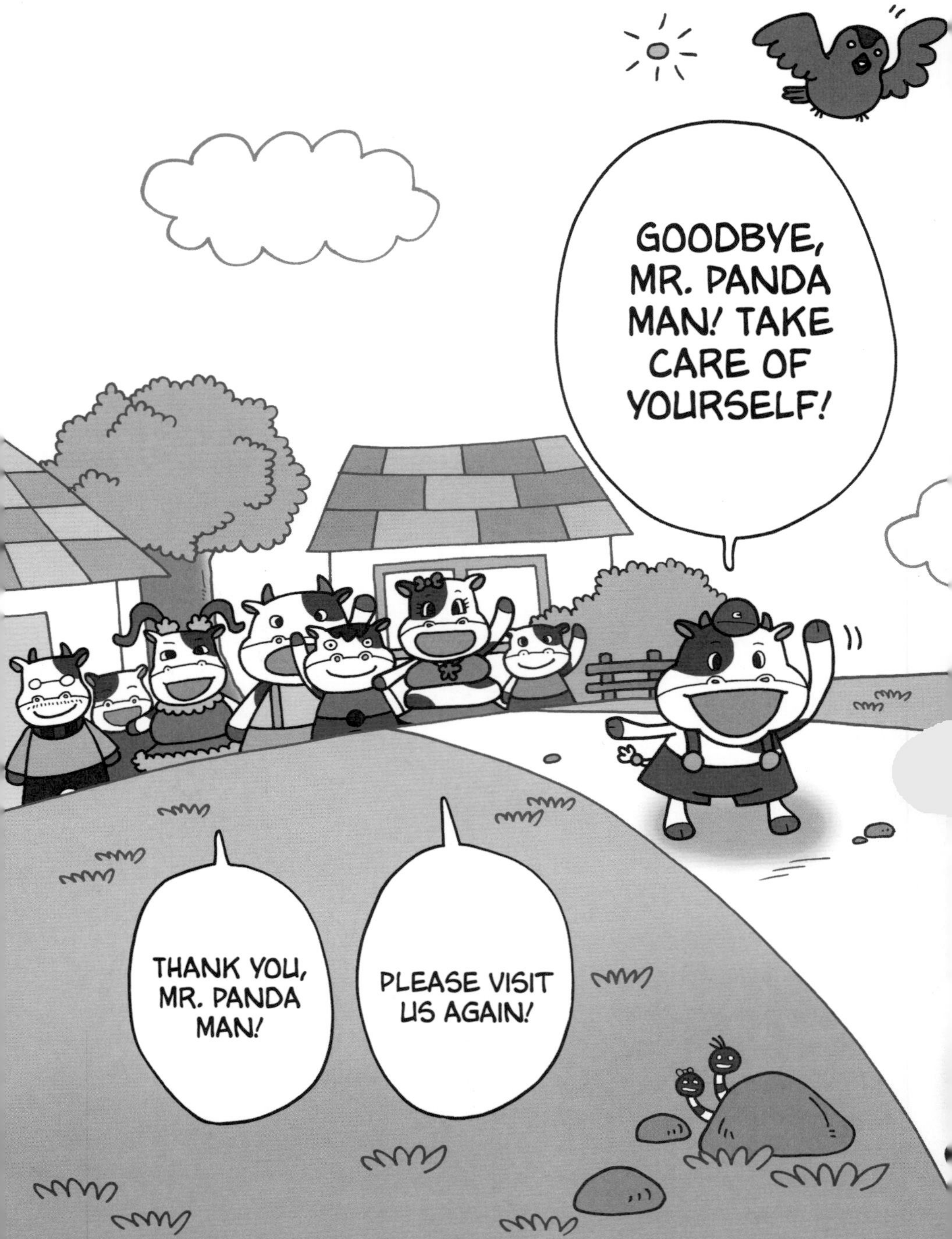
GOODBYE, MR. PANDA MAN! TAKE CARE OF YOURSELF!
PLEASE VISIT US AGAIN!
THANK YOU, MR. PANDA MAN!

There goes Panda Man, the world's greatest hero. Strong. Heroic. Brave. Wherever there's evil to defeat and good food to eat, he'll be there.

Farewell, Panda Man! Until we meet again!

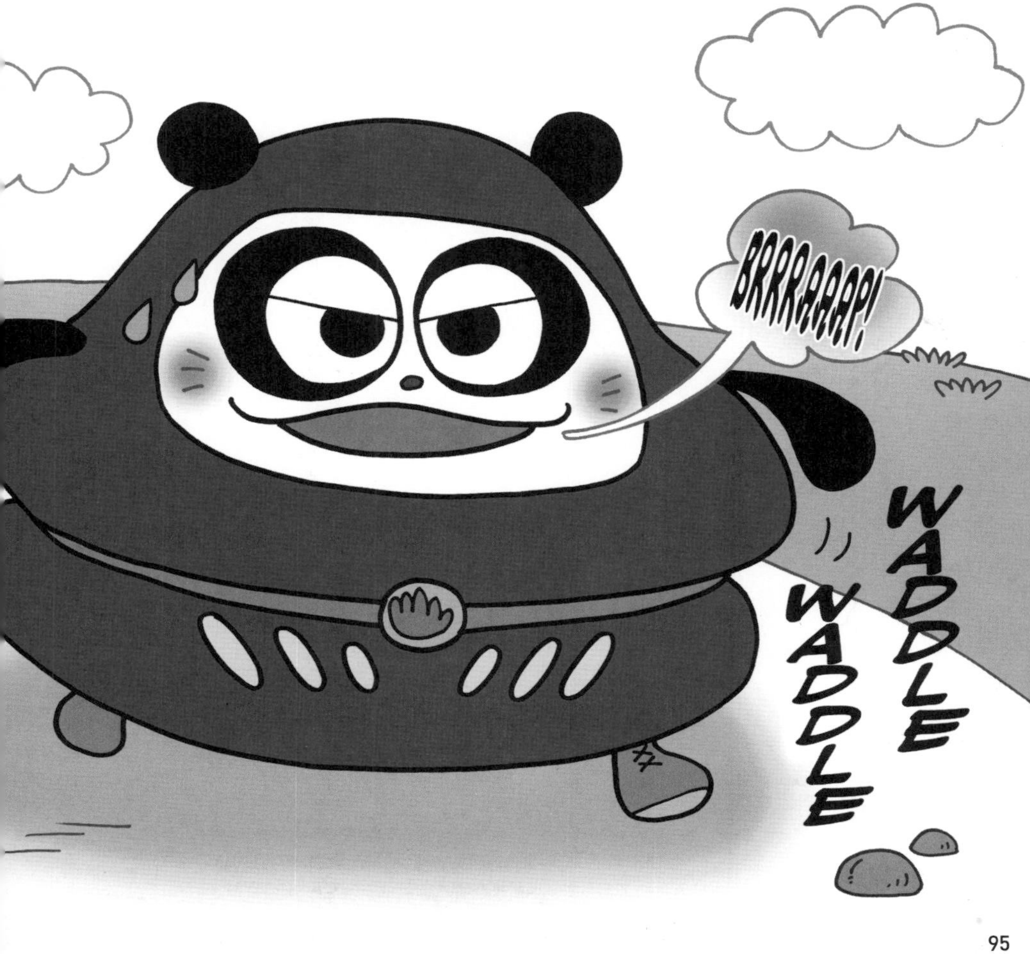
BRRRAAAP!
WADDLE
WADDLE

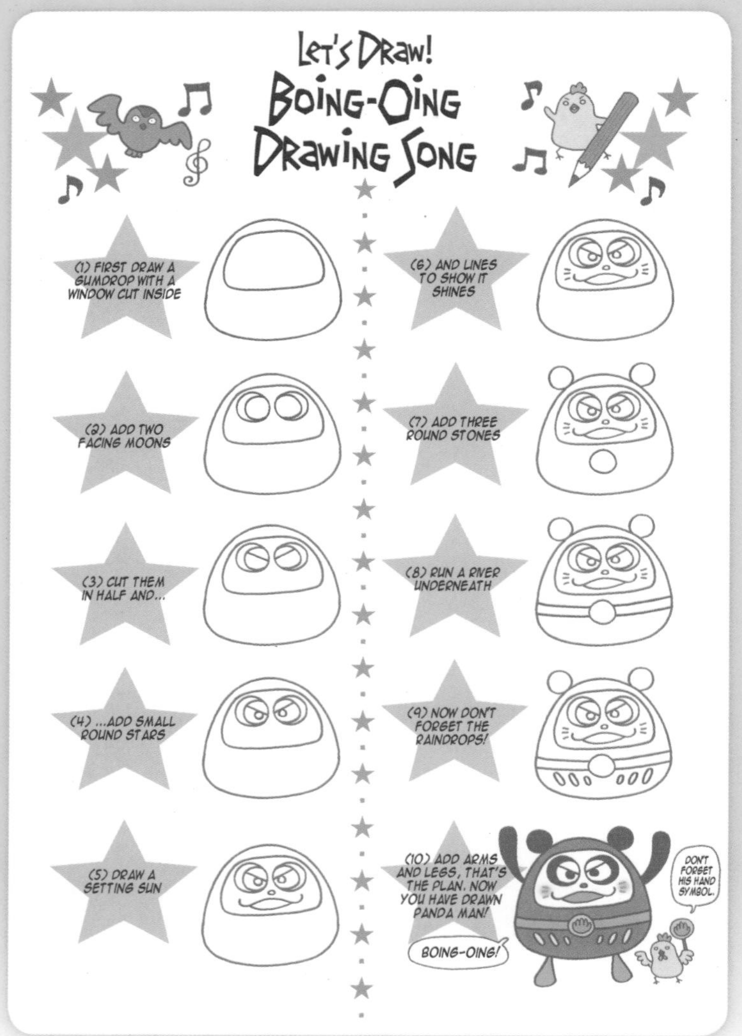
LET'S DRAW!
BOING-OING DRAWING SONG
(1) FIRST DRAW A GUMDROP WITH A WINDOW CUT INSIDE
(2) ADD TWO FACING MOONS
(3) CUT THEM IN HALF AND...
(4) ...ADD SMALL ROUND STARS
(5) DRAW A SETTING SUN
(6) AND LINES TO SHOW IT SHINES
(7) ADD THREE ROUND STONES
(8) RUN A RIVER UNDERNEATH
(9) NOW DON'T FORGET THE RAINDROPS!
(10) ADD ARMS AND LEGS, THAT'S THE PLAN. NOW YOU HAVE DRAWN PANDA MAN!
DON'T FORGET HIS HAND SYMBOL.
BOING-OING!

Panda Man to the Rescue!

VIZ Kids Edition

Story by Sho Makura
Art by Haruhi Kato

Translation: Katherine Schilling
Rewriting: Deric Hughes
Touch-up Art & Lettering: John Hunt
Graphics & Cover Design: Frances O. Liddell
Editor: Traci N. Todd

VP, Production: Alvin Lu
VP, Sales & Product Marketing: Gonzalo Ferreyra
VP, Creative: Linda Espinosa
Publisher: Hyoe Narita

BOYO-YON PANDARU-MAN

First published in Japan in 2008 by SHUEISHA Inc., Tokyo.
English translation rights arranged by SHUEISHA Inc.

Printed in China

Published by VIZ Media, LLC
P.O. Box 77010
San Francisco, CA 94107

10 9 8 7 6 5 4 3 2 1
First printing, October 2010

www.vizkids.com